Alice McDermott is an American writer and university professor of the humanities. *That Night*, her second novel, was a finalist for the Pulitzer Prize, the National Book Award, and the *Los Angeles Times* Book Prize; a film version starring C. Thomas Howell and Juliette Lewis was released in 1992. McDermott is currently writer-in-residence at Johns Hopkins University in Baltimore. She lives outside Washington, D.C. with her husband and three children.

SOMEONE

In her 1920s Irish-American enclave, the stories of Marie's neighbours unfold before her short-sighted eyes — from war-blinded Billy Corrigan, to the terrifying Big Lucy, to the ever-present Sisters of Charity from the convent down the road. As the years pass, Marie's own story unfolds against the backdrop of a changing world. Her older brother Gabe leaves for the seminary to study for the priesthood, his faith destined to be tested to breaking point. Marie experiences first love and first heartbreak, marriage and motherhood, and discovers how time can both take away and offer up so much that is precious. Stitching together the intricate tapestry of Marie's journey of the heart over seven decades, Alice McDermott reveals the delicate, bittersweet beauty that lies behind someone's — *everyone's* — experiences of loss, love and life.

ALICE McDERMOTT

◆

SOMEONE

Complete and Unabridged

CHARNWOOD
Leicester

First published in Great Britain in 2013 by
Bloomsbury Circus
an imprint of Bloomsbury Publishing plc
London

First Charnwood Edition
published 2014
by arrangement with
Bloomsbury Publishing plc
London

A catalogue record for this book is available
from the British Library.

ISBN 978–1–4448–2131–4

Published by
F. A. Thorpe (Publishing)
Anstey, Leicestershire

Set by Words & Graphics Ltd.
Anstey, Leicestershire
Printed and bound in Great Britain by
T. J. International Ltd., Padstow, Cornwall

This book is printed on acid-free paper

For David

ONE

Pegeen Chehab walked up from the subway in the evening light. Her good spring coat was powder blue; her shoes were black and covered the insteps of her long feet. Her hat was beige with something dark along the crown, a brown feather or two. There was a certain asymmetry to her shoulders. She had a loping, hunchbacked walk. She had, always, a bit of black hair along her cheek, straggling to her shoulder, her bun coming undone. She carried her purse in the lightest clasp of her fingers, down along the side of her leg, which made her seem listless and weary even as she covered the distance quickly enough, the gray sidewalk from subway to parlor floor and basement of the house next door.

I was on the stoop of my own house, waiting for my father. Pegeen paused to say hello.

She was not a pretty girl particularly; there was a narrowness to her eyes and a wideness to her jaw, crooked teeth, wild eyebrows, and a faint mustache. She had her Syrian father's thick dark hair, but also the permanent scattered flush, just under the fair skin, of her Irish mother's broad cheeks. She had a job in lower Manhattan in this, her first year out of Manual Training, and, she said, she didn't like the people there. She didn't like a single one of them. She ran a bare hand along the stone balustrade above my head. The other, which lightly held the strap of her purse, wore a dove-gray glove. She'd lost its partner somewhere, she said. And laughed with her crooked teeth. Fourth pair this month, she said.

And left the library book she was reading on the subway yesterday.

And look, tore her stocking on something.

She lifted her black shoe to the step where I sat and pulled back the long coat and the skirt. I saw the laddered run, the flesh of Pegeen's thin and dark-haired calf pressing through between each rung. The nail of the finger Pegeen ran over its length was bitten down to nothing, but the movement of her hand along the tear was gentle and conciliatory. A kind of sympathy for her own flesh, which I imitated, brushing my own hand along the unbroken silk of Pegeen's stocking, and then over the torn threads of the run.

'Amadán,' Pegeen said. 'That's me. That's what I am.'

She pulled the leg away. The skirt and the blue coat fell into place again. Across the back hem and up the left side of Pegeen's good spring coat there was a long smudge of soot that I impulsively reached out to brush away. 'You've got some dirt,' I said.

Pegeen turned, twisted her chin around, arm and elbow raised, trying to see what she couldn't see because it was behind her. 'Where?' she said.

'Here.' I batted at the dirt until Pegeen threw back her head in elaborate frustration, pulling the coat forward, winding it around her like a cloak. 'I'll be happy,' she said, slapping at her hip, 'to stop going to that filthy place.' Meaning

4

lower Manhattan, where she worked.

She paused, put her nose to the air in mock confidence. 'I'll get a boyfriend,' she said. She batted her eyelashes and drew out a sly smile. They were great kidders, the Chehabs, and no boyfriends, it seemed, had yet called for Pegeen. 'I'll get myself married,' she said, and then licked all at once the four tall fingers of the gloveless hand and swatted them against the dirty cloth.

'Amadán,' she said again. Which, she explained, was her mother's word for fool.

And then she released the skirt of her long coat and, dipping her shoulders, shook herself back into it again. She reminded me of a bird taking a sand bath. 'I fell down,' she announced. She said it in the same fond and impatient tone she had used to describe the lost glove, the forgotten library book. 'On the subway.' It was the tone a mother might use, speaking about a favorite, unruly child.

Pegeen blew some exasperated air through her pooched-out lower lip. 'I don't know what the blazes makes me fall,' she said impatiently. 'I do it all the time.' She suddenly squinted and the flush just under her downy skin rose to a deep maroon. She lowered her face to mine. 'Don't you dare tell my mother,' she said.

I was seven years old. I spoke mostly to my parents. To my brother. To my teachers when I had to. I gave some whispered response to Father Quinn or to Mr. Lee at the candy store when my mother poked me in the ribs. I could not imagine having a conversation with Mrs. Chehab, who was red-haired and very tall. Still, I

5

promised. I would say nothing.

Pegeen shook herself again, standing back and lifting her shoulders inside the pale blue coat. 'But there's always someone nice,' she said, her voice suddenly gone singsong. 'Someone always helps me up.' She struck another pose, coy and haughty, as before, her chin in the air. She touched the feather in her hat. 'Today a very handsome man gave me his hand. He asked if I was all right. A real Prince Charming.' She smiled again and looked around. Just a few doors down, the older boys were playing stickball in the street. There was a knot of younger ones on the curb, watching. Bill Corrigan was in his chair on the sidewalk just behind them.

Pegeen leaned forward once more. 'Tomorrow,' she said breathlessly, whispering now, 'I'm going to look for him again. If I see him, I'm going to get real close.' She leaned down, her hand on the banister above my head. 'I'm going to *pretend* to fall, see? Right next to him. And he'll catch me and say, 'Is it you again?''

All human eyes are beautiful, but Pegeen's were very black and heavily lashed and gorgeous now, with the sparkle of her joke, or her plan, or, perhaps, her vision of some impossible future.

She straightened up. 'We'll see what happens then,' she said, sly and confident, her thick eyebrows raised. She swung her purse slowly, turned to move on. 'That will be something to see,' she said.

At her own house, Pegeen didn't use the basement door, as usual. She climbed the stone steps, taking them one at a time, like a small

6

child. At the top, she paused again to swat at the back of her coat, only touching the dirt with her wrist. It was early evening. Spring. I could see Pegeen's reflection in the oval glass of the outer door — or at least the blue heart of the reflection, which was both the reflection of her good spring coat and the evening light on her flushed face. Pegeen pulled open the door and the thin image in the glass shuddered like a flame.

I turned back to the vigil I was keeping on the stone steps. Vigil for my father, who had not yet come up from the subway.

From the far corner, the neighborhood's men and working women were coming home. Everyone wore hats. Everyone wore trim dark shoes, which was where my eyes fell when any of them said, 'Hello, Marie,' passing by.

At seven, I was a shy child, and comical-looking, with a round flat face and black slits for eyes, thick glasses, black bangs, a straight and serious mouth — a little girl cartoon.

With my heart pinned to my father's sleeve in those days.

The boys were playing stickball down the street. Always at this time of day. Some of them friends of Gabe, my brother, although he, young scholar, remained inside at his books. The younger boys were lined at the curb, watching the game, Walter Hartnett among them. He had his cap turned backward and the leg with the built-up shoe extended before him. Blind Bill Corrigan, who had been gassed in the war, was on the sidewalk just behind Walter, sitting in the

7

painted kitchen chair that his mother set out for him every morning when the weather was fine.

Bill Corrigan wore a business suit and polished shoes, and although there was a glitch in the skin around his eyes, a scarred shine in the satiny folds of his eyelids, although he was brought to the kitchen chair every afternoon when the weather was fine by his mother, whose arm he held the way a bride holds the arm of a groom, it was to him that the boys in the street appealed whenever a dropped ball or an untimely tag sent both teams, howling and cawing, to his side of the street. They were there now: shouting into one another's face, throwing their caps on the ground, and begging Bill Corrigan to make the call. He raised one of his big, pale hands, and suddenly half the boys spun around, the other half cheered. Walter Hartnett rocked backward in despair, raising his good foot into the air.

I pushed my glasses back on my nose. Small city birds the color of ashes rose and fell along the rooftops. In the fading evening light, the stoop beneath my thighs, as warm as breath when I first sat down, now exhaled a shallow chill. Mr. Chehab walked by with a brown bag from the bakery in his hand. He had his white apron balled up beneath his arm, the ties trailing. There was the scent of new-baked bread as he passed. Big Lucy, a girl I feared, pushed a scooter along the opposite sidewalk. Two Sisters of Charity from the convent down the street passed by, smiling from inside their bonnets. I turned my head to watch their backs, wondering always why their long hems never caught at their heels. At the end of the block, the Sisters paused to greet a heavy woman with thick, pale legs and a dark apron under her coat. She said something to them that made them nod. Then the three turned the corner together. The game paused again, and the boys parted reluctantly as a black car drove by.

I shivered and waited, little Marie. Sole survivor, now, of that street scene. Waited for the first sighting of my father, coming up from the subway in his hat and coat, most beloved among all those ghosts.

★ ★ ★

Once, I stepped up to the glass case in the delicatessen in Rego Park, ready to call out my order. I was pregnant with my first child, hungry, a little light-headed. In a few months' time, I would be at death's door, last rites and all — my mother swinging her purse at the head of the priest who came to deliver them — but on this day there was only a sudden rupture behind my eyes. I fell without knowing I fell, like a sack of potatoes. And then I was faceup on the wooden floor. My legs were turned beneath me. There was an ache along the fleshy edge of my palm. Faces above me. More pain dawning, in my ankle, at the back of my skull. There was tuna salad on my hand and on my elbow and on the edge of my spring coat, where I had caught somebody's order going down. I saw only the aproned bosom of the owner's wife as I was lifted and led to a chair in the back room. There was sawdust on the floor and brown towers of damp cardboard boxes along one wall. A strong smell of salami. They sat me down in a metal folding chair that was the same color as the cardboard boxes, before a flimsy card table scored with tape. There was the slow reconstruction of what had happened. A policeman appeared, offered a trip to the emergency room, although the consensus among the other women crowded into the narrow doorway was that the slow sipping from a warm bottle of Coke would revive me. Which it did. And then the roast beef on rye I had been about to order, which the owner's German wife watched me eat in the crowded back room — the meat piled thickly and as tender as butter — until the women were satisfied enough to declare, No harm done. The owner's wife gave me a container of chicken soup and a quart of rice pudding to take home. She was a broad, solid woman with thick arms and legs. She swiped vigorously at the stain on my coat with a wad of dampened paper towel, and I remembered Pegeen then: There's always someone nice.

* * *

My father appeared at the corner. Paused for his evening paper. Topcoat and hat to mark him as a clerk, not a laborer. I only raised my head above my knees when I saw him — although surely something, some sinewy energy, some delight, tensed and trembled itself through my thin back

10

and shoulders as I gazed down the sloping street. The boys playing stickball parted once again for a passing car: it was the ebb and flow of their game. I turned away from them, raised a hand to the balustrade to get ready to spring. My father was a thin, slight man in a long coat. His step was quick and jaunty. He, too, wore shoes with a high shine.

I waited until he was halfway toward home. And then I flew, across the sidewalk and into the air as he lifted me — the newspaper held tightly under his arm the only impediment, it seemed, to an ascent that I saw in my own imagination as equivalent, somehow, to the caps the boys had thrown into the air when Bill Corrigan made his call. I would not have been surprised to hear them cheer.

My father smelled, always, of fresh newsprint and cigarettes, of the alcohol in his faded cologne. I caught my chin on his buttons as he lowered me to the ground. A brief, painful scrape that upset my glasses and made my eyes water. I walked the last few paces home balanced on his shoes. We climbed the steps together and into the fragrant vestibule — fragrant with the onion odor of cooked dinners and the brownstone scent of old wood — and up the narrow stairs and into the apartment, where my mother was in the kitchen and my brother at the dining-room table with his books.

The apartment we lived in was long and narrow, with windows in the front and in the back. The back caught the morning light and the front the slow, orange hours of the afternoon

11

and evening. Even at this cool hour in late spring, it was a dusty, city light. It fell on paint-polished window seats and pink carpet roses. It stamped the looming plaster walls with shadowed cross-bars, long rectangles; it fit itself through the bedroom door, crossed the living room, climbed the sturdy legs of the formidable dining-room chairs, and was laid out now on the dining-room table where the cloth — starched linen expertly decorated with my mother's meticulous cross-stitch — had been carefully folded back along the whole length so that Gabe could place his school blotter and his books on the smooth wood.

It was the first light my poor eyes ever knew. Recalling it, I sometimes wonder if all the faith and all the fancy, all the fear, the speculation, all the wild imaginings that go into the study of heaven and hell, don't shortchange, after all, that other, earlier uncertainty: the darkness before the slow coming to awareness of the first light.

★ ★ ★

I followed my father to the narrow closet and held the newspaper for him while he hung up his overcoat and placed his hat on the shelf. He went to the couch in the living room and I went with him, fitting myself into his side, leaning heavily against his arm — 'like a barnacle,' he said — as he read the evening paper.

The slipcover, also my mother's handiwork, was a paradise of hummingbirds and vines and deep-throated flowers, the colors, if not the

12

images, subdued by the thick brocade. Sinking into my father's side, slipping under his arm as he patiently lifted the open paper to accommodate me, I entered that paradise via my tracing fingertip and squinted eyes, until he said, 'Marie,' patiently, and asked me to sit up a bit.

He kept a long key chain attached to his belt, and perhaps to keep my bony weight from putting his arm to sleep, he pulled the keys at the end of it out of his pocket and placed them in my hands. There were two keys, small but heavy, and the metal disks with his embossed name and number from his time in the army, as well as a small St. Joseph medal tinged with green. I turned them over as he read, traced them with my fingers, tested the weight and the jingle of them. I wondered if Bill Corrigan, who had been gassed in the war, carried something of the same in his pocket.

When my mother called to me to get up and set the table, my father put his hand to the top of my head.

★   ★   ★

Slipping out of that first darkness, into the dusty, city light of these rooms, I met the blurred faces of the parents I'd been given — given through no merit of my own — faces that even to my defective eyes, ill-formed, you might say, in the hours of that first darkness, were astonished by love.

★   ★   ★

We gathered for dinner, a piece of oilcloth spread across the table now, on an ordinary night — the last concession to my sloppy childhood, because in another few weeks, after my First Communion, we would abandon the oilcloth cover at meals and once again dine on starched linen, like civilized people, as my father put it. Mashed potatoes and slices of beef tongue and carrots boiled with sugar. Canned peaches with a tablespoon of heavy cream. Then the cloth was folded back again, and once again my brother spread his blotter and his books across the cleared end of the long table.

In the narrow kitchen, standing over the steaming sink, her hands red to the elbow, my mother was unconcerned. 'Pegeen Chehab,' she said, 'has big feet.' And girls that age, she said, were always tripping over themselves, looking for boys.

She handed me a wet saucer. I was not yet allowed to dry the dinner plates. The kitchen was warm and close, the one window was steamed, and the pleasant scent in the air was of soap and of the spring sunshine that had dried my mother's apron.

For my mother, who loved romance — especially an American romance, which involved, for her, a miraculous commingling of lives across comically disparate portions of the globe — the marriage of Mr. and Mrs. Chehab was a continual source of wonder and delight. She told the story again: The place where Mr. Chehab was born was called Mount Lebanon, in a country called Syria. A desert, she said. With a

14

desperately hot sun and palm trees and dates and pineapples and sand and — she shrugged a little, her voice suddenly uncertain — a mount, apparently.

She handed me a small drinking glass and said, 'Be sure you don't put your hand inside, just the cloth.'

His own parents, she said, wrapped him in swaddling clothes and carried him away from that sunny place. They crossed over the Mediterranean Sea. They scaled Spain.

She squinted at the damp tiles above the sink as if a map were drawn there.

They climbed through France, reached Paris, which is called the City of Light, crossed the White Cliffs of Dover — there is a song — got to Liverpool, no doubt, to Dublin, found Cork, as she herself had done when she was seventeen, wearing three skirts and four blouses and carrying only a purse so her stepfather, a terrible man, would not know she was leaving home.

At the harbor, Mr. and Mrs. Chehab found a ship that brought them to Brooklyn. In Brooklyn, they put the baby into a cradle, in the cool corner of a basement bakery on Joralemon Street.

And all the while, my mother said — a trill of profound amusement rising into her voice — in County Clare, Mrs. Chehab — who was a McMahon then — was taking her own first breaths. And shivering, no doubt, in the eternal dampness of that bleak country's bitter air.

My mother looked at me from over her shoulder, her hands still in the sink.

There's a burned taste to the air at home, she said — not for the first time. A taste of wet ashes and doused fire. It can make you believe, she said, that you live in the permanent aftermath of some nearby sorrow. Somewhere in the vicinity, you're always thinking, someone's house has recently burned to the ground.

In that damp and dirty country, my mother said, Mrs. Chehab grew to be a tall girl, a girl who would have no trouble getting up the steep gangplank that led from the dock at Queenstown — a climb my mother herself had struggled with, she said, because of the rain that fell on the day she sailed, because she was alone, with no man's arm to hold on to and none offered across the whole trip, not until my father gave her his on the steps at the Grand Army Plaza.

But Mrs. Chehab would have had no trouble keeping those long feet steady against the slick and pitching floor of the ship that carried her here. Where she stopped at the Syrian bakery one day and saw a small, dark-eyed man behind the counter.

I watched my mother move her hands through the water once more, searching for stray silverware, smiling her sly smile at the delightful oddity of it all. Then she pulled the stopper from the sink, and I closed my eyes and put my fingers in my ears to block out the terrible sound.

When I removed them and opened my eyes, my mother was swabbing the counter. 'And after all that,' she said, 'and after all that, along comes homely Pegeen, with her mother's blotched skin and her father's big nose and those great long feet, God help her.'

★ ★ ★

When the dishes were put away, my father went to the narrow closet for his hat and said, 'Let's take a stroll.'

We went down the stairs together. Shined black tips of his neat shoes and perfect fall of his trouser cuffs over the smooth laces. A lilt in the tap of his step on the uncarpeted stair, the tap of our steps. Out through the vestibule and onto the sidewalk again. We were in front of the Chehabs' building when he dropped my hand and paused to light a cigarette, the smoke rising white from under the bowed brim of his hat. And then he threw his head back with the pleasure of that first exhalation of smoke. Made me look up as well to see the stars. A thin handsome man, forty years old.

It was one of his shanty cousins, the McGeevers, who would later say that a body so thin was nothing more than a walking invitation to misfortune.

★ ★ ★

He took my hand again. There was the sure familiarity of his grip, warm and firm, the palm broad against my small fingers. We walked to the other corner, away from the subway, although there was still the sound of it somewhere beneath our feet. There was as well the sound of a trolley

17

on another street, the sound of someone calling to a child, someone shouting inside a building. Lights at windows were growing brighter, growing warmer, it seemed, as the air grew cold. There was the scent of metal, whiff of tar, of stone, of dog droppings left beside the wrought-iron cage that surrounded a scrawny tree. The soft gabardine of my father's suit jacket against the back of my hand. At the corner, we turned and he tossed the glowing cigarette into the street.

'I'll be only a minute,' he said. He put his two hands on my shoulders, as if to place me more securely on the sidewalk before another stoop, and then turned to push through a narrow iron fence that led down a dim alley. The air was black, but the lights in the buildings were warm and golden. Only a few people went by, their coats drawn around them. One man touched his hand to the brim of his hat as he passed and I dropped my chin shyly. And then rose up on my toes after he'd gone, putting my face to the streetlight as if to a warm sun. I squinted, and the light burst and stretched itself yellow and white into the darkness. I heard the squeal of the iron gate and my father was beside me again, the sharp smell of the drink he'd just had in the air about him. He held out his hand. In the center of his palm there was a white cube of sugar, sparkling in the light. I plucked it up and slipped it into my mouth. I turned it with my tongue. Watching, my father pursed his lips and shifted his jaw, as if he, too, felt the sugar on his teeth. Then he took my hand again.

18

* * *

We passed the Chehabs' parlor window, where there was a lamp and a chair and the back of Mr. Chehab's dark head and broad shoulders as he smoked a cigar and read the evening news.

* * *

In the vestibule, my father shot back his cuffs and put his warm palms to my face. He studied me seriously, smiling only a little — I was a round-faced, narrow-eyed, homely, comical little thing — until my cheeks were warm enough, he said, to pass muster with my mother. And we climbed the stairs once more.

There was tea, with a slice of plain cake, while my mother, with one of his schoolbooks in her lap, put my brother through his paces: catechism questions, Latin declensions, history's dates and names. He answered all without hesitation, breaking off pieces of the cake only after he had finished a round. And then, with a jagged line of cake still left on his plate and half his milky tea still in his cup, he pushed back his chair and walked slowly to the far end of the table.

My father, at the opposite end, moved his own cup aside and leaned forward. I could see the reflection of his pale throat and chin in the table's dark wood, like a face just beginning to appear in a still pool of black water. Or disappear. 'What will we have tonight?' he said.

My brother ran his hands over his thick hair and then rested them both on the back of the

19

chair that was before him. He lifted his eyes to the wall just above my father's head. He was a handsome boy with narrow shoulders and fair hair and large brown eyes. He flushed easily. ''The Seven Ages of Man,'' he said clearly, gripping the chair. 'By William Shakespeare.'

He began. As Gabe recited, I watched my father vaguely shape his mouth around the words, unconsciously moving his lips in much the same way he had done when I turned the sugar cube on my tongue.

My mother kept her head bowed, studying her red hands in her lap while the poem wound on, looking like a woman at prayer, or hunched beside a radio.

I lowered my chin toward the table, raised my cup only briefly from its saucer. What tea was left was growing cold, but that was how I liked it. I took a small sip and then replaced the cup with more noise than was polite, which would have earned me a sharp look from my mother had the sound not coincided with the end of the poem and my parents' gentle applause.

'Some Shelley,' my father said.

My friend Gerty Hanson was made to say the Rosary with her family every night after dinner, her mother and father and all three of her big brothers kneeling on the floor around the parents' bed. I had joined them once or twice, a ritual no less tedious than this, although Gerty, at least, was given the chance to lead the prayer every fifth decade, the chance to speak out into an attentive silence — whereas here I was meant only to listen to my brother, who had won the elocution medal at his school for what seemed to me more years than I could number.

Gabe raised his eyes and directed his voice to the simple chandelier above our heads. It was new to my ears, his voice, both deeper and somehow less certain than it had been just days ago. I watched the protruding Adam's apple bob in his pale throat. ''Ode to the West Wind,'' he said. 'By Percy Blithe Shelley.'

My parents might have seen the priest in him then, the way he stood at the end of the table, offered up the lovely words.

I saw only, in my mind's eye, a picture book illustration I had found somewhere, of a cruel face in the clouds, bloated cheeks and pursed lips that blew down upon the huddled figure of a man in a great dark overcoat.

''Oh, hear!'' my brother said, reciting, and then hesitated for a moment before he abruptly lifted a palm to the ceiling — a gesture he might have been instructed to make, at school, perhaps, although it did not suit him or his steady voice.

Without raising my chin, I looked around. Gabe had left half the cake on his plate. I knew he would eat it in a single, triumphant bite when he returned to his chair. My father's slice was already gone. As was my mother's. I looked at my own plate again, knowing full well I hadn't left a crumb, and was surprised to discover there, in its center, another white sugar cube. I looked to my father, who only shifted his eyes briefly and briefly smiled. I looked to my mother, who was still studying the ruddy hands cupped in her lap, the thin gold band of her

21

wedding ring. I snatched up the cube of sugar and quickly dropped it into the cooling dregs of my tea. My father whispered the last words of the poem as my brother recited them, and then, once more, my parents were quietly applauding.

My brother said, ''Ozymandias,'' as I lifted my teacup again. I felt my mother's finger against my thigh, a quick poke to remind me to listen.

I listened, my eye on the lovely, tea-soaked dregs of sugar at the bottom of the china cup. I imagined it was the very same sweet, silver sand mentioned in the poem, desert sand, sand of Syria and Mount Lebanon. I watched with one eye squinted as the lovely stuff moved slowly across the ivory light, advanced sluggishly toward my tongue, and then, when it was too slow, the tip of my finger. I was thinking of a baby wrapped in sparkling clothes, being pushed slowly in a white carriage, slowly through the city of light, toward Brooklyn, when I felt the sting of a slap against the back of my head and then its quick echo of pain. I pulled my finger from the cup. My mother hadn't raised her eyes from her lap.

Gabe finished the poem and returned to his place at the table to drink down the cold tea and devour whole the bit of cake, his face flushed with his triumph. Patiently, my mother turned to me to ask what would happen if a teacup shattered while my fingers were inside it.

Some neighbor or faceless relation was named, a silly girl who'd 'sliced herself good' with her hand inside a glass while she was washing up. A suggested image of soapy dishwater darkened with blood following me to the bath, where I watched my mother's blurred red hand as it tested the seamless stream of steaming water.

I deployed all my excuses in a rush: the water was too hot, the house too cold, I'd had a bath last week, I had a stomachache, I was sleepy. But my mother had a grip on my arm, and my thin legs were all obedience. They raised themselves against my will, up over the cold rim of the high tub and into the steaming water, where the pain from the heat became a chill in my spine and my thin body — bright red to my calves but pale white, nearly blue, through my chest and my arms — became no more than a scrap of cloth, a scrap of cloth caught and shaken and snapped by a sudden wind. I wanted to weep. I wanted to be sick. I saw for a terrible moment that my body was a scrap of cloth, that my bones were no more than porcelain, as were my rattling teeth and the china skull that contained them. I saw how a hoop of light, the water's shifting reflection, swung up to the top of the tile wall, and then swung down again, carrying me with it, nauseous and full of despair. I sat. The warm water covered my arms and touched my chin. My mother let go of my forearm, although the imprint of her grip lingered.

There, she said. There now. After all your fussing. You just have to get used to it.

★　★　★

In those days I still slept in the crib that had been my brother's, in a corner of the small room

I shared with him. A peeling lamb painted on the headboard, a blurred line of grass and meadow flowers at the foot. Low light. Prayers. My parents' dry lips to my forehead and some single, barely whispered word at the end of the day that told me I was cherished above all things by these indistinct and warm-breathed shadows, leaning over me at the end of the day.

Gabe came in sometime later. Another blur of darkness and light — dark clothes and fair hair — coming in to take the pajamas out from under his pillow. When he returned, he was a brighter blur because he was dressed in them. Through the bars of the crib, I watched him kneel to say his prayers and then pull down his covers and climb into bed. He slept on his back, a wrist over his eyes, like another picture book illustration I had seen, of a laborer resting in a field. The light stayed on most of the night, and this gesture, his wrist thrown over his eyes, was his silent accommodation to my fear of the dark.

I woke to find the light had been put out. There were only the soft-edged, geometric patches of streetlight on the ceiling, across one wall. I threw a leg over the side of the crib, fitting my toe into the space between the bars, and carefully — I was not an athletic child — leaned to bring the other over. I lowered myself to the cold floor and then crossed it on tiptoe. Gabe opened his blankets for me in the same way he did everything: quietly, methodically, with a good-natured but stoic acquiescence to duty. A dutiful child. Wakeful himself at that hour.

I told him I'd had a bad dream, making it up

24

as I went along: a terrible, white-fisted giant with swollen cheeks had carried me to a high, precarious place I could not climb down from, and Gabe listened carefully, commiserating briefly, marveling appreciatively each time I whispered, 'And then,' adding another horror. He said, I never dream. I never have a dream that I remember. His features were a blur, although our faces were only inches apart. And yet the handsome, high-colored, precisely featured boy who was my brother during the day, the brother I saw with my glasses on, was far less familiar to me than this one of uncertain edges and soft darkness, with a spark of wet light in his mouth or his eye when he said that if I was good and didn't kick, I could stay. I made my promises, and he accepted them, but he moved anyway to the far side of the narrow bed, all the way up to the wall — the wall we shared with the Chehabs' building — turning his back to me and putting his hand on the cool plaster. The soft sheets retained their odor of sunshine against the warmer, closer scent of my brother's scalp and breath and skin. With his back turned, he told me to say a prayer to keep the nightmares away. He said if I prayed, the Blessed Mother would keep the nightmares away.

Slowly, I moved my hand under his pillow until I made warm contact with his own. He was holding his rosary. He moved his hand away until my fingertips touched only the cool beads.

He fell asleep in small starts, resisting it. As if, I imagined, the sandman had hold of his ankle and was slowly tugging him under, all against his

will. As if he struggled to remain awake. I looked at the lozenges of light on the wall, one was a rectangle, one was a crucifix. I tried out a few prayers, but since the nightmare I had described was a lie, there was nothing, really, to ask protection from. I heard my brother's knee or his hand or the ball of his foot strike the wall now and again as he was tugged under. A thump and then a thump, and then I knew he was sleeping.

In the morning, the ambulance at the curb gave up a hot breath. Children had gathered, women with coats over their shoulders, men in shirtsleeves. Across the street, curtains were drawn aside, there were faces at windows, one of them ghoulish with shaving cream. First a murmur among the crowd: women with their fingers to their lips or their hands to their hearts, men conferring softly. Then, as the minutes ticked by, the revving excitement, the pleasure of something happening that would distinguish the ordinary day: the thrill of the disrupted routine, of a dull breakfast left on the table, of schoolbooks still at the door. An excitement that sounded first in the children's voices — a sudden laugh, a loud cry — but then infected the grownups as well — a sneeze and a cheery 'God bless,' another trill of laughter — as if we had forgotten, for a minute, that some kind of crisis, some crisis at the Chehabs', had gathered us all here on the damp sidewalk at 7:00 a.m.

And then the ambulance man backing through the basement door, and then the suddenly arrested sound of human chatter gave way at once to the collective intake of breath when those assembled on the sidewalk saw that the stretcher contained a body covered from toe to head — only a slip of Pegeen's sloppy hair showing beneath.

27

From the opened door behind the second ambulance man, Mrs. Chehab's cry was a spiraling wail. Most of the women, and many of the men in the street, blessed themselves. My mother put a rough hand to my shoulder and then pulled my face into her apron, which was still a little damp from last night's washing up. All instinct, I shut my eyes and wrapped my arms around my mother's waist, gripping the apron, the rough wool of her skirt, nestling into that familiar darkness and feeling the sudden warmth of my brother's two hands as he pressed them against my ears, trying to spare me the sound of the women's prayers and exclamations, of Mrs. Chehab's lament, of the slam and the slam again of the ambulance's broad doors.

All of which, nevertheless, I heard.

*　*　*

It was the next evening that we walked in solemn stillness up the steps of the Chehabs' house and into the crowded living room. It was painful, the way my mother gripped my hand as we made our way through that forest of adults, all red knuckles, for me, and wedding bands and the hems of jackets, until the figures suddenly parted and there before the glass of the bay window was the gleaming box and Pegeen in its satin bed. She wore her white graduation dress, and her red confirmation rosary was threaded through her still fingers. There was a single taper beside Pegeen's head, its light reflected in the black window in such a way that, for a moment, I

28

believed her thin and waxy nose now bore its own flame.

I felt a pair of large hands slip themselves under my arms, warm and strong. And then I was aloft. The light grew brighter and the darkness fell away. I clutched the hard edge of the box, resisting even as I gave in, put my face to the moon-colored brightness of Pegeen's cheeks, kissed her, and then saw my own white face briefly reflected in the dark glass of the bay window as I was returned once more to the pooled shadows of the floor.

At home, my mother unpinned her hat and my father returned his fedora and his topcoat to the closet. Mrs. Chehab, they were saying, had noticed the dirt on Pegeen's coat and the tears in her sleeves, circles of soot on the knees of her good stockings, well before yesterday's last tumble down the basement stair. Pegeen had always been a clumsy girl, they said, although Fagin, the undertaker, suspected something more than the fall had killed her: Some burden in the brain, he had said.

My mother turned back the good tablecloth and my brother brought out his books. On this evening, to make up for the time lost on our visit to Pegeen, we had our tea quietly as he studied among us, the only sound in the room the ringing of my father's cup against the saucer, which I imitated with the clanging of my own. The visit to the Chehabs' had deprived us of our evening walk to the speakeasy as well.

And then my brother closed the thick book before him and reached for another from the pile beside his chair, this one worn and leather-bound, with thin pages. He turned them, and then, with his hands tucked under his thighs, bent over the book to read. I saw my parents look to him, to the top of his bowed head. It seemed to me they were watching him slyly, as if, were he to raise his head again, their eyes would dart away.

He began to read out loud. He did not read in the same clear way he recited his poems, but softly, sitting hunched over the table, the words breaking here and there under the burden of his new, thickening voice. ''Are not two sparrows sold for a small coin?'' he read. ''Yet not one of them falls to the ground without your Father's knowledge. Even all the hairs of your head are counted. So do not be afraid; you are worth more than many sparrows.''

My mother's head was bowed. My father's two hands remained folded together over the china cup, arrested in that surreptitious moment of their steadying each other against the trembling that his evening constitutional usually kept at bay. Out on the street, a truck carrying bottles rattled by. One happy voice shouted to another.

Into the silence that followed I said, 'Amadán.'

I said it as Pegeen had said it, ruefully, shaking my head as if speaking fondly of a troublesome child. I said it with my chin just above my own china cup and its dregs of melting sugar, with my eyes veering away from my brother's startled face and down into that ivory light. And then, for good measure, I said it again, into the teacup itself. 'Amadán.'

The pretty room tilted then — folded white tablecloth and black polished wood and the light of the simple chandelier — as my mother, with an iron grip on my upper arm, swung me out of my chair and into the tiled bathroom where the cup was filled beneath the silver stream of warm water and the soap dipped into it, once, then twice. 'Again,' my mother said as I tasted the bitter water and, leaning over the porcelain, spit it out into the sink.

In the dining room, my brother — the scholar — was asking my father what it meant, amadán. My father said, 'A fool. It means someone's a fool.'

Even with the water running, the cup of soapy water at my lips, I could hear my father's shout of laughter when my brother asked him, 'Who is?'

★ ★ ★

They called me 'our little pagan' after that, whenever their pride in my brother's saintliness was in need of some deflating. Self-deflating, as was their way. When the priest from St. Francis came to say there was clearly a vocation. When the letter from the seminary arrived.

'We're not so enamored of the priesthood as some,' my mother said, washing the dishes after the priest had come for tea, blushing with pride, but also holding her lips in such a way that made it clear she was not going to go overboard — as she would have put it — with her delight in Gabe's success. There were just as many men in

31

rectories, she said, who were vain or lazy or stupid as there were in the general population.

'One bishop,' my father joked, his hand to the top of my head, 'and one little pagan. We've run the gamut in just these two.'

I climbed the staircase of Gertrude Hanson's house, my hand on the wide banister. The carpet here was threadbare and there was the familiar odor of dust in the air. What light there was came through the transom above the entrance or filtered down in a single yellow shaft from the dirty skylight four stories up. Gertrude Hanson's apartment was on the third floor. I knocked on the heavy door. The corridor was warm and airless. I heard Mrs. Hanson's voice inside, laughing, and I rose up on my toes.

'Come in, Marie,' Mrs. Hanson called. 'We know it's you.'

Because this was the Saturday-morning routine, Gerty and I being even then the best of best friends. I opened the door and leaned in.

The Hansons' front room was crowded with furniture: the great black dining-room table, eight chairs with tapestry seats, a heavy sideboard, a tea cart, a china cabinet with bowed glass — indication, in those days, of a family's propriety and prosperity. Twice in my recollection I had arrived at Gerty's on a Saturday morning and been startled to find the front room starkly empty, only the lamps still there, the good dishes and the tea set piled in a corner on the bare floor. 'Repossessed' was the word Gerty used with an easy shrug. But on this morning it was all solidly in place, and beyond it I could see

Mrs. Hanson in a wide chair just outside the kitchen entry, her bare feet on a plump hassock, her hands beckoning. 'Come in, come in,' she said. 'Come in and take this poor child out into the fresh air. She's been cooking all morning.'

Mrs. Hanson had always been fleshy, with thick wrists and a broad, round face, but now with her fifth child on the way she was huge in her chair, her feet and ankles swollen, her stomach straining against the flannel of what had been her husband's dressing gown. She had tucked a handkerchief into the collar of the robe, and the bit of lace at its edge, caught between her full breasts, made her look like a woman in an old painting. As if she were a woman in an old painting, she wore her black hair partially pinned up, partially fallen over her shoulders. There was a moist gleam to her white skin, her cheeks and her forehead and her bare arms, as if they reflected some particular light. It occurred to me as I shyly approached that Mrs. Hanson was as beautiful as a woman in a painting, what with her size and her abundance, abundance of breast and hair and damp flesh, of face and feature: big dark eyes and bright teeth and wide, laughing mouth.

'You girls run out and play,' Mrs. Hanson said. She stroked her hard belly. 'Fatty Arbuckle and I will take a little snooze.'

In the small square kitchen, Gerty was drying her hands. She wore a calico apron with the strings wrapped two or three times around her tiny midriff and the hem falling well below her knees. There was the rich odor of her morning's

34

work, which was displayed on the windowsill and on a small table in the corner: a golden chicken that she was just now covering with a clean tea towel, a bowl of white potatoes mixed with celery and parsley, a homely pie, the tinges of the fork that had pierced its pale crust inexpertly spaced, perhaps, but showing anyway, here and there, a golden starburst of juice.

Gerty was boyish and matter-of-fact, easily the smartest girl in class, but also small like me and gap-toothed and thoroughly freckled. She merely shrugged when I whistled my astonishment. 'You cooked all this?'

'She's just learning,' Mrs. Hanson said. 'But she's got the knack. She'll be a great little cook someday. She'll be a great little mother while I'm away.'

Mrs. Hanson had a brogue that made her gulp air — a kind of quiet hiccup that swallowed the end of every sentence. It made her sound as if she were always on the breathless verge of astonishment, or laughter. 'It'll be like dining at the Waldorf,' she said.

Gerty took off her apron and hung it on the old gas jet by the door. A year ago, her poor head had been shaved for lice, but now her dark curls were as thick and wavy as a dried mop. She asked her mother if we could have money for a soda, considering how hard she had been working. Her mother laughed again and sent Gerty to the bedroom for her purse. Alone together for just that moment, Mrs. Hanson reached out and caught my wrist and then drew in her breath with another great gulp. Her legs on the hassock recoiled as the dark blood rose to her face and then just as suddenly drained away. 'My dear,' she whispered. She tugged me closer. I leaned over the thick arm of the chair. Mrs. Hanson smelled of wholesome things, sunshine and oatmeal and yeast, her breath as she gasped was warm and sweet. 'If you'll take Gerty around the corner,' she said, 'you'll just catch Dora Ryan going off to church. Go see. Then have a soda. Keep her out, dear. Keep her out till suppertime.' She gulped another bit of breath. 'Do that for me.'

I turned my head only slightly. I could feel the woman's breath on my face, see the mottled pearl of her teeth. All unaccountably — unless, of course, you count the woman's abundant beauty, the warmth of the small room, the good smells and the laughter and the fresh news that there was a wedding to see today — I suddenly threw my arms around Mrs. Hanson's neck and pressed my lips to the woman's damp and lovely cheek.

'My dear,' Mrs. Hanson said, and touched my back. 'Dearie, dearie,' she said. And then Gerty returned from the bedroom with the coins in her hand and cried, 'What about me?' and skipped to the other side of her mother's chair, aiming her lips, too, toward the woman's face. Suddenly we were both covering Mrs. Hanson with kisses, cheeks, eyebrows, nose, and the corner of her laughing mouth. She embraced us both and we leaned upon the hard belly to keep from falling into each other across her knees. 'You'll smother me,' Mrs. Hanson was saying, and we caught

36

even her dry teeth with our lips. 'You'll have to call Fagin,' she cried, as if with her last breath. 'I'll be killed with affection.' We now had our hands tangled up in Mrs. Hanson's thick hair. It was silky, but more substantial than silk, and we both lifted strands of it to our mouths. Laughing, Mrs. Hanson pushed us upright. 'One of you in my lap is quite enough,' she said, catching her breath, the deep color rising to her face once again, 'and Fatty Arbuckle here has already laid his claim.' She laughed, even as the deep flush rose from her chest to her neck and up into her cheeks. 'Go,' she said, swallowing air.

We traipsed out, down the stairs, arm in arm because we were the best of best friends and there was the happiness of continuing together the sudden, elaborate affection we had showered on Mrs. Hanson. Into the cool street and around the corner, and there already the black car and the crowd of girls, some with small brothers in tow. And then, as if she had been waiting for our breathless arrival, the stirring of white in the vestibule behind the glass, the door pulled open by Dora Ryan's stout mother in hat and gloves and a new blue suit, with a trembling orchid on her shoulder. And then Dora herself in her wedding dress and her white shoes, her old father beside her — for Dora was not a young bride, perhaps thirty or so, a third-grade teacher at a distant public school, square-shouldered and broad-faced, but lovely anyway, today, in her wedding dress, satin and lace and white stockings and white shoes, with only a small veil to catch what breeze there was. Her brother followed and a sister in a pink gown. The family paused at the top of the steps while a photographer crouched before them, then all swept down to the sidewalk and into the waiting car, each of us gazing silently until Gerty called out, 'Good luck, Dora!' and all the other children echoed her call. Dora Ryan waved like a queen from behind our own reflections in the car window.

It was then, as the car pulled away from the curb, that I saw Big Lucy on the other side of the street. She was mouth-breathing, holding her scooter between her red knees, the handlebar pressed harshly into her little-girl skirt. Her careening eyes fell briefly on me and I felt the bright day flatten out and grow still. Then Lucy mounted her scooter, bounced it over the curb, and took off after the wedding car, propelled by one broad white leg that seemed as solid and pale as the concrete sidewalk itself. The words she brayed were some variation of Gerty's happy salutation, 'Good luck, good luck,' but made to sound angry, even threatening, in Lucy's harsh, beseeching voice. Some of the girls put their hands over their mouths, their eyes wide. Some laughed wickedly.

And yet just as she was about to turn the corner — about to sail out of the neighborhood forever, out of the neighborhood and into an institution, because what could her poor family do with Lucy's suddenly outsized female body, her crude and childish mind, her fits of violence — I saw Big Lucy lift her leg behind her and let it hover there with a ballerina's grace.

38

By the time we reached the church, the wedding
had begun. We could hear the muffled organ
notes behind the closed doors. Lucy was
nowhere to be seen. We lined ourselves along the
curb where the hired car sat, now cool and silent.
The driver leaned against the hood, smoking
cigarettes and reading the newspaper. When the
church doors were opened again — the sound of
the organ spilling out toward us like ocean water
— we stood and brushed at the backs of our
skirts. I had expected the bride and the groom to
be the first to appear in the dark doorway, but
instead the wedding guests came out, singly and
in couples, coming down the church steps
tentatively, squinting into the sun. A man in a
suit approached us and, with a cigarette caught
in the corner of his mouth, demonstrated how he
wanted us to cup our hands: the left under the
right and the right curled into a small funnel.
Then he took a fat paper bag from his suit
pocket and poured a small stream of rice into
each curled fist. He was a smiling, joking,
wine-colored young man, made the more
charming for me by the unmistakable smell of
drink on his breath, a lovely, masculine scent, I
thought, because it was my father's.

When the sidewalk in front of the church and
the border of the church steps were filled with
wedding guests, Dora and her new husband
finally appeared. In the sunlight, and with the
perfumed crowd all around us, it was difficult to
tell if the groom was handsome. He was chubby

and squarely built in his dark suit, much like Dora herself, but he raised his free arm as he and Dora came down the steps, shielding both of them from the onslaught of rice, so it was only after they had gained the safety of the hired car and he had taken his bride's elbow to help her in that we briefly saw his face. It was a disappointment: round and smooth-cheeked, with little chin and a small mouth stretched into what was, even to our eyes, an awkward smile. He ducked into the car beside his bride and gave us only his profile, which was not promising, as the car drove away.

I turned to Gerty, and Gerty shrugged. Even without Big Lucy there, something fell away from the morning, some sparkle.

★ ★ ★

At home, my mother drew in the air between her teeth when I told her how Big Lucy had shouted after the car. She blessed herself and looked around and said, 'No good can come from that,' and then repeated the gesture and the look the next morning in church when Dora Ryan appeared between her brother and her sister, the mother and father right behind her, the dark veil of her hat pulled over her broad face. Father Quinn could not have had the attention of a single woman in his congregation on that morning, for even as they genuflected, blessed themselves, bowed their heads to pray, their eyes were drawn to Dora's gently quaking shoulders, her parents' stiff spines. My mother said later that it was possible that the groom was a lapsed Catholic, or that he was sleeping off the night's festivities, or that Dora had simply come home to catch Sunday-morning Mass with her parents before heading out on her wedding trip. It was possible, but the girl's posture, her parents' grim faces, told us otherwise. When Mass was over, the family left as they had come, the girl (who was no girl, really, well into her thirties by then, broad-bottomed, thick-ankled, and in her dark suit and hat without any of the dreamy girlishness that her wedding gown had lent her just the morning before) flanked by her parents now, her siblings trailing, but none of them pausing for the crowd outside the church, going instead — 'pell-mell' was how my mother put it, discussing this strange development over break-fast at home — out of the church and across the sidewalk and around the block.

My father said the poor fellow wouldn't be the first groom to find himself under the weather the morning after the big day, not to mention the big night, and winked at Gabe, who smiled and nodded to show he understood, but then looked at my mother and blushed solemnly.

My mother's eyes bounced from Gabe to me to my father, and then with more speed, and more intention, to me again and back to my father. 'Nonsense,' she said, and raised her chin and pinched her nostrils, once, twice, as was her way. As if somewhere in the vicinity, some scent of tragedy, as yet undefined, still lingered. 'My heart went out to Dora Ryan this morning,' she

41

said, looking over her shoulder to the kitchen that was filled with morning light. 'It really did.'

* * *

On Monday, Gerty was not in school, and when I walked by her house on the way home, a large lady was sitting on the steps. She wore an apron and scuffed black shoes and her stockings were rolled down around her mottled ankles like circlets of excess flesh. She was cooling herself with a feathered fan, although the day was mild and damp. The woman fastened her eyes on me as I approached, and in shyness, I veered away, crossed the street, kept walking. I went around the corner and would have gone on home except that just as I reached my own house, I was filled with the pleasant conviction that the strange woman on the steps had gone inside and the way was now cleared. I resolved to try again. The boys in the street hadn't started their after-school game yet, although some were already gathered around Bill Corrigan in his chair. One was swinging a broomstick, Walter Hartnett was tossing a pink Spaldeen up into the air. Mrs. Chehab was leaning out of her parlor window, rubbing the outside of the glass with a piece of newspaper. She looked over her shoulder and called, 'You've missed your house, Mary dear. You've walked right past it.' There was no reason for me to lie to the woman — the poor woman, as she was still called, three years after Pegeen fell down the stairs — but I felt, nevertheless, an urgent sense to do so. 'I'm just going back to school,' I said vaguely. 'I forgot to remember something.' There was the smell of vinegar from the doused newspaper. 'I just remembered that I forgot something.'

Mrs. Chehab laughed, with her daughter's crooked teeth in her mouth. 'Never good to forget to remember,' she said. 'Always better to remember you forgot.'

I bowed my head and hurried on, walking in a suddenly clipped and urgent way that I thought would nicely match my lie.

★ ★ ★

At Gerty's house, sure enough, the stoop was empty, and a kind of confidence in my own prescience made me take the steps two at a time. But no sooner had I gotten into the gloomy brown light of the vestibule than I saw that the fat woman was now sitting on the inside stair, halfway up, tilted over a bit to lean against the banister. There would be no getting by her without first saying, Excuse me please. But neither could I turn around, with the woman looking down at me, and dart out the door. All reluctance, I put my hand to the rail and my foot on the first step, simply because I didn't know what else to do.

From above me the woman said, 'You don't live here, do ye? I saw you pass by before.' She had a voice like a man's, deep and smoky, with a brogue — if that's what it was — that was thicker even than the accents of the McGeevers, my father's cousins, who spoke Irish to him when they came for their interminable Sunday visits and, through their narrow mouths, an unintelligible English to me. 'I thought you were coming up then, but you went on,' the woman said. She leaned away from the banister, straightened her back somewhat wearily, as if the conversation were a task she had been putting off until now. She touched one hand to the step beside her, inviting me to sit. The other hand gripped the feathered fan. All against my own will, I continued to climb the stairs. The woman's calves, even in the dim stairwell, were bright white, veined with gray and blue like marble pillars, the rolled stockings at her ankles as solid as stone. There was a basement odor about her, the odor of cold dirt. The apron that looped over her dark blouse and stretched across her black skirt was dim and gray, soft with wear. 'I take it you're a friend of little Gertrude Hanson,' she said, a small smile making her words seem warm. 'I take it you're coming to call for her.' A bit of light from the transom above the door might have caught her eyes as she cast them down at me on the stairs. Her short hair, carefully curled, had a goldish, grayish hue. She shook her head. 'But I'm here to tell you she's gone away. Her father took her out this morning. To his people in New Jersey. There's nobody home upstairs.'

Now I paused. I said, 'Oh,' and the woman suddenly leaned back. I thought at first that she was trying to see me more clearly in the gloom, but then I realized that she was leaning in order to push her apron aside as she reached for the pocket underneath, in her skirt. She stretched out one of her great ivory legs as she maneuvered her free hand beneath the apron and briefly rolled her eyes to the ceiling as if to picture what it was she was searching for. There was something of Big Lucy in the rolling of her eyes. And then she produced a penny and held it out to me. 'Do you know your prayers?' she said.

I nodded, although I knew I could not recite one if asked. The woman laughed warmly as if she knew this, too. The laughter made her look younger. With the McGeevers in mind, I had expected a toothless grin, but the woman's teeth were strong and straight.

'Give me your right hand,' the woman said kindly, and when I struggled with the school-books in my arm in order to hold out the left, she shook her head and whispered, 'The right one, dearie,' full of a peculiar sympathy. She placed the fan on her knee. She reached up to take my right hand from the banister. I felt suddenly unbalanced, there on the dim stairs.

'Get yourself down to Mary Star of the Sea,' she said. 'And light a candle.' She pressed the penny into my palm. 'Don't worry if every prayer's gone out of your head. Don't be bothered by that. A good outcome's enough to say. Light a candle and ask our Blessed Lady for a good outcome. It only takes the asking.' Her pale eyes went back and forth across my face. Despite the gloom of the staircase, I saw that the woman could read everything there: not only the fact that every prayer had indeed gone out of my head, or that left and right still puzzled me, but also that I had already determined that I would not go into the empty church all by myself. I had never gone into an empty church all by myself. If Gerty were here, the two of us would go together, we would make a game of it, as we sometimes did on Saturday mornings, laughing at the door and then tiptoeing together up the echoing aisle, lighting the flame and leaning into our folded hands at the kneeling rail with exaggerated piousness. But Gerty had gone to her father's people in New Jersey and the apartment upstairs was empty.

The woman held my wrist and pressed the penny into my palm, and knew, I could tell, that she would not be obeyed. But she asked me anyway, 'Will you do that?' And I said anyway, 'I will.'

Out on the street, I walked around the block again and climbed my own steps. Mrs. Chehab was gone, but the scent of the vinegar from her window cleaning still lingered. An Easter scent, I thought, although Easter had already passed. It was the scent of the solution we made to dye our eggs, but also the odor that pricked my nose in church when they read that part of the Passion where Jesus said, I thirst, and a sponge soaked with wine and vinegar was raised to his lips. And then the angel in the empty tomb saying, 'He's not here.'

Upstairs, Gabe was alone in the apartment, already bent over his books. He raised his head as I came in. His brown eyes with their golden lashes looked tired in the dim light. He said, 'Momma's gone out' — although I had known

46

this as soon as I opened the door, an absence in the air — and then he watched me as I placed my own schoolbooks on the table where he was already studying. 'You're late getting home,' he said. 'You shouldn't make Momma worry. She needs you to be good.'

I shrugged. I still held the black penny in my palm, and his gentle reprimand was only a small weight added to my own awareness that I was not being good: that I had taken the penny with no intention of going to church with it. That I had forgotten already what it was the fat woman had asked me to pray for, a good solution or an answer of some sort. I put the penny on the table between us. 'I stopped to see Gerty,' I said. 'She wasn't in school today. She's gone to New Jersey.'

But my brother spoke over me. 'Momma's in the city,' he said. 'You should be a good girl now' — he was repeating my father's phrase — 'and do your homework quietly until they get back.'

I reached out and picked up the penny again. It was my father's phrase, 'Be a good girl now,' but when my father said it, there was a wink about the words that also said he understood what a bland and tedious thing it was to be a good girl, little pagan that I was. When my father said it, he was asking me to pretend, at least. He was saying he would admire me all the more for my pretending. But my brother meant what he said. Beside him on the table was the single glass of water he now allowed himself in the afternoon, his sustenance between breakfast and supper, some preparation for his life in the seminary come fall.

'I have to go to church,' I told him. I said, 'A lady I met at Gerty's house asked me to light a candle for her and I promised I would. She gave me a penny.'

I held out my palm to show him the black coin, as if he might otherwise not have seen it. He looked at the penny, and then he looked at my face. I saw that he understood there was some deception here, if only in the extravagance of my gesture. I saw a subtle disappointment, a kind of sadness, cross his eyes. He wanted me to be good.

I closed my fist around the penny. 'I won't be long,' I said, and turned to leave again.

'Don't be,' he said, 'for Momma's sake.'

Outside, the boys were well involved in their game and the girls who pretended not to watch them every afternoon were gathered on the steps just beyond the Chehabs' house. Some of them were friends of mine from school, others were older girls who made me feel shy.

They were all leaning over their laps as they liked to do, their arms tucked under their knees, their skirts tucked up against their thighs to keep their underwear out of view. They called to me, and with the penny in my fist and no intention of going into the church alone, I joined them. There was a stirring of bare legs, socks and shoes, and raw knees as they made room. I sat on a low step, tucking my own skirt under my lap while the other girls leaned down to ask if I had heard the news. They were breathless as they spoke, and even those who said nothing, who only

48

leaned to listen, held their mouths carefully, as if they felt the words as an ache in their teeth and their jaws.

On her wedding night, they whispered, Dora Ryan discovered that the man she had married wasn't a man at all.

Was a woman, they said. A woman dressed up like a man.

Their astonishment was all in their mouths and their jaws. They leaned forward, their chins over their knees. Some of them had freckles, and some of them had chapped lips or pimples or sharp breath. Some were pretty, or bound to be. Someone's teeth were chattering, as if with the cold. But there was delight in it, too. In what they were saying, a giddy shifting in their eyes, a mad pride of sorts, pride in how strange and terrible life might prove to be. They hugged their thighs against their chests. Down the street, the boys were cheering in thin voices.

I shook my head. I wished above all that Gerty were there to turn to.

'How could that be?' I said. 'Who would do such a thing?'

But there wasn't a single girl among them who was as smart as Gertrude Hanson. They shifted their feet around me. They frowned, looked to one another with shallow and delighted eyes, eyes that just skimmed over the surface of things without understanding. A mean trick was the best they could come up with: simple meanness, a mean schoolyard trick, the best explanation they could offer. A lousy mean trick to pull on poor fat Dora Ryan, a woman pretending to be a man, dressing up like a man and fooling her right through her wedding day. Standing in front of the priest like that. Kissing her on the lips. Putting her hand on Dora Ryan's hand when they cut the wedding cake together. And then laughing, the way they figured it, laughing right in her face when they took off their clothes.

Which led to further speculation still, about the matter of a wedding night and the shedding of clothes. A matter mysterious and complicated to us all, in those days, but now with sheer meanness added to the vague and various possibilities of what went on between women and men.

★ ★ ★

While the girls were talking, a taxi pulled to the curb in front of my house. My mother got out first, then gave her hand to help my father, whose face was hidden by the brim of his hat, but whose legs, I could tell, were weak and watery. The girls watched silently, their attention drawn by the cab, the extravagance of it.

There was a ditty we said, skipping rope: A rich man takes a taxi, a poor man takes the train, a hobo walks the train tracks, but gets there just the same. One of the girls behind me began to say it now, all singsong, poking me in the back as I watched my parents climb the steps together.

'Marie's momma must be rich,' another said.

They felt free to tease me, I knew, because Gerty wasn't there. Because Gerty wasn't there, I was alone among them.

I put my fist to my mouth, leaning across my lap. I could taste the bitter, metallic scent of the old penny in my hand. Had Gerty been there, the two of us, best friends, would have joined arms, tossed our heads, turned away. Instead, I merely, briefly, closed my eyes.

Dinnertime was approaching and the boys in the street began to disperse, each departure marked by the hollow, melancholy echo of a broomstick hitting the pavement. Something restless stirred among the girls, some anger, some meanness that teasing me hadn't satisfied. With the day coming to an end, a halfhearted proposal went up among them about walking around to the Ryans' house. Walking around to Dora Ryan's house with the hope of maybe meeting her coming home from the subway, or seeing her at a window, with the veil of a lace curtain over her shamed face.

The older girls led the way, leaving the stoop, crossing the street. I trailed after with my penny. Two of them stopped to whisper to some of the boys just leaving the game. I heard one of the boys say, 'Go on,' and knew that Dora Ryan's catastrophe had been conveyed. Passing behind Bill Corrigan in his kitchen chair, the same two girls ran their hands over the shoulders of his suit jacket and said, 'Hello there, Billy,' languidly, nearly laughing. Bill Corrigan raised his big hand, raised his chin into the air, twisting his head a bit to look at us from beneath his scarred eyelids. I could see his pale eyes searching. Then Walter Hartnett, who sat on the curb at Bill Corrigan's feet, looked over his

51

shoulder and said, 'Get lost.' One of the girls hissed, 'Gimp,' and Walter said, 'Scram,' sneering, but turning away again.

We walked on to Dora Ryan's house. We stood across the street and studied the blank windows. The air was still damp and humid, the colorless sky felt like a dome over the neighborhood. After only a few minutes, one of the girls whispered, 'She's hiding.' We paused silently, as if waiting for some affirmation of this — a hand to a stirred curtain, a shadow behind the glass. My eyes fell to the garbage cans beside the basement door. I was hoping to see, perhaps, a torn piece of bridal veil or a white stocking waving from beneath a battered lid.

I thought of Dora's happy wedding, her satin shoes and the rice and the smiling wedding guests. I wondered if her happiness could have been preserved if the bride and groom had merely stayed in their clothes.

'So now she'll have to try to meet someone else,' one of the older girls said solemnly.

There was a chorus of whispered, even sympathetic 'Yeahs,' their cruel energies suddenly abating. I heard myself say, 'My heart goes out to her,' imitating my mother. There was a brief silence, and then, reluctantly, it seemed, one by one, the girls began to agree. 'Oh yeah,' someone said. 'Mine, too.' 'Poor thing.'

There was nothing else to do but go home. We turned away and slowly began to disperse, so that by the time I approached my own house, I was alone again. My brother was just coming down the front steps, moving quickly, his cap on and his mouth set. He threw up his hands when he saw me. On the sidewalk, he took my elbow. 'Where have you been?' he said. 'I told you to come right home.'

Inside, climbing the stairs, he said, 'Did you go to church?' and I wasn't quick enough to think of a lie. 'No,' I said.

He paused on the landing in front of our door. He took off his cap and ran his hand over his thick hair, our father's gesture altogether. 'Was that the truth?' he said. He said it firmly. 'About the lady wanting you to go light a candle?'

'Yes,' I said.

Gabe took the penny from my palm. He put his cap back on, raising his chin as he did, looking in the dim hallway light resolved and resourceful. 'What did she ask you to pray for?' he said. I shrugged. I could not call up the phrase. 'Safe travels to New Jersey,' I said. 'For Gerty.'

Gabe's eyes moved in a way that reminded me of the fat woman on the stair, reading my face. 'All right,' he said, reading everything there. 'Go on in. If Daddy wakes up, tell him I'll be home in a jiff.' And he turned back down the stairs.

I waited until the outside door had closed before I entered the apartment. There was immediately the faint odor of my father's having been sick. I found my mother in the bathroom, leaning over the sink, throwing cold water on her face. Throughout her life, this was my mother's second-best antidote — after prayer — for pain and suffering: go throw cold water on your face.

I slipped behind her, sat on the narrow edge of

53

the bathtub. My mother was still dressed in her dark suit jacket and skirt, her going-into-the-city clothes, even when she just went in to fetch my father home whenever a message came to the house, usually from Mr. Lee at the candy store or from Mr. Fagin at the funeral parlor — the two neighborhood establishments that accepted phone calls for those of us who didn't yet have a phone — a message that said he was under the weather.

I waited for my mother to turn off the running water. I wanted only to say to that broad back, to those sure hips, The man Dora Ryan married was not a man at all, only so my mother could say, Nonsense, as was her way, and thus restore the world. But my mother turned from the sink with the rough towel to her face and seemed surprised to see me there. 'Ah, Marie,' she said, looking over it, and would later apologize that she did not have the wherewithal, at that moment, to break the news more gently. 'Poor Gerty's lost her mother. Fagin's girl told me. She passed away this morning. In agony,' she added. 'God give her peace.'

There was only one small narrow window in this bathroom, high up in the tiled wall, and it faced only the airshaft, but the light through it caught my mother's face nonetheless. There were no tears in her eyes, and only a few wet strands of hair at her broad forehead, plastered to her cheeks. She began to dry her hands on the towel, in her own efficient, getting-on-with-it way. 'A little girl,' my mother was saying. 'A sister for Gerty. They're calling her Durna.'

My mother said, folding the towel neatly, returning it to the bar, 'It was late in her life to be having another child.' She said, 'There's a woman over on Joralemon, above the bakery. She might have helped the poor soul. If only she had asked.'

Sitting on the cold edge of the tub, I was aware of the vertigo I'd known when I was younger, when the reflected bathwater swung me high and shook me out and rattled the teeth in my head. Suddenly I held up my arms to my mother. I heard her cluck her tongue — either at the pity of Mrs. Hanson's death or the childishness of my pose, perhaps both — before she crossed the narrow space between us and took me into an embrace.

★   ★   ★

I faked a stomachache to avoid Mrs. Hanson's wake. Said I'd caught 'the grippe' from my father. My fear was that when I saw Gerty again she would resemble the neglected kids at school — kids with musty hair and black fingernails, with fallen hems and caramel-colored plugs of wax in their ears. But Gerty wore a new plaid coat and a new plaid tam-o'-shanter to her mother's funeral at Mary Star of the Sea, and when I once again climbed the stairs to knock at her door — grateful to discover that there was no fat woman in the hallway — she smiled to see me. Gerty smiled. Her teeth were still widely spaced, her freckles still vivid across her nose, her wild hair combed as neatly as it had ever

55

been, her curls still thick and tightly woven. She put her hand to my elbow. An older woman in dark clothes stepped out of the kitchen to see who it was, but then stepped back in again.

'Come see Durna,' Gerty said.

We went around the polished dining-room suite and into her parents' bedroom, where I had been before only to say the Rosary. It was filled with a curtain-diffused light. There was a white bassinet at the foot of the bed. The wallpaper was a close and crowded design of roses and green vines, and there were embroidered roses scattered across the bedspread. There was a tall brown dresser against one wall, Mr. Hanson's doorman's cap on top of it and, between the two windows, a dressing table with perfume bottles and jars of cream and a silver-backed brush still threaded with Mrs. Hanson's black hair. The windows here were opened behind the curtains, and sunlight, as well as the metallic odor of sunlit air, filled the room. There was the sound of cars, of people passing by in the street. Gerty took my hand. Together we approached the little bed and peered in. The baby was fair-haired, only a hint of gold across her crown, and red-cheeked, with plump fingers and a mouth like two tiny rose petals, lips the color of a pink rose.

The baby startled awake when I bumped the bassinet, and her eyes were deep blue, instantly serene. Lashes pale as wheat. She waved her arms. Her wrists and her little hands were fat and dimpled. And then a toothless smile, all for me, I thought, although Gerty, newly minted

56

expert, whispered that it was only gas. There was sunlight pouring into the room. The windows were wide open, but there was no breeze, only the sounds of cars and carts and of some children in the street. When the baby began to fuss, Gerty reached into the bassinet and lifted her, the blanket trailing. She held her on her shoulder, ran her fingertips up and down her spine, as adept as any adult. And then Gerty scooted the quieted child into the crook of her arm. She put her lips to the pretty forehead.

I felt such a rush of envy then — to be Gerty, to have such a lovely baby in my own care — that I shivered with the thought, well knowing that I had walked upon my mother's grave.

From the kitchen came the sound of a teakettle whistling and, behind it, the rattle of baby bottles clinking in a pot of boiling water. I could hear the lady in the kitchen muttering to herself, shutting the icebox, slamming the oven door. I caught the first scent of baking bread.

Mrs. Hanson would never again be found in these rooms. Or seen waiting for Gerty outside the fence at school. Or met at the grocery, or in the crowds after Mass. Her comb and brush were here, the crystal bottles of her perfume, her children and her husband were here, this lovely baby, but she had vanished forever. And although the day would come when Gerty, sitting beside me on our stoop, would suddenly bow her head to her knees and weep without sound or explanation for what seemed the better part of an hour, at that moment, in the pretty room, with the lovely baby in Gerty's arms, I believed only that the bright, bustling world had simply closed itself up over Mrs. Hanson's disappearance, and that this, then, was the way of all sorrow — Gerty's and the Chehabs' and perhaps even Dora Ryan's, once she found someone else — closed up, forgotten, vanished in the wink of an eye.

In her own last days, my mother asked, on waking, 'Am I home?' Because she didn't want to be in Ireland, but in her last days every good bit of sleep she managed to get seemed to return her to that dreaded shore. 'Am I home?' she would ask, tears standing in her rheumy eyes.

In the first days of her last illness we said, 'Yes,' Gabe and I and Gabe's friend Agnes, who was helping out — even the visiting nurses who stopped by — but when we saw how this distressed her, how she plucked at the sheet and turned her head away, we began to understand and we amended our reply. 'No,' we said, to reassure her. 'Not home. Here. In Brooklyn.'

Once, she said, 'Show me.'

I had already drawn back the bedroom curtain and raised the shade. Now, with one knee on the window seat, I struggled to open the old window in the overpainted frame. I banged at it with the heel of my palm, cursing under my breath, until my brother, who was sitting in the dining-room chair he had drawn up to the side of the bed, looked up impatiently to ask if I'd like some help.

I pushed the window open, the sound of the street, the odor of the street, suddenly, almost visibly, slipping into the room, climbing the walls, crossing the ceiling, and drifting down across the bed. The odor of car exhaust and

59

heated asphalt, of garbage and incinerator fires. 'There,' I said. 'Smells like Brooklyn.'

There was an argument going on out in the street, voices of children mostly, cursing and shouting, tinny music from a radio somewhere. 'Sounds like Brooklyn, too,' I said, and saw Gabe glance at me from across our mother's bed.

The neighborhood was in decline, the building itself much neglected. Gabe and my mother now slept with lights on in all the rooms, just to keep the roaches at bay. I had it from Agnes that when the parlor-floor apartment was broken into and ransacked — drugs were involved — one of the cops who came to the door asked my brother why he was still here, why he didn't take my mother to a better neighborhood. To Jersey or Long Island.

Gabe explained that our mother had raised her family here. That she had come here as a young bride. She'd mourn for the place, he said, should she leave it now.

'She'll get over it,' the cop said.

Gabe told him, 'My father spent his last days in these rooms,' and the cop looked around sympathetically, but raised his eyebrows in that wry, Come on, be realistic way of New Yorkers. 'I doubt he's coming back,' he said kindly.

Later, when Gabe was held up on the street by three thin teenagers, 'youngsters,' he'd called them, he asked me over the phone, 'What's happened to so harden the children's hearts?'

I shouldn't have, but I laughed out loud. 'Look where you're living,' I said.

'There you are,' I told my mother, standing in

60

the hot breeze that had entered along with the rattle of traffic and the voices in the street. 'Brooklyn.'

My mother turned to Gabe, who was holding her hand. 'Show me,' she said again.

The strain of this vigil was evident in the shape of his shoulders and the weariness in his eyes. He glanced up at me where I stood by the window and then down at her again. 'All right,' he said softly. He got up slowly, pushing back the old dining-room chair. He leaned over the bed, slipping his hands beneath her. I watched in some astonishment as he lifted her, the bedclothes trailing.

'Get the door,' he said over his shoulder as he made his way out of the room with our mother in his arms like a child. He turned to his side to fit them both through the passageway, and I overtook them in the living room. We had lined the woodwork here with boric acid, to keep the roaches at bay, and there was something of its pale dust over everything in those days. It sometimes made me recall: sand of Syria and Mount Lebanon.

I went ahead to open the door. Gabe slipped through it, our mother in his arms. I followed them down the stairs, astonished, full of objections, but unable to object. I watched him as he gently negotiated the turnings. I wondered briefly if he planned to carry her all the way to the hospital. In the vestibule, the door to the parlor-floor apartment was still patched with plywood. Gabe turned to me and nodded toward the street. My mother's eyes were closed. In my brother's arms she seemed as small and light as an infant. I went ahead to pull the first door open, and then slipped around them to get the outer door as well. There was a blast of heat. Gabe carried my mother into the sunlight and down the steps. There were kids on the stoop across the street, there was the tinny music from their transistor radios. They glared, open-mouthed. A pair of dark men passing by looked up as Gabe came down the stairs with my mother in his arms. They walked to the curb, glancing over their shoulders, giving him a wide berth. Gabe, too, went to the curb and then turned around to look back up at the house. I rushed to scoop up the sheet and the blanket that was now brushing the sidewalk.

'You're here, Momma,' I heard him say. 'Where we've always lived.'

My mother raised her head. She extricated one thin hand from the winding bedclothes and raised it to her eyes against the sun. She looked down the street and then up at our building, the blue summer light reflecting in the glass of the front door, the bowed parlor window — some plywood there, too — and then up to the fourth floor, where a bit of lace curtain, her handiwork, had been drawn through the opened window.

'Not home,' I heard Gabe tell her, reassuring her. 'Brooklyn.'

My mother called me into the kitchen. Gabe was at the seminary out on Long Island by then, a beautiful place that was reached at the end of a long train ride. There were tall trees there and sloping lawns, and the young men walked in and out of the shadows of the leaves with their heads bent, their prayer books held gently between their hands, like little boys with caterpillars cupped in their palms.

'It is time,' my mother said, 'that you learned a few things.'

On the narrow, corrugated tin of the drain board beside the sink, there was the flour bin and a bottle of buttermilk, the pale box of baking soda, a box of raisins, a box of salt, and a tin of caraway seeds. On the small table beneath the window, a bowl and a spoon and the measuring cup. There was as well a narrow card on which she had written in her careful hand the recipe for soda bread.

It was time, my mother said, that I learned a few things about cooking.

I stood in the kitchen doorway, all reluctance. Why? I wanted to ask.

My mother tied an apron around my waist. 'All right,' she said. She nodded toward the table, the bowl and the spoon and the recipe card. I looked at her. The morning sunlight through the single window lit the down on her cheeks. It showed her brown eyes had some green in them, too. And that on either side of her tall forehead her dark hair was turning gray.

'Go ahead,' my mother said. 'Get started.' And when she saw me hesitate, she impatiently put her hand on my shoulder and turned me toward the table and the bowl and the spoon. 'Read the recipe over and then gather your ingredients,' she said slowly. 'They're all right here. I'll supervise.'

I looked at my mother in her housedress and her apron trimmed with green rickrack, her wide soft breasts and her pillowed belly and her strong, firm hands. A body, a physical presence, more familiar to me in those days than my own, since my own was something I had only begun to consider.

'Don't be dense, Marie,' my mother said. 'Don't stand there gawking at me like I'm speaking Chinese. Go.' And another touch on the shoulder. 'Read the recipe over once and gather your ingredients. It isn't hard. It's high time you learned.'

Why? was what I wanted to say, but I was certain without conscious thought that the question would get me into trouble. I turned reluctantly to the table, my feet feeling heavy in my shoes. I picked up the card. It was my mother's routine to make her soda bread on a Saturday morning while I went out to join my friends. It had always been so.

'Read it over,' my mother said. And I nodded, pretending to. The sun through the single window was bright in my eyes.

'Now gather what you need.'

I picked up the flour bin and brought it to the table. I picked up the buttermilk and the raisins. I went back for the salt and the tin of caraway seeds and then stood before the bowl and the spoon and the measuring cup. Beyond the window, beyond the gray bars of the fire escape, the wash my mother had done this morning was waving on the line: sheets and pillow slips, my school blouses and my father's shirts, which were hung upside down by their hems, their arms waving in a way that made me grow dizzy in sympathy.

'Haven't you forgotten something?' my mother said behind me. I looked at the ingredients I had lined up on the small table. The sun had turned the buttermilk a kind of blue. 'No,' I said.

My mother took me by the shoulders and turned me around. 'Are you sleepwalking?' she said. 'There's the baking soda. You'll have nothing at all if you don't have that.'

I fetched the box of baking soda and then once more stood before the table. 'Now what?' my mother asked.

I shrugged. Beyond the waving clothesline were the windows and fire escapes of our neighbors, the dancing laundry of a dozen more families, the tall brown poles that held the lines, electric lines and clotheslines.

'Glory be to God,' my mother said. 'Now you read the recipe, Marie.'

I looked down at the little card. The ink my mother had used was brown. Her handwriting was lovely and neat, the capital S and the capital B at the top of the card were striking — perfectly shaped, perfectly proportioned. My mother had learned from Irish nuns. 'Marie?' my mother said.

The sound of her voice was more familiar to me then than my own; I knew the end of my mother's patience when I heard it.

'You tell me,' I said softly. 'You tell me what to do.'

Behind me, I heard my mother cross her arms over the rick-racked apron.

'There's a recipe in front of you,' she said. 'And unless I'm very much mistaken you know how to read. Read it.'

I lowered my head the way I'd seen horses do, and dogs, when they didn't want to be led. 'You tell me,' I said again.

I heard her stamp her foot. 'I won't.' Anger always stirred my mother's brogue, like meat brought up from the bottom of a stew. 'I wrote it out for you so you could read it. Now read it.'

I didn't turn around. 'Just tell me,' I said.

'A recipe is meant to be read,' my mother said.

I dipped my head again. 'I'd rather you just tell me.'

In the silence that followed, I could hear, faintly, the noise from the street, where I wanted to be: cars passing and children calling. There was also the distant thump of doors closing in the apartments below, various footsteps on the stair. There was the whine of someone's clothesline pulley. The chuckling warble of some pigeons at the window.

'Measure out your flour,' my mother said slowly, relenting. I shifted my feet a bit to accommodate my triumph: better than risking a sly smile.

I put my hand on the measuring cup. 'How much?' I said.

And now, even without turning around, I knew it was my mother who was smiling. 'You'll have to read the recipe to find out,' she said. 'Won't you?'

★ ★ ★

It was a wonder, my mother said later, in every retelling of it, that we didn't kill each other on that bright morning. Slowly, through a series of niggling concessions on both our parts — some telling, some reading, some turning away in anger, and some giving in — the ingredients were placed into the bowl and the bread was shaped and lifted into the black frying pan. When my mother brushed past me to mark the cross in its surface, her hands were trembling with anger.

'I don't know what's gotten into you,' my mother said, and banged the pan on the top of the stove, then banged it into the hot oven. 'You are the most stubborn child.'

She put away the ingredients, slamming cabinet doors, and washed the bowl and the spoon in the sink.

She turned to me again. The sunlight caught the green in my mother's narrowed eyes, as if she were peering into a deep green wood. 'The strangest child I've ever heard of,' she said. 'Refusing to read a simple recipe.'

She dried the bowl and put it away. She dried the spoon. She said, 'Can you at least, at least, keep an eye on the clock and take this out in forty minutes? I've got to meet your father downtown. Can you be responsible for that much?'

I said yes, but my eyes went to the sunlight at the window.

My mother took my chin and made me turn to the clock on the stove top.

'When the big hand comes around to the twelve,' she said, 'take the bread out. Use the cloth. Can you do that? When the big hand comes around to the twelve.'

'I can tell time,' I said sullenly, risking her anger once more.

Once again my mother studied my face, as if it were lost in a thicket of trees. 'And you can read, too,' she said, measuring out her words. 'But today it seems it's not a question of can, is it? It's a question of will. Will you do it is what I'm asking.'

I turned my face to the light at the window. I pulled off my glasses. I was a bold piece — I could hear my mother's accusation even before she said it. 'All right,' I said, and then collapsed into the single chair beside the table. 'I will,' I said, and crossed my arms over my chest, turning my exaggerated gaze to the small clock on the stove, its old glass fogged, its numbers and its two hands mere slashes of black. 'Here I am,' I said, all impertinence. 'I'm watching the time.' Knowing my mother's voice as well as I did, I could already hear her say, 'Oh, you are a bold piece.' Knowing the limits of my mother's patience, I could already feel the slap on my cheek.

But my mother merely stood beside me with her hands on her hips, studying her stubborn daughter once more, even as that daughter kept her exaggerated, myopic stare on the clock. 'I suppose this is how it's going to be,' she said softly, more to herself than to me. 'You're growing up.' And then, for a moment, she put a gentle hand to my head.

She said, 'God help us both,' and left the kitchen.

I kept my eyes on the small face of the clock until my mother came back in her hat and coat, her purse held over her arm. 'Thirty minutes more,' she warned, and I withdrew the question I was going to ask, 'Where downtown?' in order to sigh impatiently instead. 'Yes, Momma.' I heard her close the apartment door. I put my glasses back on and let my gaze wander around the solid world, to the stove top with its black burners, to the blank white enamel face of the oven door. To the sink and the drain board beside it. The tile wall and the narrow shelf above, where there was a yellow matchbox and a small statue of the Blessed Mother in her blue cloak. To the table at my elbow and a faint crescent moon of spilled baking soda that marked where the bowl had been, to the window and the light and the clothes on the line. The sunlight had already moved past fresh morning and into the steady weight of the rest of the day.

I looked around. I wanted to leave the kitchen, of course, to leave the apartment and call on my friends, which was, until this morning, my usual Saturday routine, but I resisted it. I stared at the clock once more. What I needed was a book or the newspaper, I thought. I imagined my mother coming home to find me sitting here, with the newspaper spread before me and the perfectly golden bread cooling by the window, confounding all her expectations. There would be some satisfaction in that.

I left the chair in the kitchen, rehearsing as I did the innocent look I would give my mother when she returned — convinced, of course, that the bread had burned — and discovered instead that I was sitting serenely at the table with the newspaper spread before me and the perfect loaf cooling on the windowsill.

I walked through the living room, but last night's paper wasn't there. I walked into my parents' bedroom: the trick would be to convey by my own astonished look my utter disbelief that my mother had ever doubted me. My mother's housedress and apron were thrown haphazardly across the bed. Where downtown? I wondered.

I went into my own room — my room alone now that Gabe was in the seminary. Now that Gabe was in the seminary, he slept on the couch in the living room when he came home and hung his dark clothes in the hall closet like a visitor. From my window I could see Gerty Hanson and another girl strolling arm in arm toward the part of the street where the boys were playing. I tilted my head to watch them climb the stoop four doors down, where a small knot of the usual girls were already sitting on the steps.

It would only take a minute, I knew, to run down and tell them all that my mother had me inside baking bread. That I would be with them in forty minutes' time, at most. But when I arrived at the stoop, the girls were all bent over their knees, laughing extravagantly into their laps and their hands. Gerty had just told a story, which she repeated for me, a story her father had told about a very drunk man who was throwing tomatoes at the door of a church, during a funeral no less. 'What the devil's gotten into you, man?' her father said. And the man, wound up like a pitcher on the mound, said to her father, 'To hell with the devil,' and threw the tomato anyway.

Unless you count the absurdity of good little Gerty saying 'hell' in a longshoreman's gravelly voice, I was aware even then that the story wasn't funny enough to merit the other girls' mad laughter. That the laughter itself was meant mostly to get the boys in the street to glance over from their game. To get the boys to cry out, 'Ah, shut up,' as they were doing now that Gerty's second telling had the girls roaring once more. 'Bunch of cackling hens,' the boys said to one another in their own fathers' voices, even as the girls shook their heads, as their mothers would do, and pretended they hadn't heard.

When the laughter had subsided and the boys turned back to their game, I announced that my mother had me trapped. 'Time I learned

71

something about cooking,' I repeated, which led Gerty to tell another funny story about how her aunty had recently tried to hide a pot of burned parsnips in the dumbwaiter. It was well known to us all by then that Gerty's aunty hadn't even known how to peel a potato when she first arrived from the other side to run the household.

'She still can't poach an egg,' Gerty said with some haughtiness. 'I've tried to show her a hundred times, but she just can't learn.' She held up a finger, instructing all of us. 'A touch of vinegar in the water does the trick.'

'Well, I don't want to learn,' I said. 'Once you learn to do it, you'll be expected to do it,' and was amazed at the way my own words clarified for me what had been, until then, only a vague impulse to refuse. They looked at me over their knees, this gaggle of girls: a lifetime of hours in the kitchen bearing down on us all. 'I'd rather be like your aunty.'

Gerty shook her head. 'My dad says she'd burn water if she could.' And the girls laughed again, stamping their feet and slapping their knees. And the boys playing ball in the street looked over their shoulders to shout, 'Be quiet, can't you?' There would be no veering from that future.

I returned home with fifteen minutes on the clock still to spare. I opened the oven door and used the towel to take out the heavy bread. It was, I knew, paler than it should have been, but I turned off the oven anyway, simply to dispatch the task. I joined the girls again just as they were gathering themselves to leave the stoop and walk

72

slowly down the street, pretending we only wanted to get a soda.

★   ★   ★

When I came home again, my father was at the dining-room table and my mother was bringing him his tea. My mother crooked her finger and led me into the kitchen, where the loaf, sitting on the cutting board, was darker than it had been. 'What time did you take this out?' she asked, one eyebrow raised.

'When you told me to,' I said vaguely.

'It was hardly cooked,' she said.

I shrugged, indicating both that I could not be blamed and that it was all of no matter to me.

My mother sliced the rebaked bread and carried it in to my father where he sat at the cloth-covered table. I followed with the butter. Gabe's place at the table was empty now. Now, after dinner, we listened to the radio.

The tea was poured. My father spread the butter on the thick slice of bread and winked at me before he took a bite. And then chewed, and then moved his mouth as if his tongue had been burned. He swallowed and took a drink of tea. My mother said, 'Too much baking soda,' and placed her barely bitten piece of bread on her plate. And then put her hands in her lap, her back straight. 'You must have added it twice,' she said, sternly enough to show that she understood this was sabotage. 'I don't know how I didn't see it.'

I had added it, in fact, four times, with my

73

back to my mother and my mother's impatience — Glory be to God, read the recipe, Marie, how will you ever learn — making her, on three separate occasions, turn away.

'You'll have to learn to pay more attention, Marie,' my mother was saying. 'You'll never learn to cook if you don't pay attention. A kitchen can be a dangerous place if you don't pay attention.'

'Oh, she'll learn,' my father was saying, amused. 'She'll learn in good time.'

I bowed my head and studied my hands. I would not, I knew. I would not learn. Gerty Hanson had learned, but I would not.

I raised my eyes slowly, touching my glasses back onto my nose, well pleased with myself, but careful not to give this away. The day had grown cloudy and the dining room was dim. My father had returned the piece of bread to his plate, but as if to convey his sympathy, he still held the edge of it gently between his thumb and index finger — perhaps not wanting to hurt my feelings any further by letting go of it completely. His other three fingers, held delicately aloft, were trembling. His broad hand against the white cloth and the china plate was a color I had not expected: the gray fingernails sunk too deeply into the swollen yellow flesh. His flesh was swollen, thin as he was. I looked at his smiling face. Although we were only a few feet apart, across the familiar cloth at the familiar table, I felt my eyes strain, as they sometimes did when close things seemed suddenly to contract into a great distance. In my recollection, there was something of the smell of ether in the air.

★ ★ ★

That night, I found my mother sitting on my bed when I came out of the bathroom in my slippers and my robe. She asked me, 'How are you?'

Surprised by her presence, I replied, 'Fine, thank you, and yourself?' which was how she always answered when asked the same question by people on the street. Now she looked a little surprised. She said she was fine, thank you, as if by instinct alone. Her hands were in her lap. Her back was straight.

'Although,' she said, conversationally, as if we were indeed neighborhood ladies meeting on the street, 'I'm a bit worried about your father.' She told me then that he was going to stop by the hospital tomorrow, to see if they couldn't fix him up.

I said, with street decorum, 'I'm sorry to hear that.'

I felt no threat from this news, blithe child that I was, because my thoughts were all on the strange sight of my mother sitting, idly, it seemed to me, on the edge of my bed. She came into my room often enough in those days, but always at a bustle, there to dust the furniture or mop the floor, to place clean clothes in my dresser or to turn the mattress or to scrub the bed frame with ammonia to ward off bedbugs. She came in to pull the blankets up over my shoulders every night, to kiss my forehead and remind me to say my prayers. Her stillness now, sitting here, her hands empty, made her presence particularly peculiar.

75

She asked me if I would like to come along with them to the hospital. I couldn't go upstairs to see my father settle in, you had to be over sixteen to enter the wards, but I could go as far as the lobby.

I said that would be fine.

My mother said, looking into her hands, 'In sickness and in health.' Then she raised her eyes to me, cautiously, it seemed. 'That's something you must repeat when you are married. When you make your marriage vows.'

I said, 'I know.'

She raised her chin and even smiled a little, with the kind of subtle admiration she usually turned on Gabe. 'Do you now?' she asked me. A kind of mirth entered her eyes. 'What else do you know?'

I recited the entire phrase: 'For better, for worse, for richer, for poorer, in sickness and in health, till death do us part.' Until I saw my mother impressed by my knowledge, it never had occurred to me to wonder how I knew the words, from school, from the movies, from my friends. When she asked me, I said, 'From my friends.'

My mother bent her head again and said, 'Your friends talk to you about marriage, then. About what goes on.' I believe she was blushing.

I turned away from her to pick up my brush from the dresser. I began to brush my hair, still damp from my bath. I could see her reflection in my dressing mirror, sitting straight-backed on the edge of my bed, her hands in her lap. 'Oh sure,' I said casually.

'Then you know,' my mother said, 'about what

goes on.' And in the mirror I saw I still carried the flush from the hot water in the tub. 'Oh sure,' I said, not certain even then what I was admitting to.

From behind me, I heard her sigh. 'You're growing up.' She said it much as she had said it that afternoon, both amused and melancholy, and not a little impatient. I heard the familiar squeak of the bedsprings as she stood. 'It's good that you know these things.' Her voice, like the sound of the springs, seemed to move upward into the room, as if relieved of some weight. 'We'll go downtown after Mass tomorrow,' she said. 'Get to bed now.'

In the morning, after church, the three of us took the trolley to the hospital. My father carried a small black satchel. In the lobby, he put his hand to the top of my head and said, 'Be a good girl now' — rolling his tongue the way he did, tasting the sweetness of the joke. He leaned down, and I kissed his cheek, which was smooth-shaven and smelled cleanly of bay rum. And then I nearly knocked his hat off his head as I threw my arms around his neck. He patted my back, and then placed his two hands on my shoulders as he used to do outside the speakeasy, as if to keep me there, unmoving, while he went upstairs with my mother to get settled in.

When she came down again, the two of us walked outside and crossed the street, and then looked up at the big building. She pointed. It took me some time to find the right window. And then I saw him waving to us from behind the sky's reflection.

In the sunshine on the sidewalk in front of Mary Star of the Sea, a Sunday morning in early June when I was seventeen, Walter Hartnett said, 'What's wrong with your eye?'

Our mothers were talking, purses over their arms and hats on their heads. The sun bright off the black glass of windshields, the tin fenders, the pocketbooks of the women in that after-Mass crowd, off the white sidewalk and the road and even the fading church bells. Bright off him, too, when I looked up at him: the dark hair and that pale face, and then the gray eyes turned translucent in the sunshine.

'Nothing wrong with it,' I said. 'This one just screws up on me sometimes. When the sun's strong.'

'Well, don't let it,' he said. 'It makes your whole face look funny.'

Back home, before the tiny mirror above the narrow bathroom sink, I saw it: the way the right eye, screwed closed, pulled at the corner of my mouth so that I looked like a tough with a wad of chewing gum in my cheek. How my glasses, thick bottle bottoms, stayed steady on my nose despite the contortions of the face behind them.

I was reminded for a moment of Walter Hartnett as a boy, the way he had held his hands behind his back, placid and wise beside blind Bill Corrigan. I was reminded of the sagacity with

78

which Walter would nod whenever Bill Corrigan made his impossible calls. As if only he and the blind man could see what the rest of them could not.

I opened up the offending eye. Smiled at the mirror and said, 'How's that?' Took my glasses off entirely and smoothed the skin under my eyes and said, 'Is that better?' Walter Hartnett. Mister Hartnett. Brushed my hair back — dark and thick but, like the scrinching eye, with a mind of its own — and peered into the small mirror, which showed me now only a smear of face and hair and smiling teeth, made my eyes as large as I could make them, and said out loud, 'Is that better, Mr. Walter Hartnett?'

When he called that afternoon — his voice a small and miraculous thing inside the big black receiver — he apologized if he had been rude. It was none of his business, he said, what I did with my eyes. Later, in reconstructing the conversation in what was to be the first night of my life when sleep escaped me entirely, I replied, 'Not at all,' but in truth, I'd barely murmured a word. 'I'm bossy sometimes,' he said. 'I get it from where I work. They give me a lot of responsibilities. Do you want to go out for a soda?'

When my daughters began dating, I told them, 'Here's a good rule: If he looks over your head while you're talking, get rid of him. Walter Hartnett . . . ' But by then they would throw up their hands. 'Jesus, Mom, no more Walter Hartnett stories.'

Walter Hartnett on the candy-store stool

looked over my head every time a figure appeared in the cornered doorway behind me. It got so I felt I could see them, too, the other people coming in out of the evening sun, as if I could feel their cool shadows upon my back as they stood for a moment in silhouette and Walter looked beyond me to see who it was. 'Hiya,' he would say if he knew them — I might have been in mid-sentence — 'How are you?' He'd shoot a finger up beside his face to signal a hello. Or just stare — this was for entering strangers — his eyes following whoever it was into the candy store, wondering, calculating, assessing as a man alone might do — a man alone and unguarded in the brazenness of his gaze. And then his gray eyes would drop to my face once more. There would be a second of utter indifference, boredom perhaps, and then a slow dawning — Oh yeah, you — a slow warming as his attention returned to me once again — Well, I'm happy to be here with you — sometimes even as much as a smile entering those dark-lashed eyes, and then they would flick up again, over my head, to greet with a raised chin, or only to observe, whoever it was whose shadow had fallen over my back. Then his eyes would return to my face, unseeing once more, and then the slow recognition would begin again.

It could only have been second nature to him, this veering attention. He couldn't have calculated its effect. But it was, for me, by turns, devastating and thrilling, so that by the time our sodas were finished and we slipped from our stools, I was unsteady on my feet from the dizzying turns my hopes, my heart, had been taking. My pumps caught themselves, somehow, against his built-up shoe, and in the tangle as I fell into him, he slipped his warm hand under my arm. 'Not very graceful,' he said. But we both were blushing.

Out on the sidewalk again, we walked without touching, although most of the other people on the street seemed to be couples, young and old, walking arm in arm. The Sunday-evening promenade. The sun was setting with that thick orange light, but the sky to the east was still a cool Sunday-morning blue. There was only the slightest irrhythm in his gait, a nearly imperceptible hitch, not a limp. Had he turned right and walked me silently straight to my stoop, I would have followed, my head down, and said nothing more. But he turned left instead, and I went with him. He was talking about his job. That it was steady and he was lucky to have it. He named some friends who had jobs he wouldn't wish on a dog — with the B.M.T., with the diocese, on a barge that plied the harbor. He told me to forget about lower Manhattan and head to Borough Hall when the time came to look for work. Who wanted to work in New York City? All the while his eyes following the other couples we passed, or darting to the other side of the street to see who was there.

When he stopped, I thought perhaps it was because he'd recognized someone ahead. But then he turned to me, and now, in the shadow of streetlight, his eyes reacquainted themselves with my face once again; indifference, once again, warming into deep pleasure. He pointed to the brownstone behind him.

'I've got to run upstairs for a minute,' he said, his voice full of a reluctance to leave me that well matched his newly recalled delight in my being there. 'You want to come up or wait here?'

'This your house?' I said. And he only cocked his head to convey, Whose house do you think it is?

'I'll come up,' I told him.

He and his mother lived on the top floor, like my mother and me. 'Widows in aviaries,' he would say sometime later. He let himself in, calling, 'Ma?' but there wasn't a light on in the place, except that which came from the late dusk and the newly lit streetlight at the windows. He reached for a small lamp, pulled it on. Its amber shade and the bulb beneath it swayed a little.

'She must have gone out,' he said. 'Have a seat. I won't be a minute.'

He walked through the living room, into the adjoining dining room and then into another, the kitchen perhaps. I sat. The couch was covered in a dark blue brocade, lace doilies on the arms and across the back. There was a painting of the Holy Family over the boarded-up fireplace. The Virgin and good St. Joseph and the boy Jesus in white at the center. A small glass holding fading lilacs on the mantelpiece. Two more heavy chairs in the same midnight-blue brocade faced me. Beside one there was a sewing basket. On the small table between them, four oval photographs. I stood up and crossed to them. A wedding portrait of his parents, the father looking much like Walter might with a big mustache, a portrait of Walter as a baby, wide-eyed and propped up from behind, and then in knickers and a white collar, a huge First Communion ribbon on his arm, and then looking exactly like himself, although more thoughtful and more serious — or maybe just struggling to hold in a laugh — in his graduation gown.

I felt a twinge of envy, fool that I was in these first moments of my first foray into love's irrational pains. Envy for the widowed mother who had known him all his life, who had heard his first words, dried his first tears — had they been for the shortened leg? — even envied the mustachioed father, now buried in Calvary, where my father, too, had gone, envied every happy moment Walter had lived that had no trace of me in it.

I heard his voice coming from the back of the apartment. He was on the phone. He seemed to be speaking seriously, repeating numbers. Was it his important job? Even now I can't say whether or not the phone call was a ruse. I suspect he wasn't that clever.

I returned to the couch. When he came back into the living room, he was carrying two opened bottles of beer. He offered and I refused, laughing a little at what struck me as the preposterousness of it, and he looked at the brown bottle and said, 'Oh, but it's already opened.' As if I had broken a promise. He placed the rejected beer on the radiator cover beside him and then moved to the couch. He sat next to me.

'My mother should be back soon,' he said, looking me over as if for the first time: my throat, my blouse, my belt, my hands in my lap. 'She'll want to say hello to you,' he said.

I nodded, pointed to the portraits on the small table. 'Is that her wedding picture?' I asked, and he said, 'Yeah.'

'She was pretty,' I said.

'I wouldn't mind getting married,' he told me. And then took a drink of his beer. He began to talk about his job again. What a good job it was. What a great office. What an easy thing it would be for him to begin to save his money to get a nice place of his own. When he got married. He sat very close to me. Did I want to get married? he asked, and when I said, Sure I did, someday, that slow, delighted recognition in his eyes fell on me again. He leaned away as if to see me better. We might have been the only two people in all the vast universe who agreed that we would like to get married someday, he took such pleasure in my answer.

And children? he asked. Did I want to have children?

Well, sure.

Well, sure. His eyes, darker now in the dim light of the apartment, were on me alone, were all over my face, as if I, after all, was what they'd been searching for all evening.

When he leaned to kiss me, it was both my first real kiss and my first taste of beer. He held the opened bottle against my shoulder for a minute as he pressed toward me, dampening my blouse, so that there was the strong smell of beer as well as the light taste of it in my mouth. Then he lowered his arm across my lap to put the bottle on the floor and, moving up again, put his hand over my breast. Astonished and, perhaps, afraid — already I had learned the triumph and distress of his veering attentions — I made no move. Delicately — I thought at first that he was making an 'okay' sign with thumb and forefinger just over my heart — he unbuttoned my shirt and then slipped his fingers inside. He pushed my bra aside. Exposed to the shadowy room, my breast seemed lit with its own light. He sighed and bowed his head. I felt the momentary terror of not knowing what he was going to do as he moved his mouth toward me and then felt it increase a hundredfold when I understood. He closed his mouth over my nipple. He pulled and tugged.

Of course, I had seen women nursing babies here and there, in closed-off rooms, and it was the recollection of this that muddled my emotions now. He breathed deeply, like an infant nursing, and I felt the warm air of his nostrils on my skin. I put a hand to his hair. Was this wrong? If I stopped him now, would he look at me again with that icy indifference, let his eyes drift away?

He put his hand to my spine and pressed me toward him. I felt his saliva turn cold on my skin, even as the room seemed to grow warmer around us. I felt his teeth on my flesh, lightly at first, but then in a stinging vise that made me pull in my breath. He clamped harder and I cried out, which only made him turn his head slightly as if to get a better grip on me with his molars. He might have drawn blood if there hadn't been the sudden slam of the door in the downstairs vestibule. He paused, lifted his head. Slam of the interior door and maybe footsteps across the foyer. He said, 'Cover up,' and then reached across my lap for the beer on the floor.

My poor pale breast was soggy and tender, the pink nipple distended, frighteningly transformed. I fumbled for my buttons. He leaned back on the couch, seemed to roll himself off it, the beer in one hand and the other hand pressed to his thigh. He walked, stooped, really limping now, toward the bottle he had left on the radiator. But then we heard the rattle of keys and another door opening on a floor below. He cursed and, with his back to me, hung his head, shaking it sorrowfully. And then without another word he limped out of the room again.

For a few minutes I sat alone under the shaded light. I felt it possible that he would not return. I felt for certain a warm trickle of blood was moving down my chest. When he came back, he seemed to have washed himself, hands and face, and combed water through his hair. He no longer had the bottle of beer, but he swung the second one off the radiator cover and carried it to the thick chair on the other side of the room. He sank into it and took a long drink. 'When we get married,' he said, 'you're probably going to want to live on the parlor floor. Baby carriages and all. But I think it's cheap. Everybody and his brother walking by your door. I think it's better to be up high.' He finished off the bottle in two or three long gulps and put his hand to his chest and quietly belched, as if we were already married, and perhaps had been for quite some time. 'I guess you'd better go,' he said amicably.

We walked down the stairs. I felt a panic at each turning — what if his mother came through the door now, or now, what would she read on our faces? But he took his time. On the street — the air was lovely, a slight breeze had kicked up and it felt like bathwater against my skin — he put his arm around my waist as we walked. We passed the church. Had it only been this morning that he looked down at me with the sunlight across his face and asked, 'What's wrong with your eye?'

'Well, at least,' he said, 'we won't have to fight over whose church we'll get married in, yours or mine. Both our mothers will be happy. What do you have,' he asked, 'one more year till graduation, right?'

I said yes.

'Get a job downtown Brooklyn,' he said. 'You don't want to go into New York City.'

We came around the other side of the block. Mr. and Mrs. Chehab were in the bay window of the parlor floor, their backs to the street and a two-headed lamp between them. He paused at our steps.

'Here you are,' he said. He put his hands in his pockets and shifted a little bit on his uneven legs. He may have been feeling the two quick bottles of beer. There was another couple walking down the other side of the street, toward the subway, and his eyes followed. This time, I turned to gaze at them, too. The woman wore a tight skirt across a wide bottom and her heels were clicking. The man's suit jacket was long, with a belt across the back. Together Walter and I turned to face each other again, but this time he did not go through that momentary, disinterested amnesia. Rather, he raised his chin and shot a finger into the air — as he'd done all evening when he acknowledged people in the candy store and on the street — a wordless 'I know you' — and then let his eyes fall, and linger, on my breast, the one he had exposed and suckled. He grinned. I know you.

In the first throes of my first foray into love's irrational joys, I felt both the thrill of his acknowledgment and the hot black rush of shame.

'Go on in,' he said, touching my hip. 'Go tell your mother you've got a boyfriend.'

★   ★   ★

All the thought and all the worry, all the faith and the philosophy, the paintings and the stories and the poems, all the whatnot, gone into the study of heaven or hell, and yet so little wonder applied to the sinking into sleep. Falling asleep. All the prayers I had said before bed throughout my life, all the prayers I had made my children say — Our Father, Hail Mary, Glory Be — the Confiteor if some transgression had taken place — missed the mark entirely. It was grace, the simple prayer before meals, that we should have been murmuring into our clasped hands at the end of the day: Bless us, oh, Lord, and this thy gift, which we are about to receive.

Driving back from Calvary Cemetery in the undertaker's car, pressed into my mother's side, I had sunk into the sweetest sleep I had ever known. They had put my father in the ground and my world was shattered, but the nap I had in Fagin's car driving home was like a long draft of cool nectar — sweet and deep and fragrant, washed with an ivory light (was it the winter sun passing through the window?) — the kind of sleep that came only in the aftermath of many tears. When the car pulled to the curb in front of the restaurant where the funeral luncheon was to be held, my mother gently woke me. Only Gabe, in his Roman collar, disapproved. His own eyes were red-rimmed and bloodshot; there were hollows in his pale cheeks. 'You slept?' he said. He had ridden in front, beside the driver. 'How could you have slept?'

Now, lying beside my mother in the bed we shared because Gabe had come home from his first parish, saying only that the priesthood was not for him, I passed my life's first sleepless night in joy and shame and confusion. I could not put my hand to my tender breast — bruised (I had seen in the bathroom mirror as I undressed) around the nipple, marked with two rose-colored bites — in case my mother, even in the shadows, should see what I was doing. I could not tamp down the smoldering shame. I felt it coil, wire-thin, down my spine. I felt it touch or spark something that flared and flashed and made guilt and confusion feel like pleasure, like joy. I was in love. Walter Hartnett with the gray eyes loved

89

me. Next year we would be married in Mary Star of the Sea and those eyes would never again fall on me with cold indifference. I know you.

My mother said, in the darkness, 'Do you want some hot milk, Marie?'

'No,' I said.

'Can't you sleep?'

'No,' I said.

'Can you at least try to be still?' my mother said. 'It's three a.m. I've got to work in the morning.'

'Sorry,' I whispered.

The ticking of the bedside clock had never before sounded so cruel. The windows were broad, uneven strokes of pale gray, hastily painted on the long black wall beyond the bed. The windows were opened to the cool night, but no particular breeze stirred. What sounds came from the street were distant, indistinguishable. Not even the scratching of a mouse behind the walls or of my brother's cough from the next room. Everyone else on this street was still. Everyone else had fallen into the cool ivory light, fallen asleep.

'Is Walter Hartnett a nice boy?' my mother whispered.

I said, 'Yes,' but could add nothing more. Already I felt the hot flush on my cheeks.

My mother rolled over, bouncing the mattress we shared, and then pulled the thin sheet up over her shoulder. 'I like his mother,' she said. 'Her people are from Armagh.'

★ ★ ★

90

By month's end, he was riding the extra stop on the subway every night on the way home from work, walking past our house, where he would always pretend to be surprised to find me sitting on the steps, waiting for him. He would lean against the balustrade, cock the toe of his built-up shoe into the sidewalk, and talk about his work, our wedding, the guys he wouldn't want to be, his eyes sliding, always, from my face to my breast and then rising up to my face again, his eyebrows raised as if to say, 'Remember?' As if the flush that rose to my cheeks didn't tell him I remembered.

We went to the movies together and a party once, where he drank half a bottle of whiskey and leaned heavily into my side walking home. We took a drive in a caravan of cars to a summer place owned by one Judge Sweeney, whose daughter went with a guy Walter knew. We had a picnic on a lovely lawn, but were only allowed into the house to use the john. Driving back, he said, 'Maybe we should get a place like that instead.'

I put my hand through his arm when we walked together, or he put his arm around my waist. He put his arm across my shoulders in the movie theater. At the end of the night, he would kiss me gently, always standing on the sidewalk, at the foot of our steps, never at the door, because, I imagined, he did not want me to turn and watch him limp back down the wide stair.

Even now I can't say if it was lack of opportunity or part of some plan, but the intimacy of that first Sunday evening was never repeated. And yet it was always there, in every touch that passed between us, certainly in every gesture of his pale eyes. The hours I spent on that first sleepless night imagining what I would say or do when he moved his mouth toward me again gave way to sleepless nights in which I only recollected in lovely detail everything he'd done once, teeth and tongue, his fingers on my spine. I walked beside him in a state of tremulous anticipation. I felt the pulse thrum in my veins every time we neared his block together — would this be the night he would finally say again, 'Do you want to come in?' Leaving the party where he'd had too much to drink, he'd leaned heavily against my shoulder in a dark and momentarily deserted vestibule, and for a moment his head dropped onto my chest, his hair brushed my chin, and it was all I could do not to cup my breast myself, offer it to him. On the parklike lawn of Judge Sweeney's summer house he'd stretched out on the grass beside me, propped on his elbows. He was chatting with the others, and his cheek against my forearm as he spoke and chewed and laughed, the movements of his jaw, filled me with an unbearable recollection of the dark couch and the amber lamp and the bared breast, lit as if from within.

It was the very end of summer when he called to say, 'Meet me for lunch downtown, will you?'

I hardly knew what I was hoping for, but before I left, I changed from a sleeveless polished-cotton sheath with a zipper up the back to a striped shirtwaist with buttons and a patent-leather belt. I wore new shoes and new gloves and a new slip and a new hat with red trim. I got to the restaurant before he did and sat alone at a table, which I had never done before, the water glasses throwing off trembling hoops of light because of the tremor in my legs beneath the white tablecloth, beneath the striped skirt, beneath the pink slip. I saw him come in — handsome, in a suit I had not seen him wear before, tweedy linen with a pinched waist and a belt across the back — and then I took off my glasses and smiled up in his direction until the shape of him materialized across the short table. 'Pretty hat,' he said, and pulled out his chair. 'Isn't this some place? Put your glasses back on, I don't know you without them.'

I had been here three years before, for my father's funeral luncheon, but this was not yet something I could say without my voice breaking.

I put my glasses back on and said, 'Pretty suit.'

He held out his arms. 'You like it?' He grinned. He was an ordinary-looking boy with brown hair and somewhat remarkable gray eyes. But handsome today in the suit, the white shirt, and pale tie. He had small straight teeth. Nice ears. 'I borrowed it from a buddy of mine,' he said, ''cause I'm on my way up to Judge Sweeney's summer place for the weekend.'

I leaned my gloved hands against the table edge, pressed the buttons of my shirtwaist against them. 'Whatever for?' I said.

His eyes skimmed over mine and then bounced away to follow the rise and fall of his napkin as he shook it out. 'Looks like me and

93

Rita Sweeney are getting married,' he said, and tucked the napkin onto his lap.

It was surely an image from a children's cartoon, maybe from one I had seen in the movies, with Walter or with someone else, but in my recollection of that hour, I saw the tears flow freely from my eyes and fill up behind my glasses like water in two fishbowls. Because I knew I cried, and yet no tear fell.

It wasn't just that Rita's family had some money, he explained while he ate and the food he had ordered for me sat untouched on my plate. Although she was better off than the two of us, with our two widowed mothers ending up alone in their top-floor aviaries if we got married. It was simply that Rita was better-looking, really. No flaws that he could see. Not, he said, like you and me.

'Blind you,' he said. 'Gimpy me.'

He said, as the lunch wore on, 'Don't kid yourself that everybody's equal in this country. It's the best-looking people that have the best chances.'

He said, 'I'm giving my future children the best chance I can give them. What kind of father would I be if I didn't?'

The tears rocked like the sea behind my glasses.

He said, 'You've been swell. I wanted to give you a nice lunch.'

I walked back to the subway with the tears that were trapped under my glasses washing up over my eyes. Through them, I saw the buildings and the streetlamps and the cars with their bright windshields, even the dark slips of other people, grow buoyant. I saw them float past, clashing and bobbing, unmoored by the flood.

At home, I climbed the steps, and everything that was terrible about this house and this street, about my life thus far, washed before my eyes: Here was the turn in the stair where Fagin's men had struggled with my father's coffin. Here was the couch where I had found my mother one morning last year, counting the pile of wrinkled dollars in her lap, hollow-eyed and sleepless. Here was the bed that had once belonged to my parents but that now my mother and I shared because Gabe had lost his vocation.

I sat on the edge of the bed. I wanted to take my glasses off, fling them across the room. To tear the new hat from my head and fling it, too. Put my hands to my scalp and peel off the homely face. Unbutton the dress, unbuckle the belt, remove the frail slip. I wanted to reach behind my neck and unhook the flesh from the bone, open it along the zipper of my spine, step out of my skin and fling it to the floor. Back shoulder stomach and breast. Trample it. Raise a fist to God for how He had shaped me in that first darkness: unlovely and unloved.

The door to the second bedroom opened and my brother appeared, his breviary in his hand. He wore the pants of the seersucker suit he'd had on this morning when he left for work, but he'd taken off his jacket and tie. His collar was unbuttoned and his hair was askew — anyone else would have thought he'd been sleeping — and there was an uncharacteristic stoop to his shoulders, as if he were prepared for some blow. 'My Lord,' he said, 'what is it?'

Apparently I'd been crying all along.

Standing in the doorway of the bedroom we once shared, he listened to the tale of my woe with his finger still marking his place in the breviary, the book held against his heart. I had not expected to find him home. His office had closed early, he told me, because of the heat.

He stood there, motionless in the doorway, the book pressed to his chest, while I recounted some version of what it was that had broken my heart. When I paused, gulping and whimpering, he said simply, 'Wash your face. I'll get my hat.'

In my despair, I only obeyed. Walked listlessly through the living room to the bath, my arms at my side. I threw cold water on my face. When I emerged, Gabe was waiting. He had put on his hat and his tie and his suit jacket. He said, 'It is solved by walking,' and opened the door.

He did not take my hand. Or offer his arm. We walked down the stairs together without touching, like children. He pulled open the vestibule door for me, and then the outside door. We went down the brown steps together, and on the sidewalk he slipped his hands into his pockets and nodded that we should go to the right. I went along. It was a hot day. I had forgotten how hot, because earlier, when I'd left for the restaurant, I had just bathed and splashed myself with cologne, and later when I returned, the heat was only a part of the general devastation.

But now the asphalt was as hot as a griddle.

The air had thickened with the heat. Across the street, blind Bill Corrigan's kitchen chair had been set out, but it was empty. There were only a few children on stoops. They sat on the higher steps, close to their buildings, where there was some shade. They looked limp and malnourished. I glanced up at them and then glanced down. The sun on the brim of my hat was a weight that threatened to bow my head. The hot concrete made the soles of my new shoes pliant and sticky.

The air was a wall. The heat was a reminder of what I had glimpsed when my father was dying, but had, without plan or even intention, managed to forget: that the ordinary days were a veil, a swath of thin cloth that distorted the eye. Brushed aside, in moments such as these, all that was brittle and terrible and unchanging was made clear. My father would not return to earth, my eyes would not heal, I would never step out of my skin or marry Walter Hartnett in the pretty church. And since this was true for me, it was true, in its own way, for everyone. My brother and I greeted the people we knew walking by, neighborhood women, shopkeepers in doorways trying to catch a breeze. Each one of them, it seemed to me now that the veil was briefly parted, hollow-eyed with disappointment or failure or some solitary grief.

Even in this heat, there was the smell of industrial smoke in the thick air.

My brother walked beside me. His suit jacket was buttoned and his tie was tight, but his hands were in his pockets, and this made his stride

97

seem leisurely. He paused at the first corner and then shrugged a little, turned left across the street. Soon enough I saw that he didn't really have a destination in mind — he paused at each corner, turned arbitrarily, put out his hand to make me wait for the traffic to pass — which was fine with me; I might as well do this, walk like this, as anything else. I'd had a brief fear, when I first saw him with his jacket on, and his tie, that he was going to take me to church.

On the next block, a young man stopped right in front of us, pulled off his hat, and swabbed his high forehead with a white handkerchief as large as a flag. He was slipping his hat back on as we passed him. I heard him say, 'Father,' and then, 'Father Gabe?'

My brother turned and greeted the man, whose friendly eyes seem to stagger for a moment, going to Gabe's throat, and then to me. He was short, with a round, boyish face that was florid with the heat. His shirt and pale suit were stained with sweat, his wide blue tie looked as if it had been soaked in water, wrung out, and then returned to his neck. He lifted his hat again as I was introduced, and I saw that his hatband had left a red impression across his broad forehead. Tom Commeford. He said, 'How are you, Father,' and my brother held up his hand.

'Father no more,' Gabe said. He touched his tie, as if to indicate the missing Roman collar. 'It wasn't for me.'

Now real panic crossed the young man's eyes — he looked to me again and I found myself shrugging, the two of us united for a moment by the puzzle of Gabe's lost vocation. It was the sensation of standing on a pier with a stranger, watching a familiar face disappear over the water's horizon and knowing suddenly that all kinship now was determined by the fact of earth beneath your feet or only sea. For a moment I was more kin to this florid young stranger than I was to my brother, the failed priest, at my side.

'Oh gee,' the young man said, 'I'm sorry.' It was impossible to know if he was sorry for the lost vocation or for his own, awkward mistake. He looked to me again, as if I would know. 'Once a priest,' he began to say, but Gabe spoke over him.

'How's everybody at the brewery?' he asked cheerfully. 'Everybody busy?'

'Oh, sure,' the man said. The effort he was making to recover himself was undermined by the growing flush to his skin.

'The beer's still dry?' Gabe asked, and the young man laughed as if this were a great joke.

'Oh yeah,' he said.

'Good to hear it,' Gabe said. 'Give my best to the others, will you?' He held out his hand again. 'Nice to see you, Tom.'

'Nice to see you, Father,' he said, and then quickly pulled his lips together. He did not literally bite his tongue, but it was clear he wanted to.

Gabe raised his hand, a kind of absolution. 'That's all right, Tom,' he said gently.

As we walked on, my brother explained that the young man worked at the brewery that had been part of his first parish. He sometimes came

99

to the noon Mass. A lot of the workers there did.

I said, 'Oh yeah?'

'Jeepers, it's brutal,' Gabe said. He pushed his hat back. Ran a handkerchief over his brow. The soles of my feet had begun to burn, and a blister was forming at the back of my left heel. I felt my dress clinging to my shoulder blades, felt the tickle of sweat running down my spine. Gabe touched my elbow briefly to get me to cross to the shadier side of the street, but the heat was no better there. At a corner candy store he paused and asked if I wanted to duck in for a soda. I looked up, smelled the mingling odors of coffee and newsprint and stale milk, and shook my head no.

When we reached the park, I was surprised to discover how far we had come, although by now my legs felt swollen in my stockings and the pain of the blister on my heel was making me limp. We found a bench just inside, covered in shade, and Gabe said, 'Let's sit before we head back.' He said it with an air of defeat, as if we had formerly agreed that we would not stop at all.

We sat together in the sun-spotted shade. Gabe crossed his legs and folded his hands in his lap. I reached down to take off my left shoe, feeling the thin flesh of the blister pull away with the leather and the silk. There was blood on my stocking. It was late afternoon by now and the park was full of people looking for relief from the heat. Some had already found a spot on a stretch of grass. Others were arriving with picnic baskets. There were kids with baseball bats and mitts hanging, forgotten, it seemed, from their hands. Mothers with carriages. Men with their jackets off. Some in sweat-stained undershirts. My brother took off his hat and put it on the bench between us. He loosened his tie, reached into his pocket for cigarettes and matches. There was something clean, even cool, about the scent of the struck match, the first exhalation of smoke. I watched him as he drew on the cigarette again and saw how handsome his face was — the smooth stubble of his cheek, the amber glow of his skin and his fair hair. There was something lovely about the precision of his hairline at temple and ear, about the hinge of his jaw. His hands, too, were fine, long-fingered. They'd been wrapped in white cloth on the day of his ordination. They had placed the Communion wafer on my tongue. It had been a beautiful winter day, the day of Gabe's ordination. My mother and I had ridden the train out to the seminary together. We'd gone straight to the hospital on our return so my mother could go up to tell my father about all we had seen.

I opened my purse and took out my own handkerchief. I took off my glasses to wipe the perspiration from under my eyes. My parents had said, 'We're not so enamored with the clergy as some.' They had said, 'A priest is a fine thing. But a family is, too.'

Leaving the hospital that evening, my mother had told me, 'Your father might have preferred to see him married.'

With my glasses off, I looked to my brother

once more, my eyes drawn, perhaps, by the movement of his arm, the cigarette to his lips, the suggestion, in my peripheral vision, of a blessing. Here he was again as I preferred him, the red gold of his hair and skin, the familiar blur of his profile seen through my distorted vision: the way I'd known him when we were young, when we had shared that single bedroom. He was not sitting close — the heat required a good space on the bench between us — but I was aware of the easy physical nearness we had known as children.

I put the handkerchief to my eyes and then put my glasses back on. I looked up, looked out, as my brother was doing. I watched the turning silver spokes of an elegant baby carriage go by. And then a woman walking with her lanky son, a gloved finger raised in the air. 'Get this,' Gabe whispered as two teenage girls I knew entered the park. They were dressed in stiff Roman collars and big red choirboy bow ties. 'Sharpies' was what we called them.

'Sacrilege,' Gabe said, amused. 'And in this heat.'

'They go to Bishop's,' I told him.

'They should know better, then,' he said.

One of the girls waved at me, and when I waved back, the other did the same. And then the first girl pretended to stumble. She grabbed her friend's arm, laughing loudly, throwing the laugh back over her shoulder, her eyes on Gabe.

I saw the flirtation. He did not. I felt older than them all.

We watched a young man pass by with his

jacket over his shoulder, a thick book in his hand. Then a pair of policemen with swinging billy clubs. A trio of thin sailors. I watched a pigeon strut in the dirt beneath another bench. I was only vaguely aware of birdsong in the trees, barely audible above the echoing din of the traffic in the street.

Gabe tossed his cigarette into the dirt at his feet. He lifted his hat. The space between us on the bench was wide. He leaned forward, over his knees, his hat in his hands. He spoke without turning.

'He's more to be pitied,' he said softly. 'That bad leg. An affliction like that. It can sometimes make a person more compassionate. You'd expect it would. But more often than not, it makes them cruel.'

I looked up at the trees, the thick landscape of them against the colorless sky. I had loved Walter Hartnett for the hitch in his walk, the built-up shoe, as much as I loved him for his clever smile and his gray eyes.

'More often than not,' Gabe said, 'it diminishes compassion. Makes people resent God. I've seen it. They figure, If He formed me, then why did He choose to form me this way? Why burden me with all this needless pain? It seems deliberate.' He paused.

'Once,' he said, 'we were playing ball. Walter was there, but he was just a little kid. This was long before he made himself grand commissioner of the Brooklyn street leagues.' He looked up at me to see if I laughed. I didn't. 'An ambulance came along,' he went on. 'It stopped

103

just past us, in front of the Corrigans' house. Of course we tore over there to see what was going on. The ambulance men were halfway up the Corrigans' steps when this nursing Sister comes running out of the house next door, waving her arms and saying, 'She's here, over here.' So they turn around, back down the Corrigans' steps and then up the steps next door. All of us right behind them. In no time at all they're back out again with an old woman — Mrs. Cooper, it was, I don't know if you remember her — on a stretcher. Dead, one of us says. Drunk says someone else. But the nun says, 'Mind your own business,' and shoos us all away.' He held the hat between his knees. He was slowly turning it in his hands.

'So we go back to our game,' he said, 'but we're arguing about this, the way kids argue. Each one claiming more assurance than the next. Was she dead or was she dead drunk? Then we all look at Bill Corrigan, as if this is another call for him to make. But Bill's got his fists tight on his knees and there are big tears running down his face. 'Is it my mother?' he says when we come closer, in a voice we hadn't ever heard before, cracked and whispery.'

He was slowly turning his hat in his hands. There was a bit of white satin in the crown, elegant and cool, ecclesiastical.

'I mentioned Bill in a sermon once,' he said. 'I wanted to say something about faith or second sight, but everyone laughed when I said we had a blind umpire when we were kids. So I pretty much left it at that.' He shrugged. There were more kids with baseball bats and mitts passing by even now.

'I guess it was something about those big tears. On a grown man. How many of us had ever seen a grown man cry? I guess it — the weakness of it — brought out something cruel in us.' He paused, looking out across the paths through the park.

'We said, 'Yeah, Bill. It was your mother. She's dead.'' He bit off the word, imitating the street kids they once were. 'And then we just stood there. Bill dropped his head. His shoulders lost their shape. It was only a matter of a few seconds, but for a few seconds we saw him wrecked. His whole life, the rest of his life, however he had foreseen it, blasted. Just for a few seconds. We saw we had done this. Easily. Casually. Made him suffer.' He shook his head and narrowed his eyes, and his voice came from somewhere deep within his chest. 'For a few seconds,' he said, 'we savored it.'

He shook his head. 'It was Walter who finally told him, 'Naa. We're kidding. Not her. It was the old lady next door.' Which got us all slapping Bill on the back and laughing at how we had him fooled. It took a while for him to get the joke.' He gazed out at the park, his hat in his hands. 'Some joke,' he said.

Even late in the afternoon of that day, even after all my tears, the habit of loving Walter Hartnett had not yet left me, and so I assumed that my brother told this story not to admit that he, too, had once been cruel but to prove that Walter had once been kind.

'Rescue me from my enemies, my God,' Gabe said, suddenly sitting back. 'Deliver me from evildoers.' He paused. 'I never much liked playing ball after that. With Bill Corrigan always there. I much preferred staying inside.'

He put his hand on the bench between them. 'I'm sorry this happened to you, Marie,' he said wearily. 'There's a lot of cruelty in the world.' And then he waved his hat to indicate the paths through the park and all the people on them. 'You'll be lucky if this is your worst taste of it.'

Turning away from him, I leaned once more to examine the stinging blister beneath my stocking. I didn't believe him. Didn't believe there could be a worst taste of it. I didn't consider then that my brother, too, might have longed to step out of his skin. Might have carried in those days his own blasted vision of an impossible future.

'Can you make it home?' I heard him say.

I told him I'd be fine if we walked slowly.

He raised his hat to his head, adjusted it jauntily. As he stood, I looked up at him, my right eye squinting closed against the sun. I touched his arm. Even through the fabric of his jacket sleeve, I felt him withdraw a little. Something in him, in his muscle or in his bone, withheld.

'Who's going to love me?' I said.

The brim of his hat cast his eyes in shadow. Behind him, the park teemed with strangers.

'Someone,' he told me. 'Someone will.'

TWO

Once, I woke to find that a black wheel, spoked with flashing silver, had settled behind my left eye. Tom had gotten up sometime before. He was quietly bustling as he did these dark winter mornings of our late middle age — passing shadowy back and forth across the foot of the bed, silhouetted by the dim light of the hallway. He was humming, as always, occasionally breaking into whispered song, his voice deep in his throat. 'Believe Me If All Those Endearing Young Charms.' He was in undershirt and boxer shorts, and the room was filled with the scent of his soap and his shaving cream.

Until I reached for my glasses, all of this was soft-edged and indistinct. All but the solid black image that had imposed itself over my vision. With my head still on the pillow, I put a cupped palm over my right eye and then the left. It was in the left. 'Something's wrong,' I said, sitting up slowly. 'There's something in my eye.'

He was abruptly silent. He crossed to my side of the bed, sat gingerly on the edge of the mattress. He placed a crooked finger under my chin to lift my face as he leaned toward me. I looked up to the shadowed ceiling so I would not blink. I could smell the toothpaste on his breath, the soap on his fleshy shoulders, the aftershave on his warm hand.

'I can't tell,' he said. I told him to turn on the lamp.

He leaned toward the bedside table, the mattress beneath me shifting with his weight. He turned back. Now the light cast across the ceiling was a spill of soft gold. He lifted my chin once again, gently, even coyly, the prelude to a kiss, and peered again at my eyes. 'I can't see anything unusual,' he said.

It was my own fear, as well as my surprise at the shimmer of desire that touched the small of my back when he put his warm hand to my face, that made me speak to him so impatiently. 'Give me my glasses.'

He reached for them — I could have done this myself — and I slipped them on. I cupped my hand over my left eye, and the room settled into its distinct edges. I looked at his face, which was clear again. I could see the blush of irritation from his razor, a pinprick of blood on his cheek. Even then he was smooth-skinned, although there were laugh lines, drawn as if with a pencil, in the corners of his eyes. His lips were thin and serious. His chin grown slack. It seemed a long time since I had looked at him this closely. I put my hand on my right eye and the black wheel was imposed over everything.

'Something's wrong,' I said again. I put my hand out, as if to brush whatever it was away. 'There's a black thing in my left eye.' I described a circle in the air before me and then tried to pluck at it again. I was aware of how foolish I must look — like a madwoman in my thin nightgown, with my hair sleep-skewed, grabbing

110

at nothing. 'There's flashing,' I said. 'Like spokes turning. I can't blink it away.'

I covered the left eye once more and then looked at him. I knew it was not unusual for husbands to become annoyed with sick wives. The neighborhood was filled with such tales. But Tom had tucked his chin into his throat and the lines around his eyes were suddenly deeper. There was more concern than impatience in his face, and no impatience at all in his voice. 'Better call the doctor,' he said.

I heard him humming again in the kitchen as he waited for the doctor's service to pick up, the song an insistence that he was perfectly calm, that nothing much had changed in the last few minutes, nothing disruptive or insurmountable. I heard him explaining it all to Gabe when he came downstairs for breakfast: Marie seems to have damaged her left eye, he said. Sometime in the night.

By late afternoon I was wearing a pirate patch and Tom was leading me to the admitting office of a hospital in Manhattan. Of course, churches should have been the touchstone places of our lives, a pair of Catholics such as we were. But in truth it was the tiled corridors of these old urban hospitals that marked the real occasions of our life together. The births of our four children, my mother's death, the kids' tonsillectomies and appendectomies over the years, his hernia, Gabe's breakdown, and now this surgery, tomorrow, to repair my left eye. And wasn't it a corridor much like this that would provide the backdrop for our last parting?

111

But Tom had his hand on my elbow now, and in the other he carried the kit bag that my ophthalmologist had told me to pack but that the admitting nurse contended I wouldn't need. Tom finagled a private room and, once I was settled in, a dinner tray for himself, although I was only to sip water. There was the strange domesticity of the evening, the smell of food, the sound of the evening news on TV, the scrape of cutlery, and our back-and-forth conversation about ordinary things while the hospital went about its noisy business of paging doctors and delivering medicines, and nurses came in now and again to offer this pre-op information or that.

In the morning — a brown city dawn at the room's narrow, deep-set window — Tom was there again, but he had only touched my hand and kissed my scalp by way of greeting before they came to wheel me down to surgery. They took me in the same bed I'd slept in, so that when they maneuvered it out the door and swung it around to head toward the elevator, I looked over my shoulder and waved goodbye to him as if I were a woman on a passing train. He stood alone in the now strangely empty room, not a bit of concern in his bright smile or his jaunty wave, but unabashed fear and sorrow in his eyes and across his high forehead.

What followed was ten days of blindness. They had bandaged both my eyes so that the healthy one would not go darting about, dragging along, all inadvertently, the one that had been repaired. It seemed a bit much, I told the doctor, but he assured me it was for the best — a little inconvenience now for a better outcome later. I recognized the wheedling phrase from my first labor, when, at the height of the pain, the ether was withheld. A little patience now, the eye surgeon said — after he had been reduced by my blindness to a pair of dry fingertips and the odor of whatever he had on his breath, coffee or bacon in the morning, ketchup or onion if he came in after lunch — for a well-healed eye in the future.

'My eyes,' I told him, the blindness making me raise my chin as I spoke, a bold piece, 'have never been well-heeled.' But he was some kind of Eastern European and didn't get the play on words, only touched his puffy fingertips to my chin. 'Patience,' he said.

I said, 'A patient patient,' and still he didn't respond, although somewhere in the room Tom and Gabe were laughing. Tom said, 'My wife, Doctor, will always have the last word.'

Somewhere in the room during those long days of bandaged darkness, my children sat, talking mostly to one another, mostly about where they had managed to park their cars and what time they had left home, what time they should head out again to avoid the traffic: tunnel or bridge, the Southern State or the L.I.E. I heard the bustle of their winter clothes, zip and unzip, buckle and snap. There was the jingle of car keys and the odor of exhaust. I listened to their familiar voices with a vague indifference. Rattle and clink. It was my first sense of their lives going on without me.

When I woke I was sitting up in the bed. I had no way to tell the hour. I listened, neither the clatter of meal trays nor the smell of the outdoors on visitors' clothes. Perhaps the quiet of a shift change, or the still of late night or of very early morning. The sound of city traffic was hushed and sporadic enough to mean it was either late night or very early morning. The pillows were propped behind me, and my hands lay limply at my sides, outside the thermal blanket whose texture I had begun to know as a sighted person might know a familiar face. I searched for my voice, and even the tentative way I sought it reminded me of how a blind person might scuttle her hands toward something that had fallen just out of reach.

'Hello,' I said finally, weakly enough, feeling foolish to be speaking to an empty room in the middle of the night, or a good hour or two before they brought in breakfast, but adding, nevertheless, 'Is anyone here?' Giving in to foolishness in order to avoid being overtaken by fear.

I had a terrible, lonely image of myself in the white bed, my nose in the air, the gauze wrapped around my eyes. I pictured the lightless hospital room, but since it had been so long since I'd seen this particular one — and had seen it only briefly, even so — I could not be sure if the details were real or imagined, the actual place or a compilation of all the hospital rooms I had ever been in. I imagined the building around me, the dull pulse of all the sleeping bodies it contained, room after room, floor upon floor, above and below. Something of Calvary Cemetery, of Gate of Heaven, about the rows of pale beds and all those strangers with their own troublesome eyes

114

and ears unconscious now, heads thrown back, mouths open, breathing softly into this gray light between night and day.

I heard the sound of movement, some distance from the bed, it seemed — a breath and feather sound of soft movement from an unseen part of the unseen room.

'Me,' a voice said hoarsely. And then, after a shy clearing of the throat, 'I'm here.'

I hesitated. I'll admit I was afraid. I felt my useless eyes moving behind the gauze. 'Who is?' I said. The days of blindness had made my voice impatient and wary.

I knew him, of course, by his laughter. 'Tom,' he said. 'Who else?'

Because Walter Hartnett had said, 'You don't want to go into New York City' — and hadn't poor Pegeen Chehab called it a filthy place? — I studied the want ads in the paper every morning while my mother and Gabe got ready for work and then told them, 'Nothing for me,' in the evening when they returned.

I might still be in my pajamas or a housecoat. I would be sleepy and bored, and the apartment would smell of nail polish or bath salts or the cigarettes I had taken up in my last year at Manual, hoping to look glamorous.

'There was nothing for me,' I would tell them.

My mother lifted the paper, which was always disheveled and thoroughly read, or fetched it from the garbage if I had remembered to throw it away. 'Here.' She pointed to a notice for typists or switchboard operators. 'And here,' holding the paper under my nose. 'What about this?'

I would glance down disdainfully. 'Yes, but that's midtown.' Or, pretending to be surprised at my mother's foolishness, 'But that's Wall Street. I'm not going there.'

Gabe was working for IT&T on Park Avenue. He would emerge from the kitchen with his single after-work drink in his hand, his collar unbuttoned beneath the loosened tie. 'There will be no getting her out of Brooklyn,' he would say. Or, 'She's just a small-town Brooklyn girl.'

116

Tempering my mother's anger with a wink and a nod and a gentle hand to her shoulder, which was really just a plea for peace.

All that Gabe desired in those days, he said, was the peace and quiet in which a fellow might read.

Twice since I'd graduated he'd set up an interview for me in the typing pool at his office, and twice I refused to go. Even my mother, who had found work as a seamstress at Best and Company, had given up pestering me about a sales job there. Every evening that summer and fall we faced one another in the small living room as it caught the fading light. 'Our Marie,' Gabe would pronounce, his collar open and the day's one drink in his hand, 'will not leave this sceptered isle, Momma, this Brooklyn,' charming my mother into some kind of peace, the peace in which a fellow might read. 'You'd better face the fact.'

Although when the time came, when the neighborhood as we had known it had crumbled and was no more, it was Gabe who would not leave.

★ ★ ★

In late September, I came in from Mass with my mother and Gabe and lifted the Sunday paper from the couch. As the two of them put breakfast together in the kitchen, I sat at the dining-room table with it — as was my routine — and turned the pages idly enough until one of them, as I lifted it, buckled like lace. A long column had been neatly removed. I stared, puzzled for a moment. What had been cut out was part of an ad for women's shoes and just the corner of a story continued from page 1, something about the British Prime Minister, a great hero of Gabe's in those days. I looked underneath, to the facing page, and saw that it was the first of the society pages, weddings. And that it was from this page that the long column had been carefully excised. I closed the paper when Gabe came in with the tea and a plate of toast and asked me casually, 'Anything new in the world?'

I might have said, like Joan Blondell (I had been to the movies with Gerty just the night before), What kind of fool do you take me for? except for the quick and wary way Gabe's eyes went to the paper spread out on the table.

'Nothing interesting,' I said vaguely.

Of course, it was Gabe who had cut out the column, Walter's wedding announcement. My mother did not read the newspaper — complained mightily about how much time her children devoted to it, in fact — but Gabe read it thoroughly in the early hours of every morning, especially with all that was going on in Europe. He must have gotten up from the couch while my mother and I were still asleep, gone into the kitchen for the shears. I might have said to him now, Hollywood-style, Do you take me for a fool? Did you think I wouldn't put two and two together?

I knew Walter's wedding had taken place, of course. I knew people from the neighborhood who had been invited. I had watched from my

118

bedroom window, in fact, as Bill Corrigan and his mother got into a cab, his mother dressed for church on a Saturday morning.

But something about Gabe's gesture, its generosity and its futility, made me simply fold the paper up and toss it to another chair.

'I can't be bothered reading it all,' I said. 'It's so dull.'

Gabe nodded, sheepish perhaps. But pleased.

I watched him in his rolled shirtsleeves as he took the plates and the silverware from the sideboard. He, too, had gone to the movies last night with the girl he was seeing from his office. Agnes. He had come in after my mother and I were already in bed. I had followed his silhouette as he passed through our room to get to his own, heard the fall of his shoes and the faint rattle of his belt buckle as he undressed. I knew without hearing that he knelt to pray before climbing into bed. I listened for a while until I heard his steady breathing, his reluctant sleep. When I rolled over again, I saw in the street-lit darkness that my mother was awake, listening as well.

I got up from the table to help him. As if his ploy had actually succeeded, he was suddenly lighthearted. He knocked me with his hip as I reached across him with a cup and saucer, playful and brotherly, the Sunday scent of aftershave and starch still about him. He began telling me about the news, about Czechoslovakia and Germany, and the possibility of war. I nodded, barely listening. Had I seen the photo of the flawless bride, I would have studied it, of course. I would have read, suffering all the while, the details of her attendants and her dress, her fancy schools. My eyes would have lingered on the name: Walter Hartnett, son of Elizabeth Harnett and the late, mustachioed father.

Gabe had thought to spare me that. He had thought he could.

My mother carried in the platter of fried eggs and bacon. My brother was waxing eloquent now, standing at his end of the table while my mother filled the plates. The two of us looking up at him from our chairs. This was, I thought, the language of shy men, men too much alone with their reading and their ideas — politics, war, distant countries, tyrants. Men who would bury their heads in such stuff just to avert their eyes from a woman's simple heartache.

When he finally sat down and bit into his toast, I raised my teacup and said, 'Amadán.' My mother clucked her tongue disapprovingly. Gabe laughed. Of course, he thought I meant his politics. And commended me later for my insight.

★   ★   ★

Now, an evening in late October, my mother walked into the kitchen still wearing her hat and her gloves. I was peeling potatoes at the sink. At summer's close, my mother had declared that if I wasn't going to find myself a job, I was, at least, going to be responsible for getting dinner started for the members of the household who already had one — although with my ineptitude in the kitchen so well established by then, putting the

120

potatoes on to boil or setting out the meat and sprinkling it with salt was the extent of the tasks my mother dared to assign me.

'Fagin,' my mother announced, still in her hat and her gloves and with her pocketbook still on her arm, 'needs a girl. You have an interview with him at nine o'clock tomorrow morning.'

I reached to turn off the water that was running in the sink. I looked at her from over my shoulder. 'The undertaker?' I said.

My mother nodded, smiling: the cat that swallowed the canary. 'I ran into him on the way home. His girl, that lovely Betty, is expecting. She'll be leaving him as soon as he hires someone new. Wear your good suit. If he likes you, you'll have a nice, steady position, right here in Brooklyn. Just what you wanted.' She began to take off her gloves, smiling: a job well done. 'Sit yourself down, dear,' she said generously, all past strife forgiven now that she had won. 'I'll just go change and finish up dinner,' which was the regular routine but which, tonight, my mother said as if it were yet another benefit bestowed. She turned and left the kitchen, humming. Humming.

The potatoes I had peeled were piled on the drain board beside the sink, surrounded by a little puddle of their dirty rinse water. The flesh of them, newly exposed, was sickly white and still gave off an odor of dampness and cold earth. With their blind eyes and mute yellow faces, they resembled nothing more than what they were: pale, underground creatures bred without light — sustenance.

121

Was it any wonder I hated to cook?

'I don't want to work for Fagin,' I said, but weakly. And knew my mother was pretending not to hear.

★　★　★

The funeral parlor was in a brownstone eight blocks away. Mr. Fagin, who was tall and broad-shouldered, with a small neat head, met me at the door, just letting himself in, having gone out to fetch the paper. The two of us climbed the stairs together to his office on the second floor. The parlor floor, he explained as we climbed, was for wakes, the basement was where he and his assistants prepared the bodies, and the second floor was for business. He and his mother lived on the third.

He opened the office door and put out his arm to convey wordlessly that I should go first, and it was this gesture that made me suddenly recall him from the days of my father's funeral, when he had been to me only a broad dark figure silently but effectively directing us: to the coffin or to the car or into the pew at church, and then in and out of the crowded cemetery. I had no recollection of his face from those terrible days, only his benevolent shadow.

And yet his face was, I thought now, sitting across from him, surprisingly pleasant. There were fleshy circles under his eyes, but his cheeks were smooth and rosy and he had a small but easy smile. He had been a redhead once. Although he was now mostly gray, there was the sense of sunny boyishness in his wavy hair, patted down with water. He looked more like a policeman or an athletic priest than an undertaker. The room he used for his office was not large, but it contained a good many things: the big dark desk, two velvet chairs before it, bookcases and a credenza, and a small table with a crystal decanter of sherry, a bottle of whiskey, and a bottle of gin. He sat with his back to the one window in the room, and it showed a lush tree, full of leaves turning yellow and gold. There were black binders on the bookcases, and piles of prayer books, a Bible and a dictionary, and the collected works of Charles Dickens bound in rich leather.

Later he would tell me that it was his intention to reclaim the name of Fagin from the bastard — a writer, he said, whom he loved and admired and despised in what he believed was the very way of brothers.

There was also on one of the shelves, among the books, the bodiless head of a china baby doll, curly-haired and beautiful, with a rosebud smile and what might have been human lashes on the edges of its closed eyes. A model, he would also tell me later, for the face of a child in restful sleep. It was the only thing about the place that made me uncomfortable.

He asked politely after my mother and my brother, and tried to remember precisely, in the Brooklyn way, the street and cross streets where our apartment was. He said, 'Next door to the Chehabs, who have the bakery?' And I said yes.

He nodded thoughtfully. 'Poor Pegeen,' he

said, and pursed his lips to convey, profession-
ally, both his regret for their loss and his
complete resignation to what could not be
undone. 'There was a great beauty.'

I liked him well enough by then to believe he
said this as a gallantry, not an error of memory.

'Nothing worse for a mother than to bury her
child,' he said. 'The worst days of my life are
when we have to bury some mother's child.'

His accent was all Brooklyn — nuttin, motha
— but there was also some vestige of the brogue
he might have had growing up — poorr Pegeen
— that reminded me of my father.

The job was simple enough, as he explained it.
In his twenty years of business, he had always
had, he said, a young woman on the payroll. She
would have nothing to do with the preparation of
the bodies, of course. (I said, 'Thank goodness,'
surprising myself that I spoke out loud. Fagin
laughed.) I was only to serve as a kind of hostess,
greeting the mourners, directing them to the
right room, collecting their Mass cards, and
asking them to sign the book or to take their
seats for the Rosary. At the home wakes, you
stand at the door of the apartment, he said, you
take coats, you indicate where the body is laid
out. I would be especially helpful to him when
they were holding a wake here at the funeral
parlor and another in someone's home, as the
'older ones' still preferred, when it was
sometimes difficult for him to be in two places at
once.

He laughed again and said, 'To tell you the
truth, it's always difficult for me to be in two

124

places at once. You might say impossible,' and he raised his gingery eyebrows. I felt more relief still to see that he was not a solemn man.

He placed his elbows on his desk and held his hands before him. They were large, well-padded hands that nevertheless, perhaps because they were so pale, looked weightless. 'Two things you'll do for this establishment,' he said, 'as I see it,' and moved his hands up and down as if measuring one against the other. 'The first I'll try and put' — he searched for the word — 'delicately.' And raised his eyebrows again. 'We are all men here,' he said, 'me and my two assistants, although, of course, the bodies we receive are of men and women equally. Maybe more women, to tell you the truth. Husbands and sons and brothers go up to the coffin of their female relatives and they see the work we've done: the hair, the rouge, the nice burial dress. Without saying a word about it they might start thinking — I mean some of them, not all — that a certain lack of' — he paused and glanced with some concern over his big fingers and directly into my face, which I felt was growing warm — 'privacy might have been involved in the preparation of the body.'

He paused again, looked at me for my reaction, and then smiled, as if he was satisfied that the worst of what he had to say was over. 'Of course, no one mentions this. In my twenty years in the business, not a single husband or father or brother or son has ever said a word — about this, I mean — but I figure the thought has got to be there. So I've always had a woman in the business. Not to do the work, of course. Not to handle the bodies. Holy smoke.' And he let both weightless hands sink to the desk for a second, as if to recover from the thought. 'But to provide some kind of answer for the men who might think about it, the privacy bit, if you see what I mean. They can tell themselves' — he altered his voice, making it suddenly pensive — 'Well, he has that nice young woman who works for him. Maybe she's the one who buttoned up her dress or put the lipstick on her or fixed her hair.' And telling themselves this, they're freed in a way. They don't have to think about it no further.'

He paused again to gauge my reaction. I only nodded to show that I understood, although, to tell the truth (this, I was also to learn, was Mr. Fagin's favorite refrain), I didn't, not then.

In the green and golden tree behind him, the sun-struck leaves moved with the hopping shadows of birds. A sweet autumnal breeze came through the opened window, only briefly touched with the odor of back-alley garbage.

'And then there's this,' Mr. Fagin said, once more turning his attention to the two ideas he had cupped in his broad hands. 'The vigil, whether it's long or short, is a burden on the brain. I don't mean the wake,' he said quickly. 'The wake is more of a relief than most people realize. I mean the vigil before someone dies. You probably know this from your own poor father' — poorr fadah — 'No one had to tell me when I got the body here that he'd had a terrible ordeal. I could see it for myself. And after a long sickness like that, every brain of every person

126

who stood vigil is numb. I'm sure I don't have to tell you this.' And I averted my eyes for a moment, dropped them to my lap so they would not fill with tears. I had spent the vigil for my father in the hospital's lobby, reading magazines, watching various strangers pass by, many of them carrying cones of flowers or teddy bears, some of them crying. It was my mother and Gabe who had stood by my father's bed.

'And a sudden death is no different — worse, I think,' Mr. Fagin said. 'Look at Pegeen. Because when there's a sudden death, everybody thinks about all the days before, the days that were a vigil, after all, a vigil everyone was living through but nobody knew it.' He shook his shoulders, seemed to shudder a little. 'Worse,' he said. 'But here's where you come in.' He flattened out his right hand and extended it toward me, as if to say, Here you are. 'You are the consoling angel,' he said, indicating me with his big hand. 'The very sight of you gives comfort to a weary eye.' He snapped the extended fingers into a fist, leaving only the thick thumb, which he shook at the bookcase over his shoulder. 'In Charles Dickens's day and age,' he said, 'they always had child mourners. Professional child mourners. I got the idea from him. It's in *Oliver Twist*, the book that besmirches my good name.' He smiled wryly. 'Have you read *David Copperfield?*'

And because I wasn't yet sure I wanted the job, I had no impulse to lie. 'No,' I said. I had read *A Christmas Carol* at Manual and had been frustrated to learn that no one could say, not

127

even my English teacher, if Scrooge had indeed been visited by spirits or had only dreamed it.

'You should,' Mr. Fagin said. And suddenly he stood to take the book from the shelf. He was a large, broad man in his suit, and yet his small head made him seem younger than he was. As he turned back to me with the book in his hands, one of the remaining volumes tilted softly into the empty space. It would remain just so my ten years at Fagin's until I returned the book to him on my last day — married by then and expecting my first child — apologizing that I just kept losing the thread of the tale.

Mr. Fagin sat down again and slid *David Copperfield* across his desk. I took the book in my gloved hand and placed it on my lap. It was heavier than a missal.

'They knew what they were doing in those days,' Mr. Fagin continued. 'It's rest for the weary eye at the end of a long vigil, the sight of someone young, a lovely young woman such as yourself. It reminds us of life. Life again, which is also the hope of resurrection.'

He was silent for a moment, assessing me. Now my cheeks were burning. I had never before heard myself referred to as a lovely young woman. Then he looked down into his own palms, as if to be sure he had given full measure to each one of the two things he had intended to say. He placed his hands on the desk again and looked up.

'Is that your only suit?' he asked.

The question surprised me. I said yes, and then added, not even sure yet I wanted the job, 'I

128

can always borrow another.'

'Have you got some nice dresses?' he asked.

I said yes again, but without much conviction, and he said, as if to himself, 'Probably high-school things. Skirts and sweaters.'

I said, 'Sure.'

'Dresses will be better for visiting hours,' he said. 'Wool, in dark colors, but not black. Navy or deep green is good. Trim and neat. Elegant. With a touch of perfume behind the ears. Betty uses Evening in Paris.'

He reached into his desk drawer and took out a small card, slid it across the desk. 'Muriel in the ladies' department at Abraham & Straus downtown. Go see her. She knows her stuff. She'll help you pick something out. I've got an account. Buy yourself five nice dresses and put them on my account. Bring your mother, too. Your mother knows good quality. You won't go wrong.'

I picked up the card and slipped it between the pages of the book.

Again he studied my face. 'Can you see without those glasses?' he asked.

'Pretty well,' I said, lying, because now I did want the job. I had never in my life bought five new dresses all at once. It was a struggle to get my mother to pay for just one every season. Five at once. I had never even heard of such a thing.

'Take them off,' he said, and I did. 'How many fingers am I holding up?'

The sun on the golden leaves behind him was strong enough to smear his pink hand with light.

'Two,' I said.

129

He laughed. 'Three. But you didn't squint. Good for you. Nothing worse than a four-eyed girl squinting. You can wear them here in the office, but take them off when you're at a wake. I don't think you'll fall down any stairs.'

I nodded and slipped my glasses back on. He studied me again. 'You'll be fine,' he said.

He stood and I stood, and once again he wordlessly directed me to the door. In the paneled vestibule he held out his hand. It was large and soft and gentle in its grip. The hands that had received my poor father's ravaged body. Just beyond him I could see a room with chairs and flowers and the edge of a shining coffin. I looked back at Mr. Fagin, the thick book tucked against my chest as if I had just come from church. My hand was still in his, and I knew in an instant, as if it was something I could actually recall, that it was Fagin who had lifted me to kiss Pegeen Chehab in her coffin, all those years ago.

★   ★   ★

The job proved to be as simple as he had described it. I followed Betty, a robust brunette, for a week, and from then on did as Betty had done, speaking softly but saying little and staying mostly out of the way while the friends and relatives of the deceased gathered to console and to gossip and, not infrequently, to argue with one another in hushed and furious whispers. I rode in the hearse, in the front seat beside the driver, to cemeteries all over the city — up to the Bronx, out to Queens, even to Long Island,

130

which I had seen before only during the long train ride to Gabe's seminary. I stood behind the mourners with my heels sinking into the dirt as the vigil came to a close in what felt like country sunlight or tree-muffled rain, among the gray cityscape of tombstones. I glanced into leafy neighborhoods where I resolved someday I would live, and when I came back to the funeral parlor with a bit of sun on my cheeks or grass on my good shoes Mr. Fagin joked that he wouldn't have to sponsor a Fresh Air kid this year, I was it.

On occasion I saw, and began to understand, the first point Mr. Fagin had tried to make that morning. A grieving husband or father might look on the old wife or the young daughter, nodding sadly at the words of comfort — she looks so lovely, so peaceful, her beauty restored — and then suddenly glance up and around. Even without my glasses, I could make out how their eyes fell on Fagin himself in the back of the room, or on one of his young assistants at the door, and for an instant I could almost see it, glasses or no: the unwelcome thought of what the wife's, the mother's, the daughter's body — at Fagin's we said simply 'the body' — had been through in the hours since her death. Who had touched her and how. And then they would look at me and an answer of sorts would be provided; they would, perhaps even without knowing it, rest assured.

The second point, the one that had to do with *David Copperfield*, was less clear. But I began to have a sense of this, too, as the weeks went by. I dotted Evening in Paris behind my ears and on my wrists, and the scent, along with the good dresses from A&S, and the expensive heels my mother had provided, seemed to raise my station in life, seemed to lend me a maturity I had not had before. I saw grown women, women my mother's age, duck their heads shyly when I quietly greeted them at the funeral parlor door. Old men gratefully took my hand or steadied themselves on my extended arm. Young men who might not have given me a second glance on the street touched their hearts and whispered, 'Thank you, thank you very much,' when I directed them to a chair or handed them a remembrance card as they were leaving. Once, and then twice, and then three times over the course of my first year at Fagin's, one of these young men was waiting for me when I left the funeral parlor or the apartment house at the end of the evening, waiting to ask for my name.

Never once did I have to venture to the basement of the place, although I grew to recognize the particular odor of what went on down there when it wove its way through the heavier scents of the funeral flowers, and my perfume, and the general Brooklyn air: a cloying, vinegary smell that wafted up on occasion but quickly dissipated if I opened a window or fanned the front door. But neither did I fear, after the first few weeks, the sight of the corpse laid out in its coffin at the front of the room.

If the body was a child's, rare enough but not uncommon in my time at Fagin's, I would simply leave my glasses off and avert my eyes. I learned how to drift out of the room at the sound of a mother's keening. Despite the many times, over the years, I had thought of Pegeen Chehab as I stood at the head of a long set of stairs, I never considered until I got to Fagin's the variety of missteps that might take a child from the world: burst appendix, whooping cough, consumption, pneumonia, lead poisoning, the infection from a dog bite once (an angel, Mr. Fagin had said, of the little girl), and accidents, accidents. Run over, drowned, electrocuted by a table fan; one lanky boy had tried to leap between rooftops and fell instead into the lightless areaway — even in his coffin you could see how new his body had been to him.

Later I would tell my own children when they complained that as a mother I had been overcautious about the simplest things, anxious, superstitious, plagued by dreams of disaster: 'You wouldn't say that if you'd seen what I've seen.'

But I quickly came to feel that there was a numbing sameness about the full-grown dead, young or old, male or female. It might have had to do with the particularities of Mr. Fagin's art — I'd heard the two assistants complaining more than once about his heavy-handedness with rouge — it might have been that every mortician, like any artist, from Al Capp to Leonardo da Vinci, had his own recognizable style, a style that could make everyone look alike.

But it was also, I came to believe, the very lifelessness of the bodies that made them all somehow indistinguishable and anonymous. Although it was a favorite refrain among the mourners, there was never any question in my mind that the body at the front of the room was 'only sleeping.' No natural sleep looked like that, no eyes that might flutter open again were ever stitched closed in just that way. And then there was the feel of them, of hand or cheek or arm: stiff and cold and as hard as if they'd been stuffed with horsehair. Even among the many faces I knew — I saw, in my years with Fagin, my fifth grade teacher, Dora Ryan's father, the man who sold Italian ices from a pushcart, old Mrs. Fagin, Mr. Chehab, and, of course, Bill Corrigan himself — there was little continuity between the living and the dead. I was some months at Fagin's before I found the courage to reach into a coffin to adjust a curl or a fallen pair of rosaries, or to brush away an errant bit of lipstick, but having done it once, I was quickly cavalier.

When the boys who waited for me outside the wake, and then later, the uniformed young men who began to fill the city once the war began, asked how I could bear it — being in the presence of the dead day after day — I blew smoke into the air and laughed casually. 'They're just bodies,' I would say. 'Like dolls. Like empty shells. Might as well be a sack of potatoes.'

A starting point, on more than one occasion, for the boys' own arguments, later in the evening, when they slipped their hands inside my blouse or over my stockings, 'We're only bodies, after all, just dolls.' It was an argument I was more often than not happy to let them make, up to a point. By the time I reached my twenties, my

134

heartbreak was mended, I suppose — much as the notion of what might have been still lingered: the bright wedding in the pretty church, not to mention that house in the country — but I was no fool.

★ ★ ★

I said as much to Gabe very late one evening — early morning, in fact, the dawn just striking the kitchen window, lighting up the curtain in the dining room but not yet reaching the couch where he sat in his robe and his slippers, a book in his hands, waiting up for me. I had come in from a date with a GI whose mother we had buried just yesterday. He was a quiet boy, somewhere in the middle of a pack of twelve children. The children, and the various aunts and uncles and cousins who attended them, had filled Fagin's parlor and hallway and vestibule with thunderous shouts of laughter and greeting and argument and conversation and tears. So many people that when the priest led them all in the Rosary at the end of each night, the volume of their collective response — Holy Mary, Mother of God — was enough, Fagin said, to blow the feathers off the wings of the Angel Gabriel himself.

But Rory, my date, was a subdued young man, skinny and long-faced. I had taken his cap from him when he first came in, and for the next three days he was my shadow. Homely, from what I could see of him. In uniform already, home from Camp Crowder to bury his mother and back to soldiering tomorrow — today, I corrected myself, explaining it all to Gabe. After the funeral and the drive to Gate of Heaven, we'd had dinner together, seen a movie, and then I had gone with him to his house to get his kit. There was some crisis with the plumbing, there were children in pajamas everywhere, holding their noses, crying, laughing, battering one another with what looked like broomsticks and plungers, the chaotic world happily closed up over their mother's disappearance. It seemed hardly a one of them noticed that the poor guy was leaving. So out of sympathy alone, I told Gabe, I went with him to the station to wait for his train, where we necked ferociously (I didn't tell Gabe this) and shared a bag of doughnuts and a fifth of whiskey (nor this) until 5:15.

I'd taken a cab home, an extravagance, yes, but wasn't it better to be safe than sorry?

Gabe sat in the middle of the couch, in his bathrobe and his slippers. 'I've made up my mind to enlist, too,' he said softly. 'Better to get in early.' I felt myself sway a little, still drunk. For all the anxieties that would plague me as a mother, for all the superstitions I'd absorbed as a child, my first thought on hearing this was not for Gabe's safety but for his room and his bed, which would be mine once again if he went into the army.

'Now I'm sitting here worrying about leaving Momma alone.'

I had the impulse to sit down next to him, to pat his hand, but the whiskey I'd been drinking made me hesitate. He had lectured me already.

136

Have just one drink when you go out, it's easy enough to do. A boy will respect you for it. He'll be grateful not to have to pay for more. 'If you allow yourself license in little things,' he'd told me, quoting someone or other, 'little by little, you'll be ruined.'

'Momma won't be here alone,' I said, shifting my unsteady weight from one leg to the other. 'I'm here.'

He lifted his arm, tapped on his watch. 'It's six a.m.,' he said, reasonably enough. 'You haven't been home all day. You're just getting in.'

I looked around the narrow room to avoid his frown. 'Oh come on,' I said, trying to make my tongue behave. 'This was a special case. A kid going back to camp. Just buried his mother. I couldn't leave him at the station alone. It's not like I stay out this late every night.' Although I had another date that very evening with the florist's boy, who was also joining up.

Gabe looked at his hands. 'You run around too much,' he said. 'It's not good, Marie. I know you want to make up for what happened with Walter, you want to prove something about yourself. Your attractiveness, I suppose. But this is no way to go about it. Drinking, running around. You'll get yourself into trouble instead.'

I knew what he meant by 'get yourself into trouble,' and I was astonished to discover how furious I became — a lightning bolt of black fury running across my scalp. Furious to discover that he thought of me in this way: that his thoughts had crept in this direction, sitting here in the dark with his book, his prayer book no less,

137

waiting for me to come home. Thinking here in the darkness that I was out somewhere in the city — where, the cold benches of the train station? — baring myself to a stranger, going as far as you could go just to prove Walter Hartnett wrong.

I drew myself up, only a little unsteadily. 'Damn priest,' I said under my breath, but loud enough for him to hear. I would not have said it without the whiskey. 'Holier than thou.' Nor that. 'With your filthy mind,' I said, and it was the whiskey, as well as the truth in what he had said about Walter Hartnett, that tricked me into sudden tears. 'I do not let anyone take liberties,' I said. 'I do not. And I won't let you think that I do.' I stamped my foot. 'I will not.' I saw him glance behind me, to the room where my mother slept, and I said, again, a little more softly but no less furious, 'I will not.'

I opened the purse on my arm. Inside was the empty bottle of whiskey: a memento of the evening. There was also the timetable Rory had written his address on and my handkerchief, covered with the lipstick and cinnamon sugar I had wiped from his mouth before he ran for the train. I took out the handkerchief and held it to my nose: Evening in Paris and Old Spice. It had been a lovely night.

Gabe rose from the couch and lightly, with some distance still between us, put his hands on my shoulders. More to keep me from waking our mother, I suspected, than to comfort me in my only partially righteous indignation — I had, after all, allowed some liberties. I bowed my head to avoid his earnest face. 'What do you know about anything?' I asked him, defiant. 'A lonely bachelor like you. What do you know? You're not married.'

He may have laughed a little, and his amusement was suddenly more infuriating to me than his censure. I looked up at him and said, 'Go get yourself married, momma's boy. Go marry Agnes' — and said her name the way a streetwise, mocking child might say it, the kind of child I had never been — 'then you can tell me what to do.'

Gabe pursed his lips and his face was suddenly regretful, as if the harsh words had been his own. He dropped his hands from my shoulders, held them out as if to show me they were empty. 'Some vows can't be broken,' he said evenly.

I had to look away. I understood how firmly he believed this, but I muttered, 'Nonsense,' anyway. It was all a tangle, my brother's faith, his vocation, his vows, his failure, and it only made me impatient to think of it, after such a lovely night. I wished he could be a simpler kind of man.

I stamped my foot again. 'Apologize,' I demanded.

He stepped away. I did not look up. I could hear the dawn birds, pigeons and sparrows, at the kitchen window. There was more early sunlight still across the carpet roses. I saw how the light touched his long feet in their slippers, the pale flesh of his insteps, as white as marble.

'All right,' I heard him whisper above my

head. 'I'm sorry. I suppose I didn't put it very well.' He stepped back farther still. 'I'm only thinking of your welfare,' he said. 'I'm here to be your guide.'

I put the fragrant handkerchief to my nose. The long-faced Rorys of the world, sweet as they might be, would have their work cut out for them, trying to hold a candle to this earnest brother of mine.

I raised my eyes, to his neat pajamas and the brown flannel robe crossed over his chest, and then to the pale flesh of his throat. I felt some sudden tenderness: instep and throat, were there any places on a body more vulnerable and sad? Had I said he was lonely?

He whispered, 'None of us knows the hour, Marie. Surely you understand this by now, with all your time at Fagin's.' And I shifted my weight again. 'It's as simple as this,' he said. 'I don't want you ever to be in a state of sin. Not for a moment. I don't want any of us to run that risk. I want us to be together in eternity. The way we once were.' And I saw him make some gesture toward the dining-room table and its white cloth and the simple chandelier, all of it looking distant and colorless now in the early-morning light. 'All of us together again, the way we used to be. Dad with us again.'

And I suddenly held up my hand: he would have me blubbering. 'Stop it,' I said, so firmly he took a step back. It was as if I could hear his teeth snap closed. 'You've said enough,' I told him.

Before he left the room, he showed me the

blanket and the pillow he'd placed on what we called the lady chair in the corner. 'Sleep on the couch,' he said. 'You'll surely wake Momma if you go in there now. I'll tell her you came home,' and he looked at his watch again, raising his pale eyebrows, 'much earlier.'

I nodded. But I was still angry or indignant or sorry or embarrassed enough to refuse the kindness. And the light was not so dim in his corner of the room that I failed to see how this disappointed him. 'I'm sorry,' he said again. He aimed for a jollier tone. 'Fools' thoughts are in their mouths, the Bible says. A wise man keeps his words in his heart.'

I turned my back to him. I had learned at Fagin's just how to hold myself aloof whenever someone else's sorrow threatened to send me sprawling. 'Yeah, well,' I said coolly, 'not everything's in a book.'

I heard him say, 'No doubt.' He said, 'Pray for me, anyway, will you?' reminding me — how quickly I had forgotten it — that he was going to enlist. I had to shift my weight once again. And then he turned to the short hallway that led back to my mother's bedroom and, beyond it, the room we once had shared.

'Maybe you wouldn't mind,' Mr. Fagin said early in my tenure, 'every once in a while, when things are quiet here, to go up and have a word with my mother.'

The third-floor apartment was all Irish lace: lace curtains, lace tablecloths, lace doilies on the backs and arms of every chair, lace at the throat of the old lady's dresses, and a lace handkerchief in her pale hands. She was a tiny old woman with a small, pale, pretty face. The apartment was as neat as a pin, and there were always small vases of rearranged funeral flowers on the mantel and the windowsills, on the sideboard and the tea table.

I never found Mrs. Fagin alone, which was surprising, since I so seldom caught sight of her visitors coming in. But every time I climbed the stairs and knocked gently at the apartment door, I heard from behind it the energetic scuffle of another visitor. There would be tea and cake already set out, or a light lunch, or a kettle already whistling in the kitchen. An old Sister of Charity in her pioneer cap would be there, or one of the nursing sisters, the Little Sisters of the Sick Poor, often both. Other old immigrant ladies of all shapes and sizes stepping out of the kitchen, bringing in another chair. Mrs. Fagin always sat in the middle of the high-backed couch, her little feet in black shoes barely touching the floor. She always threw up her hands in delight when I entered the room and touched the space beside her and said something charming and lyrical, 'You're as welcome as the flowers in May' or 'Here's a sight for sore eyes.'

The nuns had to turn their heads to smile at me from within their caps and wimples. I often had the impression that I had just interrupted a long, whispered story one of them was telling. They always seemed to me to be just leaning back. There always seemed to me to be a silenced breath hanging on the air. 'God love you,' Mrs. Fagin would say as I came into the neat room. 'You've just brightened our day.' Although there was no denying, as I came into the lacy, sun-washed room, that their day had already been going along quite brightly.

I sat beside Mrs. Fagin on the stiff couch, or if another old woman or one of the older Sisters was already there, I'd take a single chair. 'Now,' Mrs. Fagin would say when I had my cup, 'what's going on downstairs?'

I would name for her whoever was being waked that evening, or whose family had called that morning to inquire about Fagin's services, or whose body had arrived from the morgue and was currently being prepared. The old lady would cock her head at each name. She had bright blue eyes and pure white hair. Like her son, she might once have been a redhead. 'Oh yes,' she'd say if she knew them, or if the name didn't ring a bell, she would look to the other women in the room until she found the one who could say, 'Oh, sure,' and fill her in on the

143

deceased's pedigree. 'That's Bridget Verde's niece's girl,' they might say. Or, 'Tommy Cute's a friend of his,' or — this mostly from the nursing sisters, who, it seemed, at one point or other had had most of the bodies that came into Fagin's in their care — 'a slow death there,' or 'a weak heart,' or 'His mother, too, died the same way.' When all else failed, one of them would fetch the paper and look for an obituary.

Recollections were raised, sorted, compiled. If there was a good story attached to the life of the dead, whatever woman among them had it would be given the floor, and whatever part of the story was deemed, perhaps, too delicate for the old lady's ears (or, more likely, mine) would be acted out with a series of gestures and nods and sudden silences that I quickly came to be able to interpret as readily as the rest. A finger held to the side of a nose indicated a deception, a pantomimed bottle raised to the mouth meant there was a problem with drink, the rubbing of thumb and forefinger meant money problems (usually because someone, most likely a spouse, was cheap), eyebrows raised and words falling off into a long nod indicated sex ('and he was coming home every night while she was still losing blood and . . . ') — eyebrows, nod, and all the other women would cluck their tongues in sympathy.

Sitting among them, I sometimes recalled the whispering girls on the stoops of my childhood. I sometimes felt just as lost about the tales they proposed. But there was a sense, too, in their sorting out of recollection and rumor, of gossip,

anecdote, story — and even in their disappointment when a body came to the funeral parlor, a
stranger or out-of-towner whom none of them
could produce a single word for — of some duty
on their part, Mrs. Fagin and her attendants, to
weave a biography of sorts for the newly dead.

I say duty, but there was nothing heavy or
morbid about these conversations; there was,
rather, an eager, industrious, even entertaining,
pleasantness in all of it, which is probably why
the apartment always seemed to me to be full of
light and the aftermath of some laughter. Or
maybe it was just the cups of sweet tea that they
served me. 'What's going on downstairs?' Mrs.
Fagin would ask, wanting me to name the recent
dead. And when I did, she and her compatriots
would lean together to tell as best they could the
story of the life — breathing words onto cold
embers was how I sometimes thought of it, and,
one way or another, getting them to glow.

This is how I came to know the fate of Big
Lucy, whose mother was waked at Fagin's in the
early forties. Mrs. Meany was a huge woman,
with a goiter in her neck that Fagin had
powdered as heavily as he had powdered her fat
cheeks. But the results were unsatisfactory. Even
with the makeup, there remained something
awful about the globe of purple, translucent flesh
squashed beneath her chin. After the first night
of the wake, Fagin had gone downstairs and
come back with a broad swathe of pale green
chiffon that he wrapped around her head and
neck so elaborately that when the family
returned the next day Mrs. Meany no longer

145

resembled 'her unfortunate self' — as Mr. Fagin put it — but a kind of mummified dowager queen, which pleased them all immensely. The Meany family was what my mother would have called shanty Irish: large and broadfaced men and women, hardly well scrubbed, with a kind of dumb shyness to them as they entered Fagin's neat parlor and only reluctantly let me take their hats and coats. They whispered awkwardly to one another through the first hour of the wake, but then, as they grew accustomed to the place, began to sprawl and to laugh and to treat Fagin's chairs and lamps and good rugs with a kind of proprietary pride, pointing out a painting on the wall or the quality of the drapes to various visitors as if they themselves had selected and paid for them. Which, Mr. Fagin reminded me when I mentioned this to him, they more or less had.

Mrs. Meany, I learned in Mrs. Fagin's upstairs room, had made the trip — by subway, ferry, bus, and bus — to her daughter's Staten Island asylum every Sunday — every Sunday, it was repeated, rain or shine, for all the years since Big Lucy had vanished from the neighborhood. Lugging, the ladies said, her considerable weight and her thick legs and a shopping bag full of the cakes she had baked (not to mention the swaying baggage — as I thought of it — of that goiter) all the way out to that godforsaken place just to sit for a few hours with the girl, now a woman, who in her derangement spoke only of the most vulgar things. The poor woman, they said, poor Mrs.

146

Meany, cried herself home every Sunday, bus, bus, ferry, subway, unable to look at any of her fellow passengers, man or woman or child, the flesh of their hands and arms and legs, their bodies beneath their clothes, without the terrible images evoked by her daughter's dirty words rising to her mind like bile to the throat.

Because the devil uses dirty words, Mrs. Fagin added, instructing me, her tiny finger held in the air, to make us believe that we're only the sum and substance of ugly things.

But Mrs. Meany, see, the women went on, leaning forward, despite how her heart was broken, pulled herself together, anyway, to put on a good face for the rest of the family at home. And she went back, Sunday after Sunday, right up until the Sunday before she died. Mrs. Meany put her beautiful love — a mother's love — against the terrible scenes that brewed like sewage in that poor girl's troubled mind. She persevered, she baked her cakes, she hauled herself (the goiter swinging) on and off the ferry, and she sat, brokenhearted, holding her daughter's hand, even as Lucy shouted her terrible words, proving to anyone with eyes to see that a mother's love was a beautiful, light, relentless thing that the devil could not diminish.

Collectively, the women sat back, smiling at one another and the glowing conclusion they had wrought out of Mrs. Meany's travail.

And I, out of a certain shyness, or the deference I always felt in the presence of nuns, or perhaps out of respect for Mrs. Fagin's decorum and bright rooms, didn't bring myself to ask

147

them, what would happen to Lucy now that her mother was in the ground?

* * *

Here, too, I learned the true story of Redmond Hogan's mother. Redmond was Walter Harnett's contemporary, one of the stickball-playing boys when I was young — one of the crowd, perhaps, who had played that brief and awful trick on Bill Corrigan when the ambulance stopped at the wrong house. He was killed at Normandy, and not six months later, his mother was waked at Fagin's. Of course, a connection was made — Mrs. Hogan had six older children, but Redmond was her youngest, and thus, it was said, the apple of her eye. She died of a broken heart, was the consensus. It was said at her wake that when the news came of Redmond's death, Mrs. Hogan struggled to get into her hat and coat. She was determined, come hell or high water, to head for Penn Station and the train to Washington, D.C., where she was going to march straight up to the White House and give Mr. Roosevelt what for. It was Florence, her oldest daughter — a broad redheaded woman who even in middle age had skin like porcelain — who told the story at the wake, getting everyone to laugh at her mother's determination and how skillfully Florence had talked her out of her plan. They sat down and wrote a letter to the President instead, describing Redmond and what had been lost. Fifty-two pages of it. Pretty remarkable, Florence said, considering Redmond was only twenty-five.

148

Florence Hogan was a big, redheaded woman with beautiful skin and large brown eyes and a cashmere coat with a wide fur collar that I had tried on in Fagin's cloakroom after I took it from her in the vestibule. It smelled wonderfully of the cold, of cigarette smoke, and of some gorgeous, spicy perfume.

In Mrs. Fagin's living room the women leaned together as I repeated Florence's story about the letter, and then they passed a look, from one to another — it was eye to eye, but it was as clear to me as if it were going hand to hand — before someone said, 'Wasn't Florence the beauty, when she was a girl?' It was agreed. Mrs. Fagin said, 'An Irish rose,' although I knew from the wake that there were German cousins on Mrs. Hogan's side. 'A wild Irish rose,' another old lady said, and there was some rueful laughter.

Florence Hogan when young, the tale began, could have charmed the birds out of the trees. But she was a big girl who grew up fast and couldn't have been more than sixteen when she started going with an older man from no one knew where — White Plains, one of the Sisters offered with some authority, saying it as if the words carried the same impossible implications they would have held had she said Timbuktu or Siberia, or some other far-off place of sand or snow.

Oh, but he was good-looking, Mrs. Fagin said. Very tall and dark-haired. James Redmond was his name. There wasn't a soul in the neighborhood who could help but notice the two of them when they walked down the street

149

together, arm in arm . . . they must have kept company for a good year or so, going out together night after night . . . and here came among the women in Mrs. Fagin's living room the silence and the long nod.

And then James Redmond disappeared from the neighborhood, and beautiful Florence, as large and as beautiful as ever, was seen walking on her own.

It was one of the Little Sisters of the Sick Poor — a chubby nun with a firm and serious face — who took up the tale then, because she remembered the Sister, her compatriot, who had attended Redmond Hogan's birth twenty-five years ago. We were all leaning forward by now, although I suspect I was the only one among them who had never heard this before — a testament, perhaps, to my own naïveté or to the neighborhood's ability to leave unspoken whatever it was that one of our members wished to remain unspoken.

It was Florence, the nun said matter-of-factly, who gave birth to her brother. Poor Redmond. God rest his soul. Mary Jane Hogan's youngest child.

For a moment as I listened I feared that everything I thought I understood about babies being born was somehow wrong — the authority of the Sister's simple words, spoken from inside the immaculate white wimple, was so great. She had to turn her head and shoulders in order to see me on the chair beside her. 'The apple of his mother's eye,' she said, glaring at me to make sure I heard.

150

I was on the stair, going back to my desk just beyond the cloakroom on Fagin's parlor floor, before I understood that it was an impossible proposition: that Florence had given birth to her little brother. Although, even then, I couldn't help but think that the real truth of the matter, biology be damned, was all on the nun's side.

★ ★ ★

And then there was the bishop.

We had in one of the rooms a woman who had been the housekeeper at a nearby rectory. Margaret Tuohy. She was a small pale woman with beautiful black hair — not dyed, Fagin told me with some astonishment. She was a spinster. Her body had come from Brooklyn College Hospital's morgue, but it seemed she'd been in the care of the Little Sisters right up until the end. It was one of them who came by the funeral parlor with the dress Fagin was to put on her: a clean and simple black shift with small polka dots, a churchgoing dress for a woman her age. But later that afternoon a dress box arrived by delivery truck — from Saks Fifth Avenue. Inside was a beautiful silk suit of deep blue, a white silk blouse, and a gold cross and chain, all meant for her. And not twenty minutes after it arrived, a phone call came from a priest with a voice like a radio announcer's. He identified himself as the secretary to His Eminence Martin D. Tuohy in Connecticut. He wanted us to know that the bishop would be attending his sister's wake that evening. He asked if we had received 'the dress,' and full up as I was with all the excitement: the delivery from Saks, the visit from a bishop, I not only said yes, we had, but then went on to tell him how lovely it was, and to thank him profusely. He in turn — since we were both speaking as proxies — told me I was very welcome. He suggested that the gold cross and chain be donated to the missions when the wake was over.

The bishop had his sister's pale skin and black, black hair, and I wondered as I greeted him — as close as I had come to a man of such stature since my own Confirmation — if she'd had his bright blue eyes as well. He was the cleanest-looking human being I had ever met. He wore his black cassock trimmed with red and his long red cloak, his skullcap, but it was his white skin and his clear eyes and his beautiful white hands that impressed me the most. He wasn't a tall man — his secretary, who proved to be as handsome as his voice had implied, strong jawed and attentive, was a good head taller — but as he moved into the room where his sister was laid out, his presence changed the very air. There were other priests and Sisters there — Margaret Tuohy, after all, had long been in the employ of the Church — but none of them could retain their holy luster with the bishop in the room. He went to his sister's coffin and knelt there, his head bent. We all watched silently. Even the soles of his shoes were immaculate, as if they'd just come out of the box. We saw him bless himself and then, for the first time, it seemed, look into the coffin. He reached out to touch his sister's hand. Then, before he stood again, he looked over his shoulder to the handsome secretary and nodded, smiling a little. Expressing his approval, it seemed to me, of the lovely suit.

And then he was gone, sweeping out with the elegance and aplomb of an angel. Fagin was disappointed, I think. I think he was hoping that the bishop would stay to lead the Rosary. Instead, one of the old priests from her parish dispatched the prayers that night with mumbling speed, licking his finger and scratching at a pale white stain on his cassock through one whole decade. He was the same priest who said her funeral Mass the next day and accompanied the body to the cemetery, where a number of other Tuohys already lay. We didn't see her brother again.

In Mrs. Fagin's living room I felt the women recede as I told the story of the delivery from Saks, the handsome secretary, the clean and holy fragrance of the bishop's cloak. I was enchanted still by the excitement of his visit, but as I described it, I noticed, too, how the women looked away now and then in the bright room, turning their chins into their shoulders the way workmen or baseball players or boys in the street might do as they prepared to spit.

'Martin Tuohy,' one of the old immigrant ladies said solemnly when I was finished, 'has done very well for himself.' And the chorus of agreement with which this statement was met did not indicate approval. His family had been poor, they informed me. The poorest of the poor, they said. Coming to Brooklyn from the Lower East Side, living 'from pillar to post' in any number of neighborhoods. The father a dockworker, when he worked. The mother a washerwoman, when she could. There had been other siblings, but they had disappeared long ago. Only Martin and Margaret left by the time they came to our neighborhood, Martin being 'assumed' — I gathered they meant as in the Assumption — into the seminary not long after they arrived, still a boy.

I thought of Gabe, who was overseas by then, and the priest who had sat at our dining-room table, telling my parents over tea that there was clearly a vocation.

His sister Margaret, the women said, 'putting it kindly,' hadn't much wherewithal. Not a whit — they said — of her brother's intelligence or good looks, which surprised me, since I had seen the resemblance between the two in the black hair and the pale skin. But I also knew something by then of how thin the line could be between the best-looking people who had all the advantages and the rest of us.

She had none of her brother's instinctive refinement, either, they said.

'All dees, dems, and doses,' was how they described her. 'A sweet soul,' they added, mitigating their own unkindness. 'But you wouldn't find her dancing at the Waldorf.' Nor attending, it seemed, her brother's ordination, or elevation to bishop, or any of the elegant occasions of his rarefied career. He got her the job at the rectory, the women said, give him credit for that. But no one caught him stopping by to visit her in all these years, and when the Little Sisters who took care of her in her decline — it was cancer of the lower parts, they said — asked at the rectory if her brother the bishop shouldn't be informed that the hour of her death was near, they were told by the parish priest, 'It has been duly noted. Her brother is keeping her in his prayers.' She died without laying her eyes on anything but the big photograph she had of him in his cape and his cross, on a handful of newspaper clippings she had found here and there over the years, and on the impressive collection of Christmas tins that she kept on the mantel of her little room all year round — the tins that had held the fruitcakes her brother the bishop had sent her year after solitary year.

There was a sudden silence in Mrs. Fagin's room. I was aware of the women touching teacups to their saucers, or folding and unfolding their hands.

Not that there was a drop of resentment in Margaret Tuohy, one of the nuns said softly. Simple soul that she was. She knew her brother was an important and holy man, busy with the Lord's work.

Certainly, another said.

I felt their glances touching me from here and there. I felt them exchanging, through their glances, some communication with one another. I became aware of how rapturous I had been just moments before, describing the bishop's visit, his clean hands, the lovely clothes he had sent. They were warning one another, I could tell, not to infect my awe of the man with their own clear-eyed assessment.

I said into their silence, 'It was really a gorgeous suit. A blue like I've never seen. It must have cost a fortune.' Siding, I knew, with the elegant bishop and his handsome secretary.

The ladies murmured their responses, Oh, sure, no doubt, allowing me, I could tell, my right to be taken in.

But then little Mrs. Fagin, her feet barely touching the sunlit floor, raised her white eyebrows and smiled and crooned over her teacup, her brogue, I am certain, kicked up a notch, 'Saks Fifth Avenue no less.'

The words put a stake through the heart of the bishop's pretensions, and my own. In truth, Miss Tuohy's body in its coffin had looked a bit lost in the blue silk of the suit. Her brother couldn't have known, Fagin said, how her last illness had whittled her body to bone.

I bowed my head to take a sip of the cold, sweet tea, and when I looked up again, they were all smiling at me with their clear eyes, gracious and sorrowful and forgiving. Gently sorry, as was their way, for the silly child I was and perhaps would always be, enchanted by baubles, taken in by fools.

Of course, I couldn't help but draw a comparison between the bishop's sister's fate and my own. Walking down Fagin's dark staircase that afternoon, I imagined what the ladies in Mrs. Fagin's living room would have to say about me were I to lose my footing a la Pegeen Chehab and fall fatally down the stairs. I suspected my poorr father would be mentioned (there would be the gesture of a raised glass), my poorr mother, yet another widow in her top-floor aviary (the rubbing, perhaps, of finger and thumb). I wondered if any of the ladies gathered upstairs had ever seen me walking out with Walter Hartnett.

But it was Gabe, I knew, who would give my brief life story the kind of turn that made the ladies lean forward . . . a handsome boy, his parents' pride, and only a year at his first parish before he came back home without his collar. A mystery. I imagined them all — tiny Mrs. Fagin and her lace-curtain friends, the Sisters in their wimples or their caps — raising their eyebrows and letting their words fall off into that long nod . . . though I couldn't say then what it might have meant.

I could not have said then if Gabe's history added scandal to my own, or merely some pity. But I was certain they would know, the ladies in Fagin's upper room. They would know the clear-eyed truth of it. And they would know as well how to choose their words to tell a kinder tale.

And then, of course, inevitably, given the size of the parish and Fagin's steady business there, Walter Hartnett walked through the funeral parlor door.

It was at Bill Corrigan's wake. It was one of the long winters during the war.

Only the week before, I had come up from the subway on a wet but warm Saturday evening after a day of spitting rain. It was the gulley of water at the curb that gave the first hint of something wrong. I had been downtown shopping all day, seeing Muriel at A&S and meeting Gerty and Durna for lunch. We had sat by the window in the restaurant, we had been in and out of the stores. It had not rained very hard downtown that day, and yet there was a river rush of water along the dark curb when I got out of the subway. When I turned the corner of my own street, I saw the fire truck under the streetlights. The firemen were still putting away their black hoses as I approached, and there were small knots of people still gathered on the sidewalk here and there. There were windows open in Bill Corrigan's building, thin, pale curtains waved out from some of them. The first group I came to was made up of poor Mr. and Mrs. Chehab and some other neighbors, as well as Mrs. Shapiro, the landlady who lived on our parlor floor. I had the impression they'd been

158

outside a long time, the way they huddled, and shivered. All the women had wrapped themselves in their own arms, holding their sweaters and coats tightly around their chests, grasping their own forearms and shoulders with hands made pale by the streetlight.

'It's Bill,' Mrs. Shapiro said as I approached, hushed and astonished. 'He put his head in the oven,' she said. 'While his mother was out. Killed himself with the gas.'

Tall Mrs. Chehab looked down at me with her mouth closed tightly over her teeth and her eyes wide.

'There was a little explosion, I guess,' Mrs. Shapiro went on, 'when they forced open the door. Stupid.' She touched her forehead. 'The super couldn't see, so he lit a match. The dope.'

'Idiot,' Mr. Chehab said angrily.

'He didn't know,' another woman said.

'An explosion and a fire,' Mrs. Shapiro said again. She was a thin and wiry woman with a worn face. 'They got the fire out pretty quickly. They just took the body away.' As she spoke, the fire truck, popping and wheezing, began to move.

Across the street a group of women were gathered around the steps of the house beside the Corrigans'. Old Mrs. Corrigan, in her hat and her coat as if she had just come home, was in the midst of them, sitting like a child on the stoop. A large woman sat beside her. Another, Mrs. Lee from the candy store, was crouching at her feet. My mother was there, too, leaning toward the old woman, who was shaking her

159

head and beating her fist against her lap, a keening gesture I had come to know very well. There was a taste of the fire engine's fuel in the wet air and, less precise, the taste of scorched wood. I could hear Mrs. Corrigan's sobs from where I stood, and the women's whispered urging to come inside, out of the cold and the damp. Mr. Chehab was saying in his gentle lilt, 'Why in the world would he do such a thing? Why in the world?'

At my shoulder, Mrs. Shapiro held herself more tightly and shook her head and pinched her nostrils.

'It was a lonely life for him,' she said, finishing the tale.

★ ★ ★

Because this was one of the long winters during the war, the boys grown to men who had known Bill Corrigan for most of their lives were mostly elsewhere now, fighting. Gabe himself was at an air base in England. Bill Corrigan's wake, then, was filled with the older people from the neighborhood, and the neighborhood girls like me, but few enough of the stickball kids who had first made him their umpire, their seer and their sage. Despite this, his mother, who I learned had for family only a sister and a niece from Greenpoint, wanted the three full days of viewing.

Because he had taken his life by his own hand, Bill Corrigan would have no funeral Mass at Mary Star of the Sea, and he could not be buried

160

in Gate of Heaven, where his father and an infant brother lay. Although Mr. Fagin had turned away suicides before, Catholic suicides — no need to get on the wrong side of the Church — he reasoned that this three-day wake was all that Mrs. Corrigan would have, and he gave her the whole affair, coffin and all, gratis, in sympathy.

Bill was a veteran, after all, Mr. Fagin told me. He might have had a good life if he hadn't gone over. It's sometimes more torment for a man, Mr. Fagin said, to consider what might have been than to live with what is. There should be some accommodation for that fact, he said. Some bending. He struck his desk with his big hand.

'To tell you the truth,' he said, 'the damn Church is blind to life sometimes, blind.' And then blessed himself and begged my pardon. 'And don't dare tell anybody I said so.'

It was the beginning of the evening of the second day of the wake. Because the parish priests had to show their disapprobation, it was Fagin who had led the Rosary the night before and would do so again tonight. There would be another crowd, mostly the same neighbors who had been here last night, many of whom had been here this afternoon as well. And would be again tomorrow. But for now it was just old Mrs. Corrigan with her stooped sister and her middle-aged niece, back from dinner and resettling themselves in the front row of chairs — but not before they had, it was a ritual I had observed many times by now, looked into the

161

coffin again, as if to check for any changes while they were gone. I saw Mrs. Corrigan brush a bit of something, nothing most likely, from her big son's lapel. Only a habit of mothering.

It was during Bill Corrigan's wake that I considered for the first time what an effort of will it must have been for Mrs. Corrigan, over all these years, to keep her son in his neat suit and his pressed shirt and his polished shoes day after day. I wondered if it hadn't been the suit all along that gave Bill Corrigan his skills as an umpire, his second sight — at least as far as the boys in the street were concerned. A transformation, it occurred to me then, not unlike the one Mr. Fagin's five dresses had worked in my life.

I stood in the doorway as the three women settled in. I still had my glasses on. I had added more remembrance cards to the small stand — Mrs. Corrigan had chosen one meant for children: a small boy with a great winged guardian angel by his side, knocking on heaven's door — and I was just turning to a new page of the visitors' book when I looked up and saw a subtle shift in the yellow sidelight beside the front door. A small shadow passing under the electric lamp at the entrance that to my now-practiced eye meant a visitor had arrived. Before I had a chance to take my glasses off, the big door was slowly pushed open and Walter Hartnett limped in. It was the limp, of course, I knew, that had kept him from the war.

He took off his hat and looked around. He had not changed much. His hair might have thinned bit. His face might have been a bit fuller. A little heavier altogether, I thought, as he saw me in the doorway and smiled — same grin — and made his way across the vestibule. I smelled the liquor on his breath as soon as he spoke.

'Hello there, Marie,' he said, same wide-open grin and nice gray eyes, edged now in red, and suddenly, even before I had a chance to say, 'Hello, Walter,' filling with tears. 'May I take your hat?' I asked him. He gave me the hat, and then his eyes rose away from my face, to the room beyond me, to the women in their chairs, and then to the coffin where Bill Corrigan lay. Walter raised his chin and turned his head to where his eyes had already taken him. 'This is a hell of a thing, isn't it?' he said. And a large tear ran down his smooth cheek. 'Old Bill,' he whispered. 'What did he want to do that for?' and limped into the room.

Undone, I watched him from the door as he went to the coffin and knelt before it, the built-up shoe cast awkwardly behind him. He bowed his head, putting his forehead against the back of his folded hands. He remained like that, bent and still, for a good minute or two — old Mrs. Corrigan and her sister and her niece watching him respectfully — and then we all heard him gasp and saw his shoulders quake, rhythmically, it seemed, in a series of silent, roiling sobs.

At this point, the front door opened again as more visitors arrived, and I slipped off my glasses and turned my attention their way. When I looked back, the blur that was Walter was shaking hands with Mrs. Corrigan. He seemed to be speaking earnestly.

I watched him limp to the far corner of the room and throw himself into the farthest chair in the last row. He wiped his nose on his sleeve, ran his hands over his face and then through his hair, and then he reached into his suit jacket for a handkerchief, which he held to his nose for a moment and then returned to his inside pocket. I grew busy then, taking hats and coats into the cloakroom, greeting the same people I had greeted the night before. When I glanced back at Walter, he was once again reaching for the handkerchief inside his jacket, and this time I recognized the gesture for what it was, a reenactment of the problem-with-drink panto-mime of the ladies upstairs. I knew if I had my glasses on I'd see it was not a handkerchief he withdrew from his pocket and raised to his face but a flask. When next I glanced at him, he had slumped a bit in the chair and his head was bowed. He seemed to be staring into his own hands, cupped in his lap.

When the Rosary was completed, ending the night, Walter Hartnett didn't stir. Now I was fetching coats for the others. I had developed a strange system: I sniffed each coat when I first took it away: aftershave, perfume, mothballs, perspiration, smoke, and sniffed it again when it was called for — a strange, blind man's way of identifying an owner, but even Mr. Fagin had remarked on its efficiency. My mother was there again that night, but since I was meeting a midshipman at the subway at ten, I told her to go on and walk home with Mrs. Chehab. My

164

mother had seen Walter, of course, and she whispered to me now that I should go and give him a word of comfort, poor man. And with something of the confidence that Evening in Paris and my slim wool dress and my time at Fagin's had lent me, I slipped my glasses on and went to sit beside him.

At the front of the newly quiet room — it was the rhythm and the ritual of every wake — Mr. Fagin was now standing with the three women, who were looking down again at rosy-cheeked Bill Corrigan in his casket, saying a quiet good night one more time, his mother, once again, crying silently.

Walter, watching them, nodded when I sat down, but only briefly touched his eyes to my face, and then to the front of my dress — for which I instantly forgave him because he had wept for Bill Corrigan and, perhaps, because the scent of alcohol on a man was a charm for me still.

His eyes were on the backs of the three women. 'I never really had a father,' he said, and I knew immediately that he was very drunk. 'My old man didn't much care for me when I was a kid. Didn't like the leg. Kind of like the judge now.' He laughed, but to himself. 'He knocked my mother around when he was out of sorts, had nothing much to say to me, and then he was dead.' He gave the word two hard *d*'s, biting it off. 'And that was that.' And then looked at me again. His gray eyes had lost their focus. 'Big Bill was a friend to me,' he said. 'We' — and he seemed to seek the word and then smiled to

165

discover it — 'we conferred, him and me. That's what he'd say, 'Let's confer.' He conferred with me and I conferred with him. Nobody ever conferred with me before.' His eyes were on the past. ''Stay close to me,' he'd say when I came around every day. He'd put his big old hand on my wrist. 'We might have to confer.' He always wanted to hear what I had to say.' He looked back to the front of the room, where Mr. Fagin had now gently turned the three women from the casket and was gently herding them toward the door. I saw him glance at me. The ladies would need their coats. I had my midshipman to meet at ten.

'And you were a good friend to him, Walter,' I said. It was my consoling angel's voice. I could not have said myself if it was sincere.

His eyes dropped to my face once more, and then to my chest, unfocused and indifferent. 'We both got a raw deal,' he said, and for a fraction of a second I thought he was talking about the two of us. I thought he was apologizing. But then he added, 'Me and Bill.'

I was grateful for a moment to be compelled to say, 'Excuse me.' I met the three women at the door and in the vestibule helped Mrs. Corrigan into her coat. Mr. Fagin had arranged for one of the assistants to take all them back to Greenpoint (Greenpernt, as he said it) every evening since the Corrigan apartment had been damaged slightly by the fire and more thoroughly by the fire hoses. Mr. Fagin and I both escorted her to the car waiting in the street, and when he went ahead to open the car door, I felt the full weight of her as she leaned on my arm. I recalled how she had walked her son, her boy, down the steps every morning on the way to his kitchen chair, his hand tucked in the crook of her arm the way a bride holds the arm of a groom. I thought again of the effort it must have taken her to deliver him there every morning in his pressed shirt and his brushed suit.

When the car pulled away from the curb, I turned back. Walter Harnett was at the foot of the stoop now, his hat in his hand. Mr. Fagin bid him good night, glanced over his shoulder at me, and then went inside. I said, when Walter approached, 'I'm sorry, Walter,' in my professional way. He looked down at me. He seemed to have gathered himself together, there was something of the old swagger and charm, despite the red-rimmed eyes. He had taken a remembrance card. I could see the edge of it in his breast pocket. 'They oughta bury him with that chair,' he said, smiling again. 'Remember that chair he sat in every day?'

I nodded. 'I was just thinking about it.' It might have been the first time in my life I understood what an easy bond it was, to share a neighborhood as we had done, to share a time past. 'It's still there,' I added, as if this should amaze him. 'At least it was there this morning. No one's had the heart to take it in.'

He swayed a little. 'No fooling?' he said, and then 'Jeez.' He surveyed the street scene above my head, but without interest. 'I never come here anymore,' he said. 'I moved my mother up to the Bronx, closer to us.'

And I was surprised to discover there was a knife edge to it, the 'us.'

'I think I heard that,' I said, and moved closer to Fagin's door. 'I think my mother mentioned it.'

'Bronx's much nicer.' He was slurring his words. He touched the remembrance card, or perhaps it was the flask underneath. 'I wouldn't wish this neighborhood on a dog.'

I put out my hand. I had learned something about moving people around from Mr. Fagin. 'Good night, Walter,' I said. He looked at my outstretched hand, but didn't take it. 'I was 4F, you know,' he said. 'The gimp.'

'Sure,' I said.

'I wanted to join up,' he said. 'More than anything.'

'Sure,' I said again, and lowered my hand.

'Marines.'

I nodded. I imagined him as some kind of aide de camp, conferring with Patton or MacArthur, his hands held behind his back. 'My brother's army air force,' I told him. 'Over in England.'

Walter shifted unsteadily. The odor of cigarettes and alcohol seemed to be woven into the fabric of his suit. It was a charm to me still, alcohol on a man's breath. 'Army air force is pansies,' Walter said. 'Give me the marines.'

I shrugged. I was aware of the difference between what Walter Hartnett had become in my recollection and how he seemed to me now, in the flesh, heavier than he had been, with all his sharp sophistication worn down to a sad childishness. It was a kind of madness, to be

168

charmed by him still. 'Long as he's safe,' I said. 'That's all I care about.'

Walter peered down at me, maybe a little distrustful now. 'Do you want to get a drink?' he asked. 'Are you through working?' It occurred to me then that he had not been surprised to find me in Fagin's parlor, that he had known, somehow, before he came, that I worked here. Perhaps his mother, too, had kept him informed.

I shook my head. 'I've got to meet someone,' I told him. I saw him glance again at my chest, squinting a bit now, as if to decipher the names of the boys who had been inside my bra since his last visit. 'A boyfriend?' he asked, and when I only shrugged, he swayed a bit and said, 'I get it.'

Standing with him between the streetlight and the light cast by Fagin's door, I recognized that there was an opportunity here — opportunity for recompense — pain for pain. Opportunity to say, 'A midshipman, in fact, an able-bodied seaman,' and wouldn't that have given Walter Hartnett what for?

But Walter Hartnett had loved blind Bill Corrigan since he was a lonely little boy, conferring with him on the sidewalk beside his kitchen chair. Walter and Bill: blind you, gimpy me. It was Walter who said, 'Naa, Bill, not her,' when even Gabe had failed to be kind. Walter who had come here tonight — perhaps the only one of his contemporaries left behind — come down from the Bronx to weep like a child before the world closed up over Bill Corrigan's passing.

I held out my hand again — 'It was nice seeing you, Walter' — and this time he took it. I said,

'Let's both keep poor Bill in our prayers,' because if Walter Hartnett hadn't loved me, he had surely loved Bill Corrigan, and loving Bill Corrigan had now broken his heart.

He shook his head. 'More like him praying for us,' he said. 'Bill's retired from the game.'

I saw him grope for his breast pocket again as he walked away under the streetlights, weaving a bit. But it wasn't the flask, it was the remembrance card he was after. Just before he rounded the corner, I saw how the light caught it, cupped in the palm of his hand.

Of the fifteen or so patients in the waiting room, not one of them sat alone. I mentioned this to my daughter, who looked up from her magazine, looked around, and said, 'That's true.'

'That's nice,' I said. It was the eye surgeon's office. It was the morning he 'did cataracts.'

'They require that you bring someone to help you home,' Susan said. 'It was in the instructions he gave you.'

'I suppose you could always take a cab if you were on your own,' I whispered. Five years widowed, eight without Gabe, thirty without my mother in the world, and sixty-some-odd (sixty-six, could it be?) since my father was gone, and although I had four good grown children to depend on, I sometimes felt I negotiated this time of my life as if from a high, precarious place. For every kindness my children bestowed, every lift to the doctor's, every errand run or holiday dinner shared, I found myself imagining how I might manage if they weren't there, couldn't come, were otherwise engaged.

'No,' Susan said softly. 'The paper said you had to bring someone to escort you home. Another person,' she added.

I paused. 'I guess you could call an escort service, if you didn't have someone,' I said, and when my daughter impatiently dropped the magazine to her lap, I quickly added, 'I'm kidding.'

171

Susan raised the magazine again. 'Relax,' she said, kindly enough, but meaning, I knew, stop talking. Susan had had a rough morning with her children, or so she'd told me when she came to the house, and was not looking forward to going into work when my surgery was over. The whole firm was on edge, a huge case, a court date approaching. And now the doctor was running behind.

The patients around us were middle-aged and older, the middle-aged ones sitting mostly side by side with their peers — spouses or friends — the older ones, every one of them, with younger escorts. Children, no doubt, although the oldest woman in the room was with a black girl, Jamaican from the sound of her voice, a nurse or an aide. Hired. There you go, I thought. An escort. But said nothing.

The doctor came out in his pale blue scrubs, all the little strings of his outfit, the ones that tied the cap to his head, the ones that held the mask he had dropped around his neck, the ones that swung from his drawstring pants — which I always felt were undignified for a professional man — trailing as if he were caught in a breeze. Or running, perhaps, as no doubt he was, since he was running behind and the office was filled with patient patients and their ready eyes.

He approached one of the two women sitting alone on opposite sides of the room. 'Mrs. Something-or-other's daughter?' I didn't catch the name. The woman, in a blue dress and a suntan, attractive, sat up anxiously, but said, 'No.' He went to the other, who was somewhat heavyset and already on the edge of her chair. 'Here I am,' she said as he approached her. 'Mrs. Something-or-other's daughter?' he asked again. And she said, 'Yes.'

'It went very well,' the doctor said. 'She's in recovery now. We'll just monitor her a bit. Say, twenty minutes more. And then she'll be ready for you to take her home.'

'Thank you,' the woman said.

The doctor went back through the door from which he'd come, and another door opened in the far wall and another name was called. A man this time, maybe about sixty, leaving his spouse or sister or friend behind with only a pat of the hand. Just prep right now, in fact, as the smiling nurse told him.

Not half an hour later, the doctor's door opened again and the doctor came out, trailing his strings. He went to the attractive woman in the blue dress and asked, as if he had never seen or spoken to her before, 'Mrs. So-and-so's daughter?' and this time she said yes.

'It went very well,' the doctor said. 'She's in recovery now. We'll just monitor her a bit. Say, twenty minutes. And then she'll be ready for you to take home.'

He left, the nurse's door opened again and another name was called. The old lady with the Jamaican nurse. 'Just prep,' the nurse said kindly as the lady made her way through the door.

Twenty-five minutes by the clock and the doctor returned once more. 'Mrs. Holybody?' or some such or other — he garbled the names — he said to the man's wife, with only a brief,

173

wary glance at the black girl, who was the only other person sitting alone. 'Yes,' the wife said.

'It went very well. He's in recovery now. We'll just monitor him for a while. Say, twenty minutes. And then he'll be ready for you to take home.'

He left. The nurse's door opened again. By now Susan had once more dropped her magazine to her lap. I looked to her and said, 'My head's beginning to spin.' Susan said, 'At least he's consistent.'

And another daughter, whose mother was just going in ('For prep,' said the smiling nurse), looked at us both and shook her head. 'It's almost unbelievable,' she whispered.

By now the finished products, wearing plastic sun shades, were beginning to emerge from yet another door, their escorts rising to meet them with a muffled kind of joy. I was reminded of what I had observed at the airport last month, waiting for my son in the pickup lane, after my visit to Gerty in Florida: the cars would swoop into the curb and the waiting friend or relative would raise a hand from the suitcase, there would be smiles all around, an embrace, an exuberant shaking of hands, a particular kind of elation, not, I was certain, because of the reunion alone — certainly all these New Yorkers couldn't be so fond of one another — but because of all that had been negotiated safely: the takeoff, the landing, the coordinated meeting place, the drive to the airport, because every risk had been run, every anticipated crisis had been averted, and thus something celebratory and delightful about

174

each ordinary reunion. Something, I thought, recalling Mr. Fagin, of the resurrection and the life all about this particular bit of LaGuardia. Even Tommy, I noticed, my oldest, who had never been very demonstrative, thumped me on the back in his large embrace before he lifted my suitcase from the curb.

'Everything went very well,' I heard the doctor saying over my shoulder. 'She's in recovery now. We'll just monitor her a little more. Twenty minutes and she'll be ready for you to take her home.'

And then the 'just prep' nurse called my name.

When my own ordeal was over, Susan rose to meet me. Less exuberant, I thought, than some of the others had been, perhaps because she was now so late to work. But in the elevator Susan said, 'He knew about your detached retina, right, from back when? You told him, didn't you?' I said, 'Of course,' but I found myself slowly putting my hand to my left cheek. I recalled now that it was the cataract in the right eye he was supposed to remove. I saw my daughter raise her chin and pinch her nostrils, once, twice, although there was nothing to smell but the carpet and the bland air of the medical tower elevator. It was precisely as my mother used to do. ''Cause he didn't say everything went very well,' Susan said. I could hear her revving up her attorney voice. 'He said there was scar tissue. From a previous surgery. Like it was a big surprise. He said you'll probably need a corneal transplant, if you don't want to lose that eye.'

175

In the car, Susan said again, 'You told him you had that surgery, back when?'

'Of course,' I told her. 'They took a full history.' I had begun to feel responsible, nevertheless, for the doctor's mistake. Easy enough conclusion to reach when you were an old woman living on your own. Living on a ledge of this high precarious place. Perhaps I had confused left and right, as I had done so often as a child.

Susan banged the steering wheel with the palm of her hand. 'Fuck,' she said. 'He did the wrong eye.'

I had long ago stopped reprimanding my children for their language — quoting Mrs. Fagin with my finger raised. The world was a cruder, more vulgar place than the one I had known. This was the language required to live in it, I supposed.

Susan said, 'I told you we should have gone into the city for this. These suburban doctors are money-crazed. You saw how he ran the place. Like a factory.'

'I'll have a transplant, then,' I said casually. Knowing I wouldn't. A cornea peeled off a corpse, after all the corpses I'd seen? Not likely.

'We should take him to court,' my daughter said. 'Sue him for malpractice.'

I said, 'What's done is done.'

But Susan pushed on. 'I'm serious,' she said. 'He clearly fucked up. And now we'll have to find another doctor — we're going into the city this time — and you'll have to go through another surgery. And I'll have to take more time

176

off from work.' As if each item implied equal effort on all parts. 'There are damages here. Seriously, we should sue.'

I was thinking of the high, precarious ledge life carried you to, the ledge you lived on when you were an old woman alone, four good children or no. I was recalling myself in that ancient city hospital with my eyes bound in tape, calling into an empty room. Not empty, though, not that time.

We were pulling into the driveway. It had been years since we had gotten rid of the carport, and yet I realized I had been anticipating getting out of the car under its shade. Easier on my eyes.

'What do you think?' Susan asked.

I was thinking of the years that had passed since we'd taken down that old carport, and how foolish I'd been to have forgotten, or confused, the time I now lived in. A notion better kept to myself. I told her, 'My brother sometimes said, 'A fool's thoughts are in his mouth.' I think it was from the Bible.'

'Jesus, Mom,' Susan muttered. 'Don't quote me Uncle Gabe blade, tell me what you want to do.' There was the slap and then the sharp echoing pain. A sudden stillness in the car. I had heard my children use the phrase before, joking between themselves. I knew they meant no harm. It was how they looked at the world. 'Sorry,' my daughter said brusquely. 'But I'm serious. What just happened to you is very wrong. How much longer do you think you'll be able to live alone here if you lose an eye? It could start you on a real decline.' I felt her hand

177

against my own. 'I just think someone should be made to pay for all the inconvenience you'll be put through. I seriously think you should seek some consolation.'

I shook my head against her earnestness. There was something of my brother in her certainty about the way the world should run. 'Nonsense,' I told her. And tried to laugh. 'I don't need consolation.'

I heard her sigh with false patience. 'Compensation!' — shouting it. 'I think you should seek some compensation. For pain and suffering.'

I laughed again, sincerely this time. 'Not much chance of that,' I told her. 'Not in this life.'

Inside, she fixed me a cup of tea and a hastily arranged ham sandwich. I settled on the couch in the sunroom with a blanket and a pillow. My daughter kissed the top of my head. 'You'll be all right?' Of course, I understood it wasn't an honest answer she was looking for.

'I'll be fine,' I said. 'You'd better run.'

'Helen will be by this afternoon,' she said. 'I'll stop by in the morning.'

'You are good girls,' I told her.

I closed my eyes. I was aware of my daughter's broad frame standing over me. She wore a dark business suit. 'I didn't mean to hurt your feelings, about Uncle Gabe,' she said, but then added with a laugh, 'We're all pretty sure he was gay.'

I had heard these discussions before among my children. There was a lightness to them, a buoyant interest, as if they were talking about a character on TV. I put my wrist over my eyes to show her I was tired.

I said, 'I don't see the world the way you kids do.'

Susan said, turning away, 'Sometimes you don't see it at all,' getting the last word. I had to laugh at that. She was my daughter.

'Is it you again?' the young man said, bowing a bit before he took the chair beside me. 'I think we met before. I knew your brother.'

But my glasses were in my purse, and even if I'd had them on, I would not have made the connection between this thin blur of a young man and the chubby, florid guy who — he said now — could have bitten his tongue when he once again called my brother 'Father,' even after Gabe had so politely explained that this was no longer the case. On Court Street, before the war.

'Would it be impolite of me to ask what happened?' he said. 'Why he left? He seemed like a good priest. He always gave a good sermon.'

'Well, yes, it would,' I said, and then relented, because he had, after all, crossed the room — a crowded hotel party, a homecoming for some boy I barely knew, the friend of a friend of Gerty's — just to sit beside me. 'It wasn't for him,' I said. And then, relenting further, 'He once said it was because they threatened to throw him out of the seminary for smoking. He said after that he couldn't light up without questioning his vocation.'

He had a round, gullible face. 'No kidding.'

I waved my hand. I decided I might as well put my glasses on. I had no interest in someone with so little sense of humor.

'Just joking,' I said, and took them from my

purse. On occasion I had heard my mother say to those who persisted that Gabe had come home to take care of his mother, after our father died, What else could a loving son do? But I was not inclined to risk foolish tears, mentioning such a thing to this slip of a stranger.

Seen clearly, he was indeed thin, his collar didn't touch his neck, and as a result the knot of his tie seemed somehow unanchored. I had the impression that inside his clothes his flesh was a good inch or so away from the fabric. There were shadows in his cheeks that I had at first attributed to my eyesight, but that I could see now were actual and his own. Even the cuffs of his suit jacket and his shirt seemed too large for him. His hands beneath them were childishly pale.

'Did you just get home?' I asked, relenting again. I was beginning to recognize the look of a GI who'd had a tough time in the war.

'A while ago,' he said, and pulled his lips down in a clownish frown. Then he raised his hand and passed it in front of his face — the comic routine — and he was grinning at me. He had lovely small white teeth.

'Where were you stationed?' I asked, but he shook his head with a brief, Bogey grimace and asked instead, 'What's your brother up to now?'

I told him he was home with us, back at his old job, thinking about college.

'Married?' he asked, and when I said, 'Not yet,' he nodded as if he understood something I might not. 'Once a priest, always a priest,' he

181

said, with more wisdom than I was willing to allow him.

I swatted my hand to brush the platitude away. 'Oh, he's got a string of girlfriends,' I said, and saw by the way he dropped his eyes to the drink in his hand that I had embarrassed him.

He bowed his head to sip from his glass. There was the awkwardness of a halting conversation with a stranger in a crowded room — would it continue or would one of us soon turn away? Gerty and the two other girls I had come with were somewhere in the crowd. Were he to turn away, I would be left sitting alone.

'And what about you?' I asked him, mostly because I did not want to end up sitting here alone, but also because there was the unmistakable tug of sympathy for a guy who so clearly had had a tough time in the war.

He held up his hands and said, 'No strings of girlfriends here.' The blush was visible even beneath his thinning hair.

Which made me blush in turn. This was not going well. 'I meant work,' I said. 'Are you back to work?'

He nodded. 'Back doing my patriotic duty,' he said, saluting, 'brewing beer,' and with that the recollection stirred itself and I knew for certain what day it had been when my brother and I had met him on the street, late August, Court Street, before the war.

Later that same night I asked him, 'How did you know me? After just one meeting, after all that while?'

I was giving him the opportunity to say, Oh, I

182

knew you. I've remembered you across all these years. But he laughed and confessed he hadn't known me at all. That he'd been sitting with a group across the room and one of the girls was filling everybody in on who was who — pointing her bouncing finger here and there around the room and finally coming to me. He made the connection with the young priest he'd once known, the priest he'd once run into on the street, no collar, no longer a priest at all. He asked and learned that yes, indeed, Gabe was my brother.

And then he had crossed the room to introduce himself: Tom Commeford, although I had not remembered the name.

We were at the foot of our stoop. He had taken me home from the hotel, and we had already agreed to see a movie together on my next night off. He'd laughed when I told him where I worked, because, he said — wasn't it funny how things turn out — it was a wake at Fagin's funeral parlor that had brought him to Court Street that hot afternoon in August, before the war.

Standing in the subway coming home, he had leaned toward my ear and said, 'Aren't we in the same profession more or less: biers and beers, stiffs and getting stiff, waking and going out like a light.' He might have gone on like that if I hadn't lost my balance as the car shifted and grabbed his arm. He had patted my hand reassuringly.

He was thin, no more than an inch or two taller than I, balding and round-faced. He should have said, more gallantly, 'Oh, I've remembered you all along.'

He lifted his hat with one hand as he put out the other to say, 'I'm very glad to have met you,' there in the streetlight in front of our house. 'To have met you again,' he added.

I took his hand and surprised myself by saying, 'Would you like to come up? Gabe would love to see you.'

He shook his head. 'Oh, he won't remember me.'

I looked over my shoulder to see that the light was on in my brother's bedroom. He would be reading. He hardly slept for all his reading. He had plans to go to college. 'Gabe remembers everyone,' I said. 'He has the knack.'

And he smiled at me with his beautiful teeth. 'I'll just say a quick hello.'

Climbing the stairs behind me, he said, jovially, 'Your mother's not Italian, is she?' And I paused at the first landing to look back at him. Under the brim of his fedora, his face was flushed. He seemed a little breathless. 'I only know Italian girls named Marie,' he said, his hand on the banister, his voice trailing.

What the question revealed was that he had been thinking of my name as we climbed the stairs: not of the state of the apartment house, which was looking, I thought, a little shabby under the care of a new landlord, or the shape of my rump, or the lateness of the hour, or even of the possibility of a drink being offered once we got upstairs, but of me, my name. Four steps below me when we paused, he now doffed his

184

hat, his face raised to mine, and it was the same sudden panic that had entered his eyes when, back on that summer day, he had misspoken again, called my brother Father again. 'Was that a rude question?' he said softly, a history of his own social failings, or, perhaps, of his own failed offers of affection and friendship now in his voice. He shifted his feet. 'I don't have anything against Italians,' he said.

I couldn't help but laugh. He smiled at me, still uncertain, still in the dark, but grateful to follow my lead. 'It's George M. Cohan,' I said.

He said, 'Ah,' and nodded, as if he understood precisely what I meant, but the pretense lasted hardly a moment. His face fell again. He was, perhaps, incapable of deception. 'I don't get it,' he said.

'Don't you know the song?' I asked him. It was as if all his uncertainty had given me permission to be assured. I hummed a little. ' 'But with propriety, society will say Marie.' The way my father told it, I was going to be Mary until my mother heard that line and decided society and propriety were really what she was after — 'Blessed Virgin Mary, stand aside' — as my father said.'

And I made note, obliquely, that my voice did not catch, no foolish tears. I suddenly felt peculiarly happy, although the drinks at the party had been well watered. 'So, no, not Italian,' I said, a little more kindly than before. I smiled down at this poor young guy, shrunken inside his clothes. 'Just lace-curtain pretension,' I said. 'Both my parents were Irish born.'

The delight, and the relief, on his face made me laugh again. 'No kidding,' he said. 'Mine, too. What a coincidence.'

'Oh yeah,' I said. 'Some coincidence. Two New Yorkers with Irish parents.' And began to climb again.

'Not that I knew them,' he said from behind me. 'My Irish parents. I'm a foundling-home kid, truth be told.'

Once more I paused on the stair to look at him. I wondered suddenly if it was childhood neglect that had shaped him, not the war at all. But he was smiling. 'It's not a sad tale,' he said. 'I never knew them. My parents. They were actors. Vaudeville. My mother was a beauty with a voice like an angel. My father was a dancing man. They left me at a rooming house on Tenth Avenue and continued on their tour.'

'That's awful,' I said, and he shook his head. 'There were at least six other kids I knew growing up who had been told the same story. Vaudeville, voice like an angel, Tenth Avenue, and all. I think half the nuns who ran the place were former chorus girls.' He grinned.

'Were you never adopted?' I asked. There was the tug of sympathy, but also some wariness, I must admit. I had read far enough into *David Copperfield* by then to know a hard-luck childhood could portend a hard-luck life.

'We were only a few days from getting on a train, to be sent out West,' he said. 'Me and some buddies. I was nearly ten. I might have ended up some kind of farmer in the Wild West — can you imagine me in a ten-gallon hat? — but Sister

186

Saviour — now there's a name — held me back. She had a widowed sister in East New York who had just lost a son, older than me, her only child. A teenager. Poor kid drowned out in Rockaway. So I went out and lived with her. She had a very nice place. Very clean.' He grinned again.

'That couldn't have been easy,' I said. Standing above him just those few steps made me feel taller and wiser. Even in the ugly light of the stairway, he had the kind of face you wanted to put your palm to, like a child's.

He shook his head. 'She was a very nice lady. Very refined. God rest her soul. I got no complaints there.'

We turned onto the last landing. Going out with this guy, I thought, would involve a lot of silly laughter, some wit — the buzz of his whispered wisecracks in my ear. But there would be as well his willingness to reveal, or more likely his inability to conceal, that he had been silently rehearsing my name as he climbed the stairs behind me. There would be his willingness to bestow upon me the power to reassure him. He would trust me with his happiness.

At the door of the apartment he said, 'I'll just have a few words and be on my way. I won't wear out my welcome.' He said, as I opened the door, 'Just a quick hello.'

But he was not, I was learning, a man of a single word — of any single word. I placed him on the couch in the living room and walked quietly through the darkened bedroom where my mother was asleep. I knocked on Gabe's door and whispered Tom Commeford's name. He looked up from his book and frowned. 'One of the brewery guys,' I said.

When Gabe walked out into the light of the living room, it was clear that he did indeed remember the man. 'What do you know,' he said, pointing at him, then offering his hand.

'Small world,' Tom said, and swept his hand across the air, as if to indicate the narrow room itself. 'After all these years.'

I told them both to sit at the table while I put the kettle on. And it was the smell of the toast I thought to make for them, burning under the broiler, that brought my mother out of the bedroom in her robe and her long braid, and gave Gabe the opportunity to tell Tom, 'My sister's helpless in the kitchen. Fair warning.'

It was a kind of party, then: the three of us at the dining-room table while my mother made tea and toast and — 'Well, yes, thank you, if it's not too much trouble' — fried some eggs and some slices of ham, as if she recognized, too, in the first moments of their introduction, how little substance this stranger had under his suit.

She placed it all on a warmed platter, eggs, ham, toast, while I set the table.

The two men compared their years in the war. They had both been in England, at two different air bases, although Tom had flown, Gabe had not. There was much back and forth between the two of them as my mother and I listened. Tom had been a radio operator, he said, and with a mouth full of toast and egg, he casually revealed that he'd spent seven months in a German POW camp near the Baltic. He shrugged, glanced at me apologetically when I said, 'My goodness.' The food there didn't much agree with him, he said — you'd never catch him eating another rutabaga — but the company was good. He smiled at us with his small teeth. 'Roll call twice a day, but after that, not much to do. Terrible boredom.'

He painted pictures there, he told us. A way to pass the time. A Red Cross package had arrived with watercolors. One guy was talented. He gave the others lessons. Only Tom stuck with them. Everything he drew was lopsided somehow, but he liked doing it.

Suddenly he reached into his suit jacket and extracted a small tobacco tin. He pressed it against his tie as he pried it open, his hands pale and childish, except for a silver pinky ring, which told me there was some vanity here. There was only a thickly folded piece of paper inside the tin. He took it out and opened it up, smoothing it out on the white tablecloth before passing it across the table to me. All three of us leaned forward to see. 'That's the barracks,' he said softly, apologetically. 'Not very good,' he offered.

It was a cartoon, drawn in smudged pencil. It showed the various bunks, a prisoner lying in each, looking, each one of them, bored and idle, and yet, in each, some personality was displayed. There was a prisoner with his hands behind his head, elbows raised, looking at the ceiling. Another on his side, frowning at the book before him (a single German word, Nein, upside down on its cover), one with his knees raised and his mouth opened, a trail of zzzz's, another asleep

189

on his stomach, his backside in the air. There was a window that showed black slashes of rain and, through them, a distant guard tower, a fence. There were scraps of paper on the wall behind the bunks — intimations of pinups and calendars and days crossed off. There were only touches of color, a wash of pale yellow from the single lamp that hung from the ceiling, hints of khaki and brown and blue in the soldier's clothing, a dash of red that was a woman's dress in the tiny drawing on the wall, its edges curling.

The three of us laughed softly — it seemed called for, given the Sad Sack details, the bulbous noses, and the zzzz's, and the prisoner with his rump in the air. Tom laughed, too. 'No da Vinci here,' he said, looking fondly at his own work. 'But this is more or less the way it looked to me, if I squinted enough.'

'It's very good,' I said, although it was indeed lopsided and amateurish, with strange proportions. 'You could draw for the Sunday funnies.'

My mother said, 'I like how you can see through the window.'

Smiling, blushing, Tom carefully folded the drawing along its well-worn creases and returned it to the tin. No, he wasn't very good, he said. The guy who gave the lessons, a Southerner, was the real artist among them.

He then went on — he was a man who loved to talk — to describe the clever ways they had come up with to expand their little cache of Red Cross watercolors: boiling or mixing things, pollen and leaves, coal dust from the stove, a little ink when he could get it, beet juice, spitting

190

into their palms to dilute some mud, some clay.

He looked up and smiled and laughed a little. 'Funny enough,' he said softly, and then paused as if uncertain about going on. 'Funny thing is,' he said, 'I was doing exactly that one time, spitting into some clay' — he pantomimed, holding out one cupped palm, circling it with the index finger of the other, stirring — 'when I thought about something from the Gospels, actually something that I think you said, Gabe.' I heard the caught and swallowed 'Father.' 'In a sermon, way back when.'

The man's poor face gave everything away: he was embarrassed by where his own talk had led him, and yet driven — as if by some sudden inspiration — to go on with what he had to say.

'Shows you,' he said to me, 'what a small world it is.' And then added, dissatisfied with the cliché, 'Shows you nothing's really arbitrary in this life.' He pulled himself up, leaned over the table a bit. 'Anyway, here's the thing.' He began the pantomime again. 'I'm mixing up some paint and a little bit of clay, diluting it, and I spit into my palm, and I suddenly remember something you said, Gabe, about the blind man, in a sermon. Back when.' And he glanced at my brother somewhat warily.

I said, 'Bill Corrigan.' I indicated the front window. 'The guy across the street. He used to sit outside. His mother dressed him in a suit every day. He was blinded in the First World War. Or mostly blind. The kids used to have him call their games.'

'A blind umpire,' Gabe added.

191

'Gone now,' my mother said.

I said to Tom, 'He killed himself during the war. Poor guy. Turned on the gas.' I pointed toward our own kitchen. 'It shocked us all.' I was beginning to remember how Gabe had told me once that he'd tried to use Bill Corrigan in a sermon.

My mother said, 'He had a devoted mother.'

But Tom looked at us both, shaking his head. 'That's a shame,' he said, polite and deferential, but also frowning, determined not to be diverted. 'But I'm afraid I'm referring to something else. Not about Brooklyn, per se,' he added, somewhat nonsensically, but conveying anyway that he was attempting to be both intelligent and sincere. 'A story from the gospels. Jesus picking up some clay and spitting into it. Putting it on the blind man's eyes.' He looked to Gabe. 'Do you remember what you said? We had a conversation about it, you and I, after Mass. We had a bite of lunch together.'

Gabe's shirt collar was opened, and a deep flush had risen up from under it, up over his throat. The tips of his ears, too, had turned red.

'Nothing very original, I'm afraid,' Gabe said softly.

But Tom was shaking his head again. 'No, no, no,' he said, so earnestly that my mother and I were silenced. Tom looked at us both, still smiling, although that hopeless uncertainty once again crossed his face. He was a guy at the mercy of his own impulse to keep talking. 'You put it very well. Very profound.' He touched his balding dome as if to call forth the recollection.

192

Seemed disappointed that he could not. 'I'll butcher it if I try to say it myself.' He screwed up his mouth, drew back in his chair. 'You don't remember?'

I looked to Gabe, hoping he would be kind. Surely it would take an effort of will not to be kind to this poor guy floundering in his own sincerity. Gabe reached out to touch the cup and saucer on the table before him.

'I probably mentioned the whole profession of faith idea,' Gabe said, relenting. 'There's really no one else in the New Testament who Jesus cures without being asked. Without a profession of faith. I always found that interesting.'

'The guy was just sitting there,' Tom added happily. 'Am I right?'

Gabe nodded, generous in his small smile. 'That's right. John, chapter nine. Jesus and his disciples were having a discussion, it seems, about human suffering being a punishment for sin. The disciples pointed to the blind man begging. This man was born blind, they said, was it because his parents sinned? It was the belief in those days,' he added, young scholar, 'that blindness or deformity was a punishment for the parents' sins.'

'Grateful to be an orphan,' Tom said suddenly, and looked at my mother and me, smiling. 'Or maybe that means I'm in more trouble than most.'

'Well, we're all sinners,' Gabe said. 'But the point is, no one was asking Jesus to cure the man, they were just using him to illustrate their question. And yet, Our Lord, out of compassion alone, it seems to me, approaches the man, picks up some dirt — ' He paused, ducking his head with a wry smile. 'We all know the story.'

'Right,' Tom cried. He sat forward, even briefly lifted himself out of his chair. Then he looked at me and said, 'There you go,' as if his point had been made. 'That's just what I was doing, fooling around with some paint' — once again he pantomimed the action, circling his finger on the palm of his hand — 'a little dirt, a little spit.' He looked to my mother. 'Beg your pardon,' he said. And then added, 'Saliva,' correcting himself. He seemed utterly delighted by yet another connection being made, between that lonely time in the prison camp and this homely one here at our dining-room table, between Gabe's words and his own. He looked into his palm. 'And I thought about what you said, how the guy's just sitting there, not asking, not wearing himself out with asking, you said, and, bingo, Jesus cures him. Just because he feels sorry for the guy. We had lunch together. We talked about it.' He looked up. 'I don't know,' he said cautiously. 'It was a good thing to remember, over there. That you didn't necessarily have to ask. Or even believe. It gave me hope.'

We were silent for a moment, and I could see reflected in his face the uncertainty with which the three of us had received his tale.

'And I don't mean Bob Hope,' he said suddenly, as if this had been his hidden punch line all along.

We laughed, and he brushed his hands together, ridding them of the imagined earth and

194

paint and saliva. 'So that's my war story,' he said with a grin.

'And how did you come to be there?' Gabe asked him. 'In the camp?' He said it softly, as if he were speaking to a penitent. His own time on the army air force base in England had been, as far as my mother and I could tell, a triumph. He'd been promoted twice. A glorified paper pusher was how he put it when he returned, all modesty.

Tom shifted in the chair, glanced at me, and smiled. 'Jerry caught us on a return run,' he said lightly. 'Battered us but good. We had to bail.' He made a stage grimace. He might well have had some vaudeville in his blood. 'That's when I figured I was done for.'

His parachute training, he said, had been short and perfunctory, and after a few easy missions, he'd stopped even imagining himself jumping out of a plane. When the order came, the plane shuddering — like a subway car going over cobblestones, if you can imagine it, he said — he was pretty sure he couldn't do it. He gripped the door. He seriously considered just hanging on. Going down with the ship. But then he felt a push from behind, and then he dropped into the worst nightmare anybody ever had: cloud, smoke, the thick smell of the fuel. A dream's endless falling.

He laughed telling it, as if it were a joke and the joke was on him. Through the years, he would always tell it this way. It was the way even our children retold it.

He said he remembered only *after* he had

pulled the parachute cord — touching his forehead in a comic gesture of despair — that he was supposed to count to ten *before* he pulled it. And then he counted anyway, a second too late, foolishly, all apologetic, as if he thought that if he counted with enough sincerity, the parachute wouldn't notice he was counting too late. And then he counted again. All the way down, he kept counting to ten. He surprised himself, he said, thinking back on it. He surprised himself that he kept counting like that, going down, when what he should have been doing was saying his prayers.

And then out of the noise of the worst and loudest sound he had ever heard and hoped never to hear again he fell into dead silence. Nothing at all, he said — and held out his hands and made his eyes wide to replicate his astonishment.

So suddenly quiet that he thought his ears were blown out for good. He saw the air was now blue and there was a serene patchwork world beneath him. Even children running across a churchyard, into a field, and he thought — 'I kid you not,' he said in his the-joke's-on-me way — 'Now, this isn't so bad. I could get used to this.'

He was floating peacefully; there was some sunshine. The children with their open mouths were like a voiceless chorus beneath him. The terror had vanished, so too the bitter trembling. He thought, he said, 'This might be even better than living.'

The children were the first to reach him when

he fell, tumbling back to the hard earth, busting up his shoulder, breaking his wrist.

'But those kids,' he said, 'that was the luck of the Irish, it turned out.' And he gave a kind of salute to my mother, as if she had arranged things.

Because, he said, the next thing he knew, a mad old Kraut was pointing a Luger at his head, so close that he could smell the hot metal, as if it had just been fired. 'He was in a tizzy,' Tom said. 'Mad as hell,' and he apologized to my mother again for his language. 'I couldn't understand anything he said but *Kinder*, waving the goddamn gun' — he apologized again — 'and telling me, I guess, that he'd like to blow my brains out except for the kids who were there, all around us. He even tried to chase them away, but they were having too much fun, throwing little handfuls of mud in my direction, yelling their heads off. So much excitement. You know how kids are.' He laughed and touched his fingers to the teacup. 'The crazy old Kraut had enough decency not to want to shoot me in front of them.'

My mother put her hands to her lips and said, 'Glory be.'

Tom gave a self-deprecating wave of his hand. 'Well,' he said, 'to make a long story short, a German officer showed up — officer, hell, he looked all of eighteen, like a choirboy — and gave the old man Hail Columbia in German, and then told me in English, in so many words, to get out of the harness and follow him — *mach schnell* — if I wanted to live. It took me a few

197

minutes to get it. I thought I was already dead.'

He laughed again, his face flushed under the light of the chandelier. He was enjoying our attention. He was a man who loved to talk.

'This fellow grabbed me under the arm. I was still wobbly-kneed, shaking like a leaf, but he got me the hell out of there. He told me the old man was crazy, crazy with grief. He'd learned just the day before that his son, his only child, a German airman, had been killed by the Allies. So he was out for revenge. He would have put a bullet in my head if those kids hadn't been there.'

'An eye for an eye,' Gabe said.

Tom sat forward. He shook his head. 'But here's the thing,' he said. He was smiling oddly, with less mirth than before. 'Here's the way I looked at it. And believe me, I had plenty of time to look at it. If the old guy had shot me, then and there, it wouldn't have been the same. It wouldn't have been equal.'

He turned to my mother, as if she alone needed an explanation. 'I was an orphan, you see,' he told her. 'A foundling-home kid. I had no father to grieve for me.' He looked to Gabe again. 'So it wouldn't have evened out, if he'd shot me right then and there. There would have been no counterpart, no American counterpart, so to speak, to match that poor old Kraut and his grief. There still would have been more pain on his side of it. The pain of a father losing a child. There wouldn't have been any pain like that on my side, since I had no father. So it wouldn't have been equal.'

Suddenly he lifted his eyes to the chandelier

198

above the table, and I was both embarrassed and dismayed to see the light there reflect a sudden tear. I saw his throat move as he swallowed with some difficulty. There was, I thought, something unmanly about all this, not just the sudden emotion, but the stream of talk. I was used to more reticence at this table. And yet, there was also the unmistakable tug of sympathy for a guy who had been through so much.

There was an awkward silence — even with all my expertise I struggled to find a word of comfort. And then Gabe said softly, 'We're all of equal value in the eyes of God.'

Tom turned to him with some admiration. I was relieved to see that the tear in his eye hadn't fallen. He brushed it away with his knuckle. 'Well, that's a nicer way to think of it,' he said. He said, 'That's a good point to consider,' and smiled again before he added, 'But that don't mean some of us won't leave this world without anyone much taking notice.'

The platter at the center of the table was empty, and I stood to gather the plates. With some intention, I touched my hip to Tom's arm as I leaned to reach his. He turned his head a bit, smiling, his ear somewhere in the vicinity of my breast and my heart. There was the unmistakable tug of sympathy for a guy who had known such loneliness.

I took a few minutes in the kitchen, rinsing the plates, refilling the kettle, resisting something I couldn't define. I heard my mother telling him, 'Only these two. But my husband used to say we've run the gamut, seeing how different they

199

were. Different as night and day.'

When I returned to the table with another pot of tea, Gabe was saying, 'Amadán was what she called me when she was a kid. Fool. Although the Bible has it that whoever calls his brother a fool will be subject to fiery Gehenna.'

Tom stood as I came in, held out my chair. He was laughing again. 'Gehenna, no less,' he said, relishing the old family story of how I had squelched Gabe's boyish piety with Mrs. Chehab's leftover Irish. 'You're in for it, Marie,' he said, relishing, perhaps, my name.

My mother put her hands to the table and slowly rose. Tom stood, moved to help her with her chair. She touched him gently on the arm, although she was never one to go about touching strangers. 'I'll leave it to you, Tom,' she said, 'to stand between these two. I'm going back to bed.'

So I had my wedding in the pretty church, after all.

Squinting at myself in the narrow bathroom mirror, lovely in my makeup and my veil, I confess to recalling another time: How's that, Mr. Hartnett, I thought, making eyes at my own reflection. Mr. Walter Hartnett.

Gabe walked me down the aisle and surprised me at the last minute by not merely kissing my cheek when we reached Tom but pulling me into a firm embrace. We all joked about it later, at the reception. 'Like he was sending you off to the Foreign Legion,' Tom said. Gabe laughed quietly. Admitted, blushing, that he might have been a little overcome, there was so much to think about on such a day. 'I am the fool of loss,' he said.

'You haven't lost a sister,' Tom told him. 'You've gained me. God help you.'

That night, Tom lifted the blanket and I closed my eyes completely, even though the light in the hotel room was already dim, only a thin shaft from along the bathroom door and the low glow of streetlight behind the thick curtains. 'There's not much to you, is there?' he said.

I was on my back, my hands folded together over my chest so that I was aware of both the new wedding ring on one and the feel of my own heartbeat beneath the other. I wore the white

201

nightgown, satin and lace, that my mother had sewn. It was the centerpiece of my trousseau, and the provocative way my mother had worked the lovely lace into its bodice had come as some surprise to me. My mother, it seemed, knew things she had never spoken of.

'Take it or leave it,' I told Tom with a laugh. I was dizzy with the champagne we had drunk.

And Tom said, 'Oh, I'll take it. If I may.'

There was the stirring touch of alcohol on his breath. The taste of champagne and sweet cake at the back of my throat. The faint, lingering scent of bleach on the hotel's sheets and pillowcases. And it was either an indication of some expertise I didn't know he had, or of my mother's skill with fabric and needle and thread, that I was out of the lovely gown without the slightest effort on my part, without even opening my eyes.

I was naïve enough, drunk enough, to be surprised to find that a body could become a new thing altogether, shed of its clothes. Just as I was surprised to discover, not then, of course, but over time, that in the dark it would all remain unchanged — skin, hair, and limb, bone and blubber, scent and heartbeat and rhythm of breath. Unchanged as far as mouth was concerned, lips were concerned. A mystery revealed only to the long married.

In the morning, in the pale hotel room, what a lot of strangeness. I reached for my glasses to see the time. Just after 7:00 a.m. There was a brown-edged cigarette burn in the wood of the night-stand that I associated somehow with the

202

narrow headache that was searing the center of my brain. My mouth was as dry as ash. Experience told me I would not go back to sleep. Whatever charm the room had had last night, with its low light and drawn shades and elegant silver bucket of champagne, hadn't exactly fled — I had never before, after all, spent a night in a place anything like the St. George Hotel — but there was a weirdness about it all at this hour of the morning — the light behind the pale green curtains and the rattling of the dark radiator, a door slamming somewhere, the revving of motors in the street, a disappointing sense of an ordinary day, even here in the lovely hotel, an ordinary day simply going on. Tom, this stranger, with his thin hair curled like a Coney Island Kewpie doll's above his pink face, was serenely asleep beside me.

I found my nightgown on the floor, slipped into it — hardly a wrinkle, I was happy to discover, good fabric, as my mother had said. The robe was on a chair in the corner. In the bathroom, I threw cold water on my face to relieve the headache. I brushed my teeth and rinsed my mouth, combed my hair, and put on a little lipstick. In the movies, there would be room service, a bellhop pushing a cloth-draped table into the room, ostrich feathers on my sleeves, but it was Sunday morning and we had to fast, since we were meeting my mother and Gabe for ten o'clock Mass. My mother would give us breakfast back home, with all the wedding party invited. There would be some quiet kidding, no doubt, Tom's friends from the brewery especially. At the reception one of them had crooned, 'Oh, how we danced on the night we were wed, we danced and we danced cause the room had no bed.' One had left a jar of Vaseline on the seat of the hired car when we left the reception — which Tom knocked to the floor and I pretended I didn't see.

We were taking a train to a resort outside of Albany, a place Gerty had recommended that would prove to be less elegant than we had hoped.

With my head aching, I recalled something my father had once said, about someone not being the first groom to feel under the weather the morning after the big day. I figured I wasn't the first bride to feel this way, either. And then I remembered it was Dora Ryan's husband he had referred to. The woman pretending to be a man. I was grateful that I hadn't thought of her before this, especially last night, as we slipped out of our clothes.

When I went back to the room, Tom was awake and looking at me with some concern. His hair still stood up above his bald scalp like a pale flame. 'Are you all right?' he whispered as if I were some delicate thing, and although I was a little sore — I'll admit I had wondered at one point if the Vaseline would have helped — I said, blasé, 'Oh, I'm fine, thank you. And yourself?'

He said he suspected a glass of tomato juice with a shot of Worcestershire would help, after Mass. And I quoted my father to him, Not the first groom, after the big night.

He moved aside a bit, as if he needed to make

room for me to get back into bed, and I climbed in beside him.

Strangely — here I was in my satin and lace nightgown and him in his undershirt, in bed together for the first time in our lives and talking as if we were fully clothed and sitting at my mother's table drinking tea — we went over our plans for the day, Mass, breakfast, the subway to Grand Central, or should we splurge and take a cab? Why not? Our packed suitcases were at my mother's — I said 'my mother's' purposefully, self-consciously, not 'my house,' or even 'home,' as if to remind myself of where I now belonged — even if it was only a small apartment in Rego Park that I had barely seen, that Tom had secured only two weeks earlier. I said 'the old neighborhood,' although it had been my neighborhood just the day before.

Because she was on my mind, or perhaps because we were a married couple now and such subjects were no longer impolite, I told him the story of Dora Ryan's travail, back in the old neighborhood: a woman pretending to be a man.

'More to be pitied,' Tom said. He in turn told me about a fellow he worked with, Darcy Furlong, from the South. 'A nice guy,' he said, 'but a window dresser, if you know what I mean.' Some of the other fellows had given him a hard time until the boss put a stop to it — the guy's tormented enough, was the way the boss, Mr. Heep, had put it to Tom.

(At our reception, Mr. Fagin and Mr. Heep had stood before me, arm in arm, laughing and pointing at each other, shouting about what they called the 'irony of it,' that they both had names out of Charles Dickens. I thought it only a meaningless happenstance, but Tom, who had learned his catechism from former chorus girls, saw every such coincidence as God's winking reminder that He was a regular Ziegfeld, orchestrating everything. Tom raised his glass to the two men and said, 'Beers and biers,' which got everybody roaring.)

'You've got to have some pity for them,' Tom said. 'People like that. It's got to be a lonely life.'

And we drew closer together, in our new and unaccustomed intimacy, under the hotel sheets that smelled faintly of bleach and now of our own sleep-warmed bodies.

For one of us at least, we knew, we were certain — this is how we saw the world — there would never again be loneliness in life. For Tom, as it turned out.

He shifted in the bed and put his arm around my waist, put his face to the satin and lace of my lap. There was the sound of water running in another room, another door closing somewhere nearby, and short voices in the hall. The ordinary, rushing world going on, closing up over happiness as readily as it moved to heal sorrow.

I reminded him that we didn't have much time, we had to get going if we were going to make it to Mass. His cheek against my bare arm was rough with the night's stubble. The taste of champagne lingered on his breath. To hell with time, he said, and I marveled to discover that this was something we might also do in daylight.

The figure in the doorway was squarely built, broad-shouldered in his long white T-shirt and with a wide dark head, but not tall, and decidedly pitched to the right.

'Can't you sleep, Marie?' he said.

'No,' I told him.

'Would you like some hot milk?' A smiling lilt to the words.

'No,' I said, resisting the charm of it.

I heard him sigh. Saw him tilt a little farther to his right, leaning, I supposed, against the door frame.

'Is there anything at all I can do for you?' he said. There was some golden light, hallway light, behind him. There was the lamplight from behind my chair that touched his white T-shirt. He had told me at some point that he'd found a cardboard box of them, size XXL, on the side of the Grand Central Parkway, and now he wore them every day to work, fresh and clean, a little too long, perhaps. He was not a tall man, but broad and strong, although somewhat mis-shapen. He had had scoliosis as a child. He had told me this, too. Like most of the workers here, caregivers they called themselves, he was from one of the Islands and spoke with a lilt that was often both beautiful and incomprehensible.

'I'm fine,' I said.

If you're the caregiver, I sometimes said, am I

the caretaker? But they didn't understand the joke.

'Would you like to get back into bed?' he asked, and I lifted my hand. Sleep eluded me in the way so many things had begun to do: recollections, sounds, vision. I had grown weary of waiting for it. 'No,' I said, 'I'm better off in the chair.'

'I think you would be better off in the bed,' he said.

And I told him I had four children, six grandchildren, and each one of them did an excellent imitation of my mother. He should try another tactic.

I heard him laugh. He said, 'But your mother couldn't teach you to bake the bread.'

I said, 'That's true.' It surprised me to recall that I had told him the story. 'I thought if I learned to cook, my mother would die. The way it happened to my friend. I was a stubborn child,' I added. ''A bold piece' is what my mother called me.'

With the way my eyes were, and the way the hallway light shone behind him, it was impossible to see his face, but I heard his laughter, which was meant to tell me I hadn't changed. Two small children, who were not real, stood beside him, leaning against the hem of his oversized shirt. It was a trick my eyes had begun to play on me: figures appearing here and there, mostly in my peripheral vision: strangers, children in old-fashioned clothes, sometimes nuns in long habits or women with babies in their arms. A clean and lacy light all about them.

When I told my own children about this, they either nodded impatiently — well, if you'd had that transplant — or commiserated with false enthusiasm: maybe it means you're regaining some vision. Even with my diminished eyesight, I knew they were exchanging 'Let's be tolerant' looks. Once, I asked them, impatiently — an impatient patient — 'Why do you think every mystery is just a trick of the light?'

But my caregiver here in the doorway, in his oversized T-shirt, found in a cardboard box on an access road off the Grand Central Parkway — I knew all his stories just as he knew mine — called these illusions angels, the consoling angels that appeared to only the few, in their old age. He said I saw them because I had once saved someone's life. Some Island superstition, I thought, or a tactic from the caregivers' manual. But closer to what I wanted to believe, to tell the truth.

Still, I told him he was very much mistaken. I said I'd worked at Fagin's funeral parlor until my first child came along. I was the consoling angel in those days, I said. I helped bury the dead. I didn't save a one of them.

Now he asked me, his hands held to his sides as if to place them on the illusory children's heads, 'Will you call me when you're ready to get into the bed? Will you do that at least, so I can help you?'

I said, 'I will,' and the silence that followed told me he knew I lied. I saw the children move into the room.

'If you ask,' he said softly, 'you know I will do

it for you. You only have to ask.' And then he disappeared from what was left of my vision, because my eyes suddenly brimmed with foolish tears.

I suppose I stood then, because he caught me as I fell.

The doctor was red-faced. His hands were abrupt. 'Mrs. Commeford,' he said, 'you are not cooperating.'

Although I could not see it, I knew there must have been perspiration beaded on his forehead, because as he leaned to shout at me, a drop of it hit the sheet beneath my chin. I didn't see it fall, but somehow I heard the sound it made, and in my pain I imagined that out of that sound, the sound of a raindrop on a dry roof, there rose more profoundly the scent of the hospital laundry, the scent of bleach on the sheet that nearly reminded me, too, of some experience in this life that I might have liked, might have loved, even — my first night with Tom, under sheets that had not been dried in the sun or on a line in my mother's kitchen — but the pain was a swelling black tide that engulfed the brief, bright recollection in the same way it began to absorb the doctor's red face and the hovering nurses in white and the light in the room — daylight or electric, who could say. I had been in labor for hours and hours by then, days perhaps.

I had not understood, I had not been told, the extent of the suffering involved, from the cramps of the enema to the scrape of the razor to the endless searing rise and the long aching fall of each contraction.

I had sent so many entreaties to heaven by

then — first, that my baby would be healthy; then, that I would please not die; now, only that the pain might end — that I had begun to see myself as some kind of Fuller Brush salesman knocking on a solid door, a door without hinges, without knobs. Hours, days, could it be weeks, into this ordeal, I'd given up the hope of getting an answer, and so turned my pleas instead to my own father, who had loved me and would have wept to see me here, trussed up like a beast in a slaughterhouse, trapped under the weight of my belly, racked with pain, and now, among so many indignities, this man, this doctor, shouting angrily into my face.

'I am cooperating,' I managed to say, and wanted to add something shocking and bitter and profane. But the black tide was surging across memory, too. I couldn't reach the words I wanted: bastard, son of a bitch, amadán, damn fool.

There was, somewhere beside my ear, a hiss of air. The white nurse leaned in. She held in her hand the rubber mask, offering the ether, but the doctor brushed her away with a wave of his hand. She seemed to disappear into the light. 'Oh, please,' I heard my own voice, not roaring out those curse words as I had imagined, but pleading, whimpering and thin.

The man leaned down again. This was not my own doctor but one, I recalled, brought in sometime in the last few hours or days, red-faced, imperious, with abrupt, impatient hands. 'A little pain now,' he said, 'for a good outcome later. For your baby.' A good outcome.

212

A bitter drop of his perspiration fell on my lip, and then he leaned across me and his white chest absorbed like cotton the black wash of my pain. He was going to smother me, the only antidote, of course, for my suffering. Fool that I had been to think otherwise. No other relief but dying, letting go of this poor body at last, sloughing it off, a shell, a doll. They could stuff it with horsehair. I would make no more entreaties: I would fall effortlessly against the solid and unyielding door.

They tore me in two. Later, making a joke of it, I said I was run over by the Coney Island Express, the parameters of the pain, from breast to thigh, just about the distance between the black steel of the subway tracks. The odor of blood that filled the crowded room like the underground scent of hollowed rock and cold steel. I heard, in fact, the walloping, beating rhythm of passing subway cars just as the red-faced doctor sliced me apart without sufficient anesthesia, without any at all, I was certain. And pulled the baby out. And sewed me up again so that I felt every stitch. Pain like the walloping beat, light and dark and pounding air, of a passing train, steel against bitter steel, a train passing over me, cracking my hip bones and rattling the teeth in my china skull.

'Unnecessarily withheld,' two of the nurses said later as they bathed me and changed my dressing and returned my limp body, still mine, it seemed, to a bed on the ward. They spoke softly, looking over their shoulders to the door and the hallway outside. 'He had his training in the army,' they told me. 'He had a bad war.' 'Cruel,' they said of him. 'Brutal.' They said, 'He thinks women need to be more stoic about these things.'

But when the doctor came into the room again, they only smiled and bowed and then scattered like pigeons when he shouted his demands.

I saw my mother in a chair by the window when I opened my eyes again. My mother wore her hat and her pale broadcloth summer suit, and she held her purse on her lap. The slatted sunlight had washed her of all color. I thought for a moment that we might both have died during the long days and nights of my ordeal, not because of the pale light in the blank room, but because of the sweet assurance I felt, waking and seeing my mother there, that I was loved, cherished beyond all reason. The peace of this, the stillness of the room, the temporary suspension of pain, seemed evidence enough that I had come to the end of time. I felt a strange elation. And then I closed my eyes and slept again.

It was evening and the light was low and Tom was in the chair when I next opened them. And then a parched morning, the sound of trays and rolling bassinets and babies crying here and there, the sound of the nurse's voice as she leaned over me, all of it furred and fiery. I had an unshakable image of red-flocked wallpaper growing like fungus over my tongue and down my throat. They threw whatever covered me aside, but there was no relief in the chill I now felt on my damp skin.

The wide bandages were ripped from what was left of the poor pale flesh suspended between the thin bones of my hips. There was the sweet, pungent odor of pus. There were barked orders from the military doctor, or perhaps this was another one. More indifferent hands running over my flesh; no indignity in it anymore, I had grown so accustomed to it now. A broad nurse with gold curls beneath her cap washed my naked body with a large sponge, running the thing up and down over my extended arm — extended because the nurse had lifted my hand and clamped it under her own armpit, in the casually efficient way a busy woman hanging clothes holds a clothespin in her mouth. She ran the sponge up over my shoulders and between my breasts. The nurse wore a damp apron over her uniform, and her fat arms were as cool and solid as gray marble. There was the faint smell of vinegar in the air.

Later I heard my mother's voice raised in anger, but had no strength to assure her that there was no need to object: a body, after all, was a paltry thing, and really, Momma, all modesty had long ago gone out the window.

And then there were murmured prayers. A bald priest in a black cassock with a green-and-gold stole, with a missal in one hand and the other reaching for the small container Gabe held out to him in his cupped palm. Gabe, too, in a pale suit, standing at the dark priest's elbow, but presiding somehow, elegant and assured, none-theless. I focused on Gabe's hands. His beautiful hands. And then I felt the flesh of the priest's thumb against my forehead and my palms. And then someone fumbled with the blanket at my feet and I whispered, or so I was later told, 'Oh, honestly.' It was Tom who laughed then. I knew him by his laughter.

Later, he put his dry lips to my cheek and held them there.

'Please,' he said, later still.

'A beautiful boy,' he said, and kissed me again.

He said, 'You're doing fine.'

And another time, 'Home soon.'

I heard the loudmouth doctor say, 'Built like a child to begin with,' and kept my eyes closed, pretending to sleep.

Then another morning, and when the doctor came in, I was sitting up in the bed and had just finished a light breakfast. He folded the blanket down to my thighs to examine my incision, but this time with a polite caution I had not seen before. He even said, 'If I may.' He touched the bandages with his fingertips. It occurred to me that I had become accustomed to looking down across my body to find his head hovering there. I knew his bald spot as well as I knew Tom's. He said, 'That's fine, much better,' and then quickly, almost shyly, covered me again. He was, I thought, giving my body back to me. I felt a peculiar regret, the end of some intimacy.

He put his hand on my forearm. He was red-faced and gray-haired and strong-jawed. He looked like an old general. Someone had told me he'd had a bad war. Brutal. 'Don't have any more children,' he said. And then turned to the nurse in the doorway. 'Bring this little mother her boy.'

★ ★ ★

At home — it was agreed that I would go back to my mother's house until I was fully recovered — my mother said, 'There is the ring. There is the sheath. You can take your temperature every morning and keep a record. You can sleep in separate beds.'

The baby, little Tommy, was plump and healthy, alive in my arms, and he woke every three hours. Once again, my mother and I were sharing the big bed. My mother was up at the child's first whimper, always the warmed bottle of formula at the ready. The ordeal that had almost killed me was reduced now to the hot red incision that split my belly — so jagged and roughly sewn that my mother, seeing it, had whispered, 'I'd like to wring his neck.' If I moved the wrong way, the pain from it would flare across my entire midsection, make me stoop to catch my breath.

My long ordeal, as I'd come to call it, reduced as well to the ache in my breasts that my own doctor had assured me would soon go away as my milk dried up. He was gentler than the general, but still he spoke of my breasts and the milk they were producing with a dismissive smile, as if the whole process was some vestige of a primitive time — an immigrant custom, as one of the nurses on the ward had called it when my mother, who kept asking why I didn't nurse the child, was out of the room — a persistent biological habit that these young mothers, had they only the wherewithal, would have long ago managed to break. None of my friends nursed their babies, and the infection I'd had in the hospital would have precluded it, anyway. Not that this satisfied my mother, who watched the child rooting against my shoulder and said, 'He knows what he's missing.'

A married woman now, nearing thirty, with a beautiful child alive in my arms and a body that had been flayed, publicly, indifferently exposed, not to mention a memory of that solid, unyielding door — death's door, yes, as I thought of it — remembering for a moment, with a stir in my spine, the exposed breast, lit as if from within, and Walter Hartnett's mouth moving toward me.

★ ★ ★

Tom came to the apartment after work and had dinner with us, usually with the baby in his arms, and then sat in the living room holding my hand, chatting and chatting in his cheerful way, only, reluctantly, lifting his hat and kissing us both goodbye when I got up to go to bed. I followed him to the door — I was still to avoid stairs — but more often than not, Gabe walked him to his car. Gabe said, in the first days of this routine, he did it because Tom seemed such a lonely soul, going back alone to our apartment in Queens, but I began to suspect my brother had another intention in accompanying poor Tom

218

down the stairs. There was the matter, after all, of the doctor's injunction. I must not have another child.

When we were alone in the apartment, my mother said, 'There is the ring. There was once a woman who lived on Joralemon, above the Chehabs' bakery, who you could go to for the thing. But the right doctor could tell you as well. There is the sheath, if Tom will oblige. You can take your temperature every morning and keep a record. You can sleep in separate beds or separate rooms, and if he comes to you in the night, you can say' — she lifted her nose into the air — ' ''And who'll raise this baby when I'm dead?'' You can sleep with a soup spoon under your pillow and give him a whack with the back of it — I don't have to tell you where.' Which got us laughing like girls. My mother knew things she had never spoken of before.

In the kitchen, the bustling sounds of diapers boiling, bottles roiling in the speckled pot.

My mother said, 'When the priest came to your bed that night, I told Gabe to send him away. All day I'd been watching out the window, and it may be that I had sun spots still in my eyes, but I didn't like the look of him, that priest. In his black suit with his tiny bag. I'd been looking out the window all day. I watched the sun grow strong and I counted the shadows as the whole day went by, and I had on my mind that it was nighttime when your father died in this very same place. While you and I were home and asleep, and Gabe was asleep at the rectory. Slipped away in the night when

219

none of us was near. I know I was afraid of the night coming, as frightened as any child. I was afraid that it was in the night that you would slip away from us, too.'

We were at the familiar table, my mother in her usual chair, folding the diapers she had just taken from the line. The summer heat had abated, but the window was still open. I was sitting at Gabe's end of the table, to avoid the draft. I had the baby on my shoulder.

'The priest, to my eyes, seemed very dark in his suit,' my mother said, 'with his little black bag, standing in the doorway and then coming toward your bed. I told Gabe to send him away. He was upset with me. He steered the man by his elbow, just out into the hall, and then he came back in and said that this was something we must do for you, to assure you'd get into heaven. The last rites. He was very serious. You know how he can be. A sacrament, he kept saying, as if I had forgotten.' She raised her chin, in some imitation of the defiance with which she had met Gabe's words. 'I hadn't forgotten,' she said. 'I just didn't like the looks of the man, coming toward your bed like that. A black-suited banshee. I was desperate with the fear that I'd lose you.

'I said to Gabe, 'She's a young woman just after giving birth to her first child, who's going to keep her out of heaven?' I said to him, 'How do you know she won't see him praying over her and give up the fight?' I said to him finally, 'You're a priest, aren't you? You're still a priest. Send that blaggard away and give her the

220

blessing yourself. Didn't you do as much for your poor father?''

My mother, telling it, put her fingertips to her lips. The morning sunlight touched her downy cheek and crossed her lap where the white diapers were neatly arrayed. The lace curtain, her handiwork, stirred. 'Which was terrible of me,' she said. 'Reminding him of that heartache.' She looked at me. My mother wore glasses by then, and her salt-and-pepper hair was neatly permed. No longer for her the long graying braids of the immigrant. 'He was barely ordained,' she said. 'It was a terrible thing to have asked him to do at the time, and it was a terrible thing to throw in his face just because that mincing black priest made me angry.' She took another clean diaper from the basket on the table, folded it neatly.

The baby began to fuss, and I stood. I rubbed my fingers up and down his spine. I hadn't known this, that it was my brother who had given my father the last sacrament. It made perfect sense, of course — Gabe was at his first parish then — but the time was a blur and I would not have thought until now to turn my imagination to it. Once, early on, my father had stood at a hospital window and waved to me out in the street — just a pale image behind the high-up glass — but my last real glimpse of him had been at this table, with the sabotaged soda bread, my own childish effort to stop time, in his hand.

I said to my mother, 'I didn't know.'

My mother nodded. 'It was a terrible thing to have him do,' she said. And she dropped her hands into her lap, as if from sheer weariness. 'Terrible for him.'

She said, 'He was all of what, twenty-three? Barely ordained. And your father so wasted by then. His bowels coming up to his throat, if you want to know the worst of it.' She fluttered her thin hand from her breast to her chin to illustrate.

I didn't want to know the worst of it.

'Even as Gabe was putting the holy oil on him, the poor man was heaving and choking. Cruel. That cancer. Cruel of me to make Gabe go through it. I should have banned him from the room.'

'I don't remember,' I said, moving to a corner of the dining room to avoid the draft from the open window — ever vigilant now against drafts, missteps, scalding water. I was a mother now and all the terrible things that could maul a child, snatch him from the world, had bared their teeth and trained their yellow eyes on me. The baby was warmly asleep against my shoulder. 'I hardly remember that time at all,' I said.

My father a pale figure in the hospital window. All those strangers passing through the lobby, some crying, some carrying armloads of flowers. And then Fagin's benign shadow. The McGeevers with their mouths full of broken teeth standing over the coffin in the living room, telling someone in the crowd that a man so thin was a walking invitation to misfortune. And then that sweet sleep in the car on the way home from Calvary, one of the sweetest sleeps I'd ever known. Gabe in his collar then, looking

222

down at me, his red eyes puzzled. 'You slept? How could you have slept?'

'A blessing for you,' my mother said. 'Not to remember.' And she once again touched her lips. 'It was my fault, asking him. The poor child's hands were trembling and the tears were running down his face. And your father was choking back the black bile, trying to encourage him. Trying to help him with the Latin.' She put her fingertips to her chin. 'Moving his lips like he used to do when Gabe said his poems. Moving his lips because he couldn't speak. There was a terrible odor. Rot and bile. The man's body wasted to nothing. Radium was what they gave him to drink. Poison. His face a skull. The dear man.'

With her hand to her chin she paused and closed her eyes again. I could hear the water boiling in the pots on the stove. I could hear the traffic in the street outside.

'I think your brother's vocation was squashed right there and then, in that room, if you want to know what I think.' And she opened her eyes again. Behind her thin glasses they were black with her anger.

'I think it was the end of that poor boy's sweet faith, to see your father suffer the way he did. To see his body suffer. Here he was, newly minted, full up with all the words they'd given him out there, at the seminary, all the prayers, and here was the sight of his father's body reduced to a whimpering, suffering thing.'

She paused and lifted one of the white diapers, struck it against her lap, once, twice, three times. A keening gesture I had come to know. 'How was

223

he to go back to his parish,' she said, her voice low, 'and stand in the pulpit and tell the people looking up at him that there was any mercy in this world? How was he to console them?' She glared at me, although it hardly seemed it was me she was speaking to. Her lips were wet with her fury. 'His vocation ended right there in that hospital, if you ask me. I've always thought it. I've thought it for a long while.' And then she suddenly looked at me directly. 'But don't you dare tell him I said so.'

I shook my head. I would not.

My mother began to fold the diapers once more. 'So it was terrible for me to bring it up again, at the hospital, when that priest showed up with his black bag. Terrible of me to throw that memory in your brother's face when what he was trying to do for you was what he still hoped was right. The very best thing he knew, still. Trying to assure me that you'd get into heaven after all your pain. But I wouldn't be consoled. I didn't want you in heaven, I wanted you alive, on earth, with your child. When the priest came in again, I swung my purse at his head.'

'Your mother did get her Irish up' was how Tom described it later, in his own version of the scene.

In both versions, Gabe simply put his hands on my mother's shoulders and said, 'Now, Momma, quiet down.' He showed her his empty palms, as if it should be apparent that whatever they once had held, they held no more. I knew the gesture. 'Let Father bestow the sacrament,' he said. 'He's a good priest. I'll stand by his side.'

'And wasn't he right?' my mother said, smiling at me, changing allegiance, or so it seemed to me, simply by wiping the spit from her lips and shaking the anger from her eyes. She folded and smoothed and patted down the clean diapers on her lap. 'Weren't you better the very next morning? Almost a miracle.'

I nodded. I thought of that solid door and the slip of my shucked body falling against it. I supposed I now had in my own life an equivalent experience, perhaps, to Gabe's dark night in our father's hospital room or Tom's long fall from the plane, or any of the lonely journeys the dead had taken, journeys that couldn't be shared or even sufficiently described. Now I had my own mystery, mine alone, my singular experience never to be shared or even sufficiently described, try as I might, over the years: death's door, I would say. Like being run over by the Coney Island Express. None of it sufficient enough to convey what I had been through. Now I knew the quick work pain could make of time, of a lifetime. Now I knew what it was to abandon modesty, body, the entreaties of those who loved you, who wanted you to live.

'It was just that the infection cleared up,' I said. 'That penicillin did the trick.'

And my mother, now that she had soothed herself, shaken off the memory of her anger at the priest, at Gabe, at the injustice of my own suffering, glanced at me with sly eyes, with that secret smile about her mouth that warned against the risk of drawing too much attention to the deepest joys. My mother reached out and put her hand to the baby's back. He was curved warmly against my shoulder. 'Nonsense,' she said.

★   ★   ★

On a Saturday in cool October, two months after my ordeal, Tom put the bassinet and my suitcase into the trunk of the car, tying the lid half closed with rough string. He was giddy, going in and out in his good overcoat. My mother went before us down the stairs with a shopping bag full of the meals she had cooked, Gabe was behind us with the baby in his arms. Tom put one arm around my waist and gripped my right hand with the other as I leaned against the banister, taking one step at a time at his insistence. 'I'm really fine,' I said, although the cold air and the sunlight on the sidewalk made my head swim. He eased me into the front seat of the car, only a twinge in my abdomen as I sat — an echo of the insult. Gabe leaned down to place the baby in my arms.

As Tom and I pulled away from the curb, I waved to the two of them, my mother and my brother. They were standing on the sidewalk together — my mother looking very small beside him. Gabe as handsome as ever. I knew they would watch until the car rounded the corner, and then they would go up again together to finish out the suddenly quiet day.

★   ★   ★

At the apartment in Rego Park, all was Spic and Span and lemon polish and the lingering odor of the apple pie Tom had taught himself to bake that morning, only the beginning of his efforts to make up for a wife who would not learn. There were roses in a vase on the table in the small kitchen. The crib was ready in the single bedroom and our bed was crisply made. He carried up the bassinet and the bottles and the shopping bag of food, while I changed the baby's diaper and fed him a bottle and put him into his crib. Then Tom made tea and cut two pieces of the pie. I admired the roses while we ate at the small table. Tom told a funny story about the two ladies in the grocery store who had advised him about the best apples to choose.

'While the baby's asleep,' I told him, 'I might go lie down.'

He brought my suitcase in, and I changed out of my dress and took off my stockings and put a housecoat over my slip. I put my glasses on the bedside table. He smoothed down the bedspread for me and took a throw from the closet — all wordlessly, so as not to wake the sleeping child. He lowered the shades while I stretched out on the bed, and when he leaned down to kiss my forehead and whisper sweet dreams, I took his wrist and said, 'You lie down, too.'

He walked around the bed, sat at the edge, and untied his shoes. He lay back, somewhat cautiously, I thought, and, with as much distance between us as there could be in a double bed, reached over and took my hand. He gripped it, briefly, to assure himself that I was there, perhaps, or maybe simply to convey that he was grateful for the assurance. I heard him sigh and knew without turning my head he had closed his eyes. I lifted his hand and brought it to my lips.

It was not that my life was less valuable to me now that I had glimpsed what it would be like to lose it. My love for the child asleep in the crib, the child's need for me, for my vigilance, had made my life valuable in a way that even the most abundantly offered love, my parents', my brother's, even Tom's, had failed to do. Love was required of me now — to be given, not merely to be sought and returned. My presence on earth was never more urgently needed. And yet even the certainty of that fact seemed reason to throw away caution, not to heed it.

I kissed his hand and moved it to my heart. We turned to each other.

'Oh, Marie,' he whispered. 'We have to be careful.'

'Why?' I asked.

And I saw that he couldn't resist a smile at my answer. I was a bold piece. He made his eyes and his mouth grow serious. 'You can't endure another child.'

'Who said?' I whispered.

He shook his head. I still held his hand against my heart. 'Your doctor,' he said. 'Your brother. Even the priest who came to the hospital, who gave you last rites.'

'Fools,' I said. 'Which one of them has ever had a baby?' But Tom closed his eyes and put his hand to his forehead. 'What a terrible night that was,' he said. He whispered, 'They gave you last

228

rites,' as if the memory of it still took his breath away.

Gently, I touched his cheek to make him see me. I squinted in an effort to see him. 'It was only the silly infection,' I said, and moved closer. I felt the ache in my abdomen, the muscle closing up around the ragged scar. 'Next time I'll know better,' I said. 'I'll bring my own ether.'

I began to unbutton his shirt. 'Everyone says the second baby's easier.' Put my lips to his bared throat — was there any place on a body more lonely and vulnerable? 'A girl next time,' I said. 'One of the nurses told me to have a girl next time. Someone to take care of me in my old age.' But he was still shaking his head.

'I'm not afraid,' I told him. I wasn't. I had conceived our first child without any notion of the suffering involved. Now that I knew, desire — which was still there, of course — seemed small enough incentive to conceive again. It was courage now that was delightful to me. I was a bold piece. I had stood at death's door. I had withstood pain. I knew I could make a stand against it, against time, bold and stubborn, a living child in my arms.

When he ran his fingertips over the scar that split my belly, he paused. I heard him catch his breath. 'This is foolish of us,' he whispered.

I said, 'I suppose it is.'

THREE

The first strange thing was that Tom brought him in through the front door, which we never used. I had been sitting in the kitchen, waiting for the shadow to cross the lace curtain over the window in the back door, the shadow that meant the car had been pulled into the carport, when I heard instead the rattle and bang and then the odd wheeze of the door at the front of the house. I heard Tom's voice — loud and buoyant. 'Come in, come in,' a jovial innkeeper — and another series of small crashes that was my brother's suitcase being wrestled into the narrow hall.

Susan was at the sink, making something complicated out of the simple task of brewing iced tea — there was wild mint involved, weeds from the yard, as far as I was concerned, honey, and lemon rind — and the two of us glanced at each other at the sound of the front door opening, the sound of the storm door clutching at the threshold, with the same surprise we might have shown if Tom had led Gabe in through the drier vent. 'What in heaven's name?' I said.

Gabe was standing alone in the middle of the living room. He had his hands at his side. Even as a boy, he had sometimes stretched his smile too wide like this. Conveyed, all inadvertently, the effort he was making to express a pleasure that was, nevertheless, authentic and sincere. It was a shy, dutiful boy's picture-taking smile, held

233

a beat too long. 'Hey there,' he said.

He had lost weight. Something of his natural color had left not only his face and his hair but also the backs of his long hands, his polished dress shoes, the clothes he wore — a white polo shirt buttoned to the neck under a blue Windbreaker, despite the heat, and a pair of gray dress pants. Meticulous as always, yes, his broad long face was clean-shaven, his fair and graying hair carefully combed, but altogether less vivid than he had been, less present, somehow, in the world. I crossed the living room to him, Susan behind me, Helen following. Tom was already halfway up the stairs with the suitcase, and he called to Gabe over the banister. 'Look out,' he said, 'the gang's all here,' as if to remind my brother that the women must be humored.

I reached up to put my palms to Gabe's hollow cheeks. His skin was prickly, glazed with perspiration. He raised both his hands to my elbows. For a moment, we brought our faces together in the modern way, but then we stepped back, into the more comfortable distance we had known growing up. There was the scent of the institution about his clothes: cafeteria food and hospital disinfectant under his aftershave. 'How was the traffic?' I said, and Gabe said, 'Fine' — even his eyes had lost some vividness — while Tom cried out from the top of the stairs, 'Southern State backed up through Hempstead going out. Poor fools won't hit Jones before sunset.'

I turned to the girls behind me. I hadn't

intended it to, but it felt like a turning away.

'Here's Susan and Helen,' I said brightly. The two girls had paused just inside the arched doorway of the living room. Each of them raised a hand and wiggled its fingers, Helen ducking her head as she did so, lifting her shoulders shyly — she was a hunchback of shyness in those years — and Susan showing in her smile that she knew she could, if she wished, unmask us all: her jovial father, her cautious mother, her uncle just out of Suffolk — the mental hospital out east that had been the stuff of childhood insults for as long as she could remember:

Where do you go to school, Suffolk?

Hey, Suffolk called, it's time to go back.

The men in the little white coats want to give you a free ride to Suffolk.

He was, perhaps, the first adult about whom she knew something she was supposed to pretend she didn't know, and I understood then that this set her well above us all in those first hours of Gabe's return.

Tom came tapping down the stairs again, his hand hovering over the banister. 'You wanted to tell the poor P.R.s,' he said, loud and jovial, perspiring as well, his broad face and bald dome flushed pink, 'to take their coolers and their transistor radios and head back to the Bronx.'

Now he was at the foot of the stairs, in the small foyer where the front door — the door we never used — was still open. He pushed it closed, and a measure of sunlight fell away from the foyer, from that end of the living room as well. We all stood there for a moment in the dimmer light, sealed in together by the shut door.

Although the house was small enough, we didn't use the living room much either: we opened Christmas presents here, and took Easter photos, and when we entertained, we sat in here with cocktails and bowls of salted peanuts. There was only one double window, dressed with white, crisscrossed sheers and venetian blinds that were closed now against the morning's heat. There was the sturdy upright under the stairs, the gold brocade sectional along the far corner, a coffee table, a pair of Waterford lamps. At the beginning of every summer, I rolled up the good wool rug strewn with roses that had been my mother's, sent it off to storage, and left the wood floors bare until September. My voice echoed faintly, then, as if on a stage, when I said, 'Come on in, Gabe. Make yourself at home.'

★ ★ ★

I led him back through the dining room and into the kitchen. It was a pass-through kitchen, aqua and pink, a narrow, impractical space, catty-cornered between the dining room and the hallway that led to the two downstairs bedrooms. There was only a small table with two chairs, and Helen darted in and took the farthest one, sitting on one folded knee as she liked to do, as if folding in on herself and yet ready to spring. Susan went back to the counter where she'd been assembling her iced tea. I followed and then turned to my brother. Gabe stood in the doorway, reluctant and uncertain — a good foot taller than Tom, who was behind him, still talking about the drive, the beach traffic this morning going out, the relative ease with which they'd gotten home. 'Please,' I said, indicating the chair, 'have some tea.' I blushed at my own awkwardness. 'Or do you want to wash up?'

Gabe said, 'I might do that.' And I showed him to the small powder room, as politely as if he had been a stranger.

In the kitchen, Tom slapped his pockets and asked loudly what he had done with his car keys, and then — 'Here they are' — held them up between his thumb and forefinger, laughing as if he had conjured them. He said he really should go right out and move the car out of that hot driveway and up under the carport so the seats won't melt and the paint won't fade in this heat. He'd been telling Gabe, in fact, he said, telling him on the drive back, how well the old Belvedere was holding up and how cautious he was about keeping it in good repair.

He jingled the car keys, and they caught Susan's attention as they had done when she was an infant. This was the summer she learned to drive.

'Shall we?' he said, but Susan shook her head. 'You go ahead. I'm still making the tea.' Tom shrugged. I recognized the brief struggle he made to convince himself of the unreasonableness of his hurt feelings. She had never before turned down the opportunity to get behind the wheel with him: she was, understandably, curious about this mad uncle of hers, newly arrived.

★ ★ ★

When Tom was gone, out through the side door, as was usual, Susan turned to me and said, 'Why didn't he just pull in to begin with? Why'd he come in through the front?' I offered something about getting Uncle Gabe's suitcase up the stairs, although I understood by then that Tom hadn't wanted Gabe to feel he had become a back-door guest.

'Weird,' Susan said, and then looked over my shoulder, to Gabe coming back into the room. She suddenly grew busy with her lemons and her mint.

'Sit down,' I said, turning to him. 'You must be parched. Susan's putting together quite a concoction.'

Gabe moved through the small kitchen. I noticed his weight loss once more. It was not a healthy loss. He took the other seat at the little café table, across from Helen, who was studying him unabashedly.

'It was awfully nice of Tom to pick me up,' he said as I served him the tea. Nothing had been added to, or subtracted from, the short smile he wore. 'Coming out all that way.' His voice, too, had lost some of its luster. It had always been quiet and even-toned, but now it had a scarred quality to it, as if he had weathered, and recovered from, a disease of the lungs or the throat. 'More often than not,' he said, 'people leave Suffolk in cabs.'

The girls were watching him silently. I had been prepared not to mention his time at Suffolk at all.

'Which I would have been happy enough to do,' he added.

'Nonsense,' I said.

He had his legs crossed, his arms crossed over his lap. He still wore his Windbreaker, although it was warm in the house in those pre-air-conditioning days. I offered to take it from him, but he raised his hand to say he was fine. His shoes were brand-new wingtips. 'It is a lonely sort of way to go,' he said. And laughed a bit. 'To leave, I mean,' he said. The skin of his throat had grown corded, the chin loose, although it was clear that he had carefully shaved. 'I've seen some of the poor loonies walk out to the cab looking for all the world like they'd rather stay.'

The word — 'loonies' — startled and pained me. I could feel both my daughters straining against their instructions to remain mute. Helen, of course, was too shy to say a word, but Susan already had the questions on her tongue: Was it awful? Were there strait jackets? Were you in a padded cell? — the same questions she had asked us when we called her and Helen, quietly, into our bedroom the night before and explained to them both in serious, whispered phrases that Uncle Gabe was coming to stay for a while. Not a sick man, Tom had said — he had been visiting the hospital regularly and knew well the psychiatrists, the experts, he called them — only, he said, for a while there, a man overwhelmed.

239

'Swamped' was the word he used. 'Like by a big wave,' he told the two girls. 'Like at Jones Beach.'

In fact, nearly a year ago, Gabe had walked naked out of the apartment at dawn. He had walked all the way to Prospect Park — weeping — the police report said, which was probably why he wasn't charged with indecent exposure, only sent to the hospital, and then, after our own family doctor intervened, to Suffolk.

The scene had been described for us in the admitting room of the hospital on the evening of the day Gabe was picked up by the police. There had been a small crowd, apparently, kids mostly, following behind him as he stumbled along. Some of them had thrown mud. There were traces of it on his shoulder blades and buttocks. Others had thrown thin branches torn from trees, or bits of garbage, newspaper, or lunch wrappers, from the street. He was naked and crying. His feet were bare, one was bleeding. Someone in one of the apartment buildings had called the police. The officers approached him warily. They called him 'Buddy.' They asked him where he lived, if he had any family, but he was crying and could not speak. They had nothing in their patrol car to wrap him in, and they would have put him in the car as he was, when an old woman from one of the apartments appeared, breathlessly speaking in Italian or Yiddish, the officers couldn't agree on which it was. She had a blanket in her hands. She didn't know him. She couldn't give them any information, but she had, apparently, been following him for quite a few blocks, the blanket held before her.

It was a hot autumn day. They were at the dusty edge of the park, which was much neglected then. There was the clamor of the children's taunts and the foreign woman's words and the cars going by, some slowing, some emitting their own jeers. The sunlight itself was clamorous. Exposed to it, my brother's fair skin would have been mottled and pale. The officers were perspiring in their uniforms, the guns in their black holsters absorbing the heat. One of them, not the one who was speaking kindly, calling him Buddy, but the other — Officers Fernandez and O'Toole, I had no way of knowing which was which — had a nightstick in his hand. My brother stood naked among them, pale and thin, his own hands at his side. He was weeping, unable to speak. They cuffed his hands behind his back. They wrapped him in the blanket the old woman had brought. He let himself be led away.

Tom and I, together in a small room somewhere inside the hospital, had listened, had flinched, had lowered our eyes even as the doctor described the scene, read off the names of the officers, said 'weeping' and 'crying' interchangeably. Walking out together down those awful corridors to see Gabe, I let out a single breath and shook my head. Tom took my hand. 'Did you see that toupee?' he whispered.

'Every time I saw a cab pull up,' Gabe was saying, 'I thought of that scene from *Harvey*. The one when the cab driver comes in to get paid but the sister can't find her wallet. And while they're waiting, he tells them how the nutty people are

241

all friendly and happy going out to the sanatorium, but then all angry and impatient when he drives them back, after they're cured.'

He paused, bent forward from the waist, politely, as if to see if we had heard and understood him. As if to gauge whether he had too suddenly said too much, or had spoken at all. I remembered the look, the slight, questioning, polite leaning forward from his boyhood. His hairline was receding and the light in the kitchen caught the curve of his skull in two places.

Helen said, 'I love that movie.' She was sitting opposite Gabe at the small Formica table. She was not sitting up straight, she never did sit up straight. She was hunched over her glass, her pointed little chin nearly touching the rim. There was so much weedy mint in her tea it looked like an amber-lit terrarium. 'Harvey made the wallet disappear,' she said.

'The pooka,' Gabe said softly, nodding. He turned toward her politely, but with some surprise, as if he had not expected her to speak.

'So Elwood wouldn't get the shot,' she said.

He nodded again. 'Elwood P. Dowd,' he said. It was the gracious wariness of an adult unused to conversing with children. 'Right you are.' The cuff of his Windbreaker had ridden up a bit, exposing the pale skin. There was a hospital bracelet on his bony wrist. He looked at me. 'Someone stays up to watch *The Late Show*,' he said, and Helen's chin dipped farther, touched the rim of her tall glass.

Susan laughed. 'And *The Late Late Show*,'

242

she said. There was both big-sister mockery in her voice and, perhaps because of Gabe's presence here, a new forbearance. There was a way her body had, in those days, of bobbing and weaving as she spoke: as if a more assertive, adult Susan — the lawyer she would become — was elbowing past the shy child she, too, had once been. Although she'd once been as skinny as Helen was now, she'd recently begun putting on weight. I was aware of the cool heft of her fleshy forearm. She was standing against the sink, her palms hooked behind her, but her body bobbing forward. I nudged her aside a bit as I opened the utensil drawer and took out the kitchen shears.

'She even tries to stay home sick when there's a good movie on in the morning,' Susan was saying. 'She plans her whole life around the TV schedule.'

'I do not,' Helen said into her glass. 'I never do.'

'Are you kidding?' Susan cried, goading her. Showing off, too. 'Who circles all the old movies in the *TV Guide* every week? And puts those reminders on the bathroom mirror, like *National Velvet*, Tuesday?'

Helen dropped her chin yet again, drew her raised shoulders nearly up to her ears. 'No, I don't,' she said softly, while her sister said, 'Of course you do, don't lie,' and laughed.

I crossed the narrow room and took my brother's hand from his knee without a word. Without a word, he gave it to me. 'I'm of the same mind,' he said to the girls. 'A good old movie on TV can make my whole day.' His flesh

243

was cold and there were graying, golden hairs on the backs of his pale fingers. I slipped the kitchen shears between the plastic cuff and the blue underside of his narrow wrist. I neatly cut the thing in half, then touched his knee before I carried the bracelet to the trash.

'Guess I won't need that anymore,' he said, and I tried to sound lighthearted. 'We know who you are,' I said.

Gabe turned to Helen. 'What's the movie today?'

Helen raised her eyes to the clock on the wall. She had a narrow face and small dark eyes, black-lashed and lovely. She had perfect vision, both girls did. A blessing from their father. 'A Hitchcock,' she said. '*Shadow of a Doubt.*'

'Joseph Cotten,' he said. 'Another good one.'

Helen said, 'I don't know who that is.'

Something authentic entered my brother's smile. 'Joseph Cotten,' he said. He shifted in his chair, reaching into his pocket for his cigarettes. He looked at me. 'Whatever happened to Joseph Cotten?'

I shrugged, aware of, grateful for, the grace of this ordinary conversation. 'Who knows?' I said airily. 'All those old actors. Probably making commercials.'

'Probably dead,' Susan said.

'It's from nineteen forty something,' Helen added. 'The movie, nineteen forty-one or nineteen forty-two.'

'Ancient history,' Gabe said. 'Your mother was still a babe in arms.'

I laughed. The air in the warm room had

244

grown a bit lighter. 'Hardly,' I said. 'I was working at Fagin's by then.'

Gabe smiled a warmer smile. There was as well the grace of a shared past. 'The consoling angel,' he said. He tapped the crushed pack against his palm, extracted a single, filtered cigarette and then the matchbook inside the cellophane. I took an ashtray from the windowsill and crossed the room to put it on the table. Again, I touched a fingertip to his knee. 'I don't know about that,' I said. 'I did get five new dresses out of the deal.'

And I saw my daughters glance warily at each other: they knew this story, too.

Gabe bent his head as he struck the match and then waved it in the air when the cigarette was lit. He blew the first smoke toward the ceiling. 'We were all great fans of the afternoon movie out there in the insane asylum,' he said.

The side door burst open and Tom bustled in once more, talking. He was saying how earlier that summer he had hung two tennis balls from the rafters of the carport, a parking guide for Susan, to keep her, he said, walking into the tiny kitchen, swinging his keys, from knocking us all off our chairs in the middle of dinner when she put the front end through the dining-room wall — as women drivers, no doubt, were apt to do. In fact, just yesterday, he said — and look at all this lovely mint, will you, Gabe, grows wild in our own yard, we should make mint juleps — just yesterday, he went on, he saw a woman take out a hedge on the corner of her own lot as she backed down her driveway at what must have been forty miles an hour, her husband standing on their front steps with his hands in the air.

He demonstrated, throwing his hands straight up and then letting them fall back in despair to his own bald head.

He turned to Susan, who was leaning against the kitchen counter, tolerating him, but fondly, fondly. There were times through my daughter's adolescence that I would have been grateful to have some of that fondness. 'I'll probably get an extra year or two in purgatory,' Tom said, 'for adding another woman driver to the world.'

He poured himself a glass of iced tea and loaded it with sugar, even though Susan told him there was honey in it already. 'So here's the thing,' he went on, addressing Gabe. 'I put those g.d. tennis balls up there myself, and yet every single time I pull into the carport, they hit the window and I jump about a mile. They about give me a heart attack every time.'

The girls started laughing. He about had a heart attack, they repeated, laughing, every single time. Jumps a mile and cries, Jesus H. Christ.

'Sometimes worse,' Helen added.

'Sometimes he says, ''Holy shit,''' Susan said, and I cried out, stamped my foot, as if to crush the scuttling word. Susan said, 'I'm just quoting.'

'I don't know why I can't remember they're there,' Tom was saying. 'They get me every time.'

This, was, of course, a lie. They had startled him once, but never again. The rest was an act, a comic set piece he had honed over the past few weeks. I knew this. The girls knew it, too. The

246

sudden start, the cursing, the hand to his startled heart, were all part of the joke. One of his jokes on himself, meant to get us laughing at him, meant to get his daughters' impulse to mock him seem only a weak afterthought to the way he mocked himself. I knew this. The girls knew it.

Gabe was smiling at us all through the smoke from his cigarette.

'He thinks it's the roof caving in,' Susan said. 'Or meteorites.'

'Yellow flying squirrels,' Helen added, giggling. She looked at her father. 'Well, that's what you said yesterday. You said, Goddamn yellow flying squirrels.'

Tom turned his straight face to Gabe. 'You see what I put up with here?' he said calmly. 'With the boys away, I'm the only man in the house, and this is what I have to put up with. Thank God you're here.'

The smoke poured out from Gabe's small smile, it rose up from the cigarette in his hand. His legs remained crossed, his arms crossed over his lap; the wrist of the hand that held the cigarette, bare now, was long and blue-veined and covered in pale hair. The distance between the boy he had been, my brother, and this stranger sitting here now behind a veil of smoke seemed vast. I felt a sudden vertigo, looking across it, and leaned against my daughter's bare, damp arm as Tom began to tell Gabe a story about some flying squirrels that had once invaded the crawl space behind the upstairs room ('Where you're staying now, Gabe, but

247

don't worry') and the comical pair of exterminators — 'Mutt and Jeff' — who had captured the things and taken them home for pets. One of them, the little one, coming to the door some days later wearing the baby squirrel on his shoulder like some kind of mountain-man pirate — 'I kid you not.'

He was a man who loved to talk.

'Did you see that toupee?' he had said as we left the room in the ancient Brooklyn hospital where Gabe's nightmare had been described for us. He shook his head and let out a single sigh as we headed down that bleak corridor.

He said, 'You'd think a guy like that could afford a better rug.'

He said softly, leaning to speak softly into my ear, 'A psychiatrist, for Christ's sake.' He held my hand. 'Wearing a rug like that.' He chuckled. 'Talk about a cry for help' — the very words the doctor had said about Gabe — 'terrible-looking thing. You wonder his wife doesn't tell him. Must itch like hell.' Sailing us both down that bleak hallway until we'd reached the door of the ward where Gabe was lying, sedated, his back to us, his face to the wall.

Helen said, 'May I be excused?' when her father came to a pause, never an end, to his flying-squirrel story. It was five of four.

'The movie,' Susan said, all wisdom and forbearance.

Tom did a theatrical stagger. 'Tell me you're going to watch a movie . . . on a nice summer day?'

'It's hot,' Helen said, and Susan cried, 'Dad,

248

she does this every day!'

I added that she had been swimming in the Graysons' pool all morning.

But, of course, in those days Tom was never home from work at this hour to know this was his daughter's summer routine. He'd only taken the day off to drive out to Suffolk to fetch Gabe.

'And where is Lucy Grayson?' Tom asked, looking under his elbows. He explained to Gabe, 'The neighbor kid, Helen's best friend. Her shadow. They're usually joined at the hip, those two.'

'Her Gerty Hanson,' I told Gabe, bringing him in.

'She's home,' Helen said quickly. And before I could catch his eye, Tom asked, 'What? Did you have a spat?'

Helen lowered her chin and Gabe leaned forward again, over his crossed knee and his crossed arms.

'I hope she hasn't stayed away,' he said, 'because of me.' And then, in the sudden awkwardness that followed, he turned toward the table to put out his cigarette, as if to give us all time to rearrange our faces. I had indeed asked Helen not to bring Lucy over until we had Uncle Gabe well settled in.

'Believe me, Uncle Gabe,' Susan said kindly, 'you're not missing anything. This girl has the most annoying voice you've ever heard. Like Minnie Mouse if Minnie Mouse smoked a carton a day. Right?' she asked Tom. She was quoting him.

Tom laughed and said, 'Right. A twelve-year-old with a voice like a consumptive hooker.' And I cried out another objection.

'Can I go?' Helen whispered, her eyes to the clock just over the kitchen doorway. 'It's starting.'

Gabe leaned to return his cigarettes and his matches to his pocket. 'I'll watch it with you,' he said. 'If I may.'

There followed a sudden bustle in the crowded little room. Helen rushed to the basement stairs to get the TV turned on — it was an old set and needed a few minutes to warm up. The rest of us followed. The basement was ten degrees cooler than the rest of the house. It smelled heavily of damp earth and heating oil. Helen already had the set on and had taken her usual place in the worn chair closest to the TV. I directed Gabe to the old couch. Susan, saying she would watch only for a minute and then go wash her hair, took the rocking chair beside them. Tom didn't have the patience to watch television in the middle of the afternoon — and could never watch any movie silently, anyway — but stayed long enough to see everyone settled. He had some errands to run, he said, and showed me a prescription from Suffolk cupped in the palm of his hand. 'Enjoy the show,' he said, and then climbed the basement stairs, his step light, his hand held lightly over the banister.

I went back to the laundry room to empty the drier and start another load. I finished my ironing, carried the fresh clothes to the

250

bedrooms upstairs, and put them away, then went down again to put the new load into the drier. Susan was still watching the movie with Helen and Gabe — there was forties movie music and the voice of a young actress. Only Gabe noticed me as I came down the stairs, and he raised one hand from his thigh.

★   ★   ★

When I went upstairs again to start dinner, I found Tom reading the paper on the screened porch in back. I peeled the potatoes and set them to boil. Then I poured a beer into a pilsner glass from the freezer and brought it out to him. He said, 'Thank you, dear,' and offered me the first sip. This was our routine. First and best, he sometimes said. I tasted the foam, the icy beer underneath, and then handed it back to him. 'Should we offer one to Brother Gabe?' he asked.

I shrugged. 'What do you think?'

'Drink's never been his trouble,' Tom said. And paused. 'Although there was some discussion, out there, about your father being a drinker. Sins of the father, you know. All that Froodian stuff.' He widened his eyes, mocking himself and the doctors simultaneously.

I looked into my hands. It was Tom who had driven out to Suffolk every Thursday night to sit in on the therapy sessions in the men's ward. When we visited together, we drove out on Sunday afternoons. We brought Gabe cigarettes and candy and sat outside when we could. We talked about meaningless things and saved our pity for the other patients, whose trouble was evident in their puzzled faces or the defeated slump of their shoulders.

I told Tom once that there was something of Gabe's old seminary about the place. He had laughed and said there was also something of the stalag.

Tom said now, 'It's just their way of trying to find someone to blame for his trouble.'

Through the screened wall behind him I could see the early-evening sun casting long shadows across the back lawn, the small patio and the flower beds and the ocean blue sides of the pool. I could hear the gurgle of the filter and the metallic pock and shallow calls of the kids in the next yard, playing ball.

It was a homely room. The floor was painted concrete and the screens stained here and there with rust. Even then, the cushions on the wrought-iron garden chairs were yellowing beneath their painted vines, splitting along the seams. There was a sickly-looking Wandering Jew and a spindly spider plant in the corner, a basket of old pool toys no longer used. Beside it, Tom's easel and paints and a nearly finished painting of the bed of impatiens in the front of the house. Both inexpert and pretty.

'Will we ever know,' I asked him now, 'Gabe's trouble?'

Tom placed his beer on the glass-topped garden table. Were I to dream again, I would dream myself into this room, at this hour. I would take the fading cushion beside him.

'We only know what the doctors tell us,' Tom

said. 'Depression.' In those first weeks, he had come back from his visits to Suffolk and joked that this was the first time he had ever heard the word used without the 'the.'

'Which pretty much tells us nothing,' he added.

'What's the prescription for?' I asked him, and he said gently, 'Only to help him sleep.'

I said, 'He never was an easy sleeper. Even as a kid.'

And then Susan appeared in the doorway to say, 'Well, that was ironic.'

I looked at her over my shoulder. 'What?'

'The movie,' Susan said, moving into the room. She had stayed to watch it all. 'Do you know what it's about? It's about Uncle Charlie. He comes to visit his *sister*' — she bobbed forward a little as she said it — 'his sister and his *niece*, his sister's *daughter.*' She bobbed again. 'The niece thinks Uncle Charlie's the most charming guy in the world, just worships him, until she finds out he's a murderer. That he murders old women and steals their money. And their jewelry. So of course, he tries to murder the niece, too. He even looked a little like Uncle Gabe.'

I said, 'Susan,' because Helen was already behind her. Gabe following. They both seemed a little subdued.

'How was the movie?' I asked brightly, and Helen said, 'Good.'

Gabe said, 'Not very fair to the bachelor uncles of the world.'

I glanced at Susan, who was blushing beneath

her freckles, her eyes cast down. 'So I hear,' I said.

'I'll be forever suspect, I'm afraid,' he said. And smiled that short smile. He still wore his Windbreaker. There was a gleam of perspiration along his lip.

I offered Gabe a beer and then went into the kitchen to pour it. I suggested he take off his jacket and sit outside with Tom, to catch whatever breeze there was through the screens. While the girls set the table and I finished making dinner, I listened to the voices of the two men as they shared the paper and talked about the news.

★   ★   ★

I served mostly cold meals in the heat of those summers: sliced ham and coleslaw from the deli, cucumbers in vinegar, potato salad, and bakery rolls. Gabe sat at our older son's place. His manners, as always, were meticulous and elegant. They had been meant, after all, to belong to a bishop. Watching him at my table, I briefly entertained the notion that the lace-curtain pretensions my parents had taught us might well have been meant as a way (frail at best, but a way nonetheless) of cosseting, corralling, patting down, and holding in, whatever it was that had undone him last summer.

I made note to mention this to the girls when they slumped (Helen) or licked the back of a spoon (Susan), that good manners, gracious

254

conversation, might well be all we have, finally, to cosset and confine confusion.

Our two boys, Tommy and Jimmy, our Irish twins eleven months apart, were working in Hampton Bays that summer. Having a fine old time, Tom explained to Gabe over dinner, bringing him in. Attracting girls like flies at their age, he said. Two college boys, he said. Two Mr. Party Guys. Both brown as a berry, last time we saw them, what with lying out in the sun all day. Jumping into the ocean to cure their hangovers, no doubt, and then working in the restaurant at night. Not a care in the world, Tom said. 'Not like you and I were, Gabe, at that age.'

'I worry about them,' I added. 'What with all that's going on. Drugs and whatnot. And the way the girls are these days.'

I knew Susan was rolling her eyes.

Tom waved his hand, dismissing my words. 'They're just sowing some wild oats,' he said. It was an ongoing argument between us. 'Enjoying themselves while they're young.'

'Oh sure,' I said. I did not like to be dismissed.

Gabe looked at me and smiled. He had taken off his Wind-breaker, and in his white polo shirt he seemed both younger and frailer than he had when he arrived. Maybe more like himself as a boy. Or maybe more like our father, although Gabe was now older than our father had lived to be.

'Do you know the prayer of St. Augustine,' he asked me, 'the one he said when he was their age?' Gabe pronounced the saint's name with a soft ending, in what I thought of as the priestly

255

way, which may be why I felt there was suddenly something reverent in our attentiveness. Even the girls grew serious, or perhaps wary. Despite our best efforts, they were no more pious than I had been at their age, little pagans.

'No,' I said.

There was a warmth in my brother's brown eyes. ''Grant me chastity and self-control,'' he said, quoting the saint, ''but please, God, not yet.''

We all laughed — the girls with some relief, perhaps, to discover that he was not a solemn man, Tom with all the old affection and admiration for this intelligent brother of mine.

'He's your guy, isn't he?' Tom said, 'St. Augustine,' and he pronounced the name with a layman's hard ending — like the city in Florida. He did so, I knew, more out of humility than ignorance. In his mouth, Gabe's finer pronunciation would have been a pose. 'You've mentioned him before.'

'I'm an admirer,' Gabe admitted. 'The man struggled mightily.'

I stood to clear the table. 'I don't know about that,' I said. 'I only know I sleep better when the boys are at home.'

★ ★ ★

Over ice cream, Susan dissected the four o'clock movie. She outlined its flaws in logic and probability, budding lawyer even at seventeen. How could it be that no one knew, she said, and really people weren't that naïve, and surely that

256

was way too much of a coincidence.

'What's the point of watching a movie,' shy Helen asked her sharply, 'if you're going to spend the whole time looking for reasons not to believe it?'

'It is called *Shadow of a Doubt*,' Susan answered.

'Well, I'd put my faith in Alfred Hitchcock,' Tom said.

Gabe said, 'At my first parish,' and nodded to Tom, who would remember, 'there was a widow with three children, the youngest twins, who was at ten o'clock Mass every Sunday. I asked our pastor about her when I first got there, thinking we should do something for her, for her kids, at least, and he says to me, 'There's a hard case. She's a drinker.''

Susan and Helen both laughed a bit, and Gabe glanced at them and smiled.

'No, seriously,' he said. 'That's what he told me. It was well known to everyone in the parish, he told me. She had a drinking problem, three kids and all. She was as neat as a pin in church on Sunday, so were the kids, and the couple of times I'd said hello to her she seemed fine to me, but the pastor told me I was wet behind the ears if I couldn't see it. She was a real alcoholic, he said. I couldn't get over it. I started to look for her. She always looked cold sober to me. The kids were quiet in church. They always had money for the plate and never came late or left early. I asked the pastor again how he knew, what the evidence was, had he seen her stumbling or weaving or whatnot, and he called me a puppy, said I was naïve. Said once more that it was well known. I couldn't figure it out. There was no one else to talk to. I didn't want to fan any rumors by asking around. But then I noticed that every Sunday morning, as she and the kids were walking to church, she ducked into the candy store just down the block from the rectory. The three kids would wait outside, she'd duck in and out in no time. Maybe, I thought, she was taking a nip then. Maybe that's what she did.'

'What a shame,' Tom said, but Gabe held up his hand.

'So one Sunday morning when I'm not scheduled to say the ten, I walk down to the candy store at about nine forty-five and go inside for a cup of coffee. While I'm there, sure enough, she comes in. She buys a roll of Life Savers and pays with a dollar bill and goes out again. After she leaves, the owner, the candy store owner, turns to me and says, ' ''There's a project for you, Father. She's in here every Sunday morning buying mints. Covering up the alcohol on her breath. Before Mass.'

' ''Did you smell alcohol on her breath?' I asked him, and I could see by his indignation that he hadn't. 'Sure,' he says. 'Why do you think she's buying the mints?''

'Why?' Helen said.

Gabe smiled. 'To cover the smell of the drink, or so he thought. But I had a hunch. I followed them into the church. I asked the ushers to let me help with the collection. I passed the plate, and sure enough, she adds a quarter, the boy adds a quarter, and the twins each put in a dime.

258

At the second collection only the mother puts in a quarter. Three quarters, two dimes every Sunday. Ninety-five cents. Life Savers were a nickel then.' He sat back. 'She'd been doing it for years, breaking a dollar before she went into church. And that, as far as I ever knew, was the sole source of the rumors that had her an alcoholic.'

Tom laughed. 'Never assume,' he said. He drew the word in the air, circled the first part and the last: this was not a new routine. 'You'll make an ass,' he said, circling, 'out of u and me.' The girls were bearing with him, love and pity in their eyes and their smiles. 'You ever explain it to the old pastor?' he asked Gabe.

'I did,' Gabe said. I wondered at the bond between these two, strengthened further, perhaps, by those weekly conversations in the men's ward. 'But he wasn't much interested,' Gabe added. 'We had bigger fish to fry by then.'

Helen said, hunched over her dish of ice cream, the spoon in the air. 'How come you're not still a priest? You didn't like it?'

I felt what would have been my mother's impulse to grab her by the upper arm and lead her from the table. Susan said, delightedly indignant, 'Helen,' confounding the rudeness of the question by acknowledging it. But Helen's face took on Tom's look of innocent uncertainty. Guileless. Was that wrong?

Gabe said, kindly enough, 'It was the greatest privilege of my life, to be ordained.' The rest of us were silent. He was looking at Helen alone. 'But after my father died, I couldn't see leaving

259

my mother, and your mother, to live alone. Someone had to be there,' he said. He put his tongue in his cheek, moved his mouth as if he tasted something sweet. 'Your mother couldn't cook, you know. And she had some wild oats of her own. Someone had to be there to guide her.'

'There you go,' Tom said happily. He nodded, as if the matter was settled, now and forever. It only took the asking. 'And think about this,' he said to the two girls. 'If it wasn't for your uncle coming back home, your mother and I would never have met, which means you wouldn't be here, we wouldn't be here,' and he gestured, dramatically, taking in the whole house. 'So say thank you to the man. Thank him for changing his plans.'

The girls, laughing, puzzled, bowed their heads. 'Go on,' Tom said, encouraging them, overdoing it, I thought.

'Thank you,' Helen murmured, smiling, into her plate. Susan shook her head and said in a singsong, mocking way, 'Thank you, Uncle Gabe.'

★   ★   ★

After dinner, I invited him for a walk around the neighborhood. It was dusk. Sprinklers were going on the darkening squares of green grass, and neighbors on webbed lawn chairs raised their hands as we passed by. Gabe smoked. I reminded him of the long walk we'd taken when I was seventeen, when Walter Hartnett had broken my heart. 'Seventeen,' he said, and shook

260

his head. He remembered it. He looked straight ahead as we walked, and he held his cigarette low against his thigh, cupped inside his hand. 'I can't imagine anything I said was any help to you.'

'It was,' I said.

'Walter Hartnett,' Gabe repeated the name. 'The kid with the bad leg. Bill Corrigan's right-hand man. Poor Bill.'

And I added, 'Poor Walter, too.'

Gabe said, 'You can't blame a man for saying he's had enough pain.'

I supposed he could have been referring to either one of them.

There was the suburban smell of cut grass and honeysuckle, the sounds of televisions and radios, there were the halos of lampposts, house lights coming on. It is solved by walking, he had said. He had walked out into those ravaged streets of the old neighborhood, naked, weeping.

'You're welcome to stay, you know,' I told him. 'The upstairs room is yours for good. When you go back to work, you can drive to the station with Tom. Susan will be off to college in the fall and Helen's soon to follow. The boys are on their own for the most part. You'll be company for me and Tom. You'll keep Tom from talking my ear off when he retires. We'll be company for one another.'

Gabe smiled. 'Thank you,' he said simply. He thought for a bit and then said, 'I'll have to go back to pack up the apartment. I'll have to break the lease.'

I wished he had said 'the old apartment.'

261

'Tom's been over there,' I told him. 'He's already taken out anything worth saving, which wasn't much.' Gabe's clothes, some pictures, all of his books. Even before my mother died, we had moved anything of value out here. 'You should be happy to break the lease,' I said. 'The building's worse than ever these days.' And then I added, only half joking, 'These days, I wouldn't wish Brooklyn on a dog.'

He smiled again, but less sincerely. Still loyal.

As we turned the corner to start home, we came upon a group of children, five or six of them, running across three lawns, catching lightning bugs. Among them was Helen's friend Lucy Grayson, and she paused as we passed by, dragging her bare feet in the grass as if to stop her momentum. 'Hi, Mrs. Commeford,' she said in her voice like stirred gravel. She was a skinny girl with nut-brown legs beneath her cutoffs, wide eyes, and a perpetually opened mouth. I waved and said, 'Hiya, Lucy,' and then saw how the other children were slowly stopping, too, gathering around Lucy as if her sudden inertia had pulled them in. Each of them said a small greeting, at odd, firefly-like intervals — 'Hi, Mrs. Commeford.' 'Hi.' 'Hi.' — until we had walked past. And then I heard one of them shout, 'Suffolk called.' It was a boy's voice, choked with laughter. It was followed by a twitter of hushes, and then more laughter still as the children scattered again across the blinking grass.

Gabe looked straight ahead, smiling that short smile. I touched his arm, just a fingertip to the inside of his elbow. He tossed his cigarette into the street.

'Uncle Charlie's come to town,' he said, and it took me a few seconds to realize he was referring to the old movie. 'Another bachelor uncle with a shadowy past,' he said. 'Forever suspect.'

'Nonsense,' I told him.

*　*　*

When we returned to the house, there was a strange car in the driveway. Strange to me, because Gabe said, 'This might be a fellow I know.'

The front door was open once again, the porch light lit above it, and we went in that way and found Tom and the girls and a strange man sitting in the living room. There were two glasses of beer on the cocktail table and Helen was just placing the nut bowl beside them. The man stood as we entered. He was tall and broad through the shoulders. He wore a pale blue short-sleeved shirt and gray dress pants like my brother's. He had short dark hair, heavily Brylcreemed, graying at the temples. He said a jaunty 'Hello there' as he stood, and then another 'Hello, there' as Gabe introduced him. 'Matt Cain, a friend of mine.' From his days at IT&T.

I sat on the edge of a slipcovered chair and made small talk as best I could, although our voices in the rugless room echoed and rang. I felt beads of perspiration running down my back. Matt Cain knew the street in Rego Park where

263

we'd had our first apartment. He himself lived in Bay Ridge. Still with IT&T on Park Avenue, yes. He had a wide thin mouth and too much gook in his hair, although, to be fair, he might have just come from the barber. There was a ghost of white skin along his hairline. A thick handful of wiry black hair at his throat, as well. Twice he offered his cigarettes all around, and twice Tom and I raised a hand to refuse them. Although Gabe took one and leaned forward from the other side of the couch as Matt Cain held the match to it.

I excused myself and went into the kitchen. The girls had washed the dishes but left them piled in the drainer. The pot I'd boiled the potatoes in was still dirty on the stove. I washed it, and washed out the sink. And then put the dishes away, not bothering to muffle the ring and clank of my lifting and stacking and returning, one by one, the forks and knives and spoons to the utensil drawer. I was being rude, I knew. Purposefully. And I wasn't sure why. I drank a long glass of water at the sink, held my wrist under the running faucet to cool myself down. I dried my hands and put a smile on my face and returned to the warm living room to ask brightly if the men would like another beer — or, if it wasn't too hot, some coffee?

Gabe, it seemed, had been telling them about Suffolk. His routine there. Tom and the girls — Susan perched on the arm of her father's chair, Helen on the floor at his side, her legs crossed and her chin in her hands — were watching him solemnly. Matt Cain had leaned himself back against the corner of the couch, his arms spread out along the back and the side, his legs splayed — he had thick legs, long, with heavy thighs; he was altogether heavier than he seemed on first impression. He had his head turned a bit; he was picking a bit of tobacco from his tongue, but he'd been listening, too — amused or moved, it was hard to tell.

And I interrupted, breezing in to offer them another beer, coffee if it wasn't too hot, meaning — intending, I knew, although I would not have said, in the moment before I spoke, that this was my intention — to graciously bring the night to a close. And wanting to kick myself in the second after I spoke when I saw, or heard, as if in some fading echo of the conversation I'd brought to a halt, that Gabe was telling them about his life at Suffolk and I had missed it.

Matt Cain pulled in his great big legs and leaned to the coffee table to put out his cigarette. 'None for me, thanks,' he said. He placed his hands on his thighs and turned to my brother. 'I should go,' he said. There seemed to be a thousand meanings conveyed in it. Gabe said, 'I'll walk you out.'

Matt Cain insisted on carrying his and Gabe's beer glasses to the kitchen. He shook hands with me there, and with Tom and the two girls. I knew the smell of whatever he used on his hair would linger. As he started back through the dining room to the front door, Gabe caught his shoulder. He indicated the door to the carport. 'Susan tells me this is the preferred means of egress and ingress,' Gabe said, and winked at me.

'I'll put on the light,' I said.

Through the curtained glass in the door, I could see the two men pause. Gabe pointed to the ceiling of the carport and Matt Cain playfully bounced the hanging tennis balls off the windshield of Tom's car. I heard them laugh, and I hoped in my heart there was no mockery in it. Not of Tom, I thought, who had lost a day of work to drive all the way out to Suffolk to fetch him. Who had driven out there a dozen times this year to sit in the men's ward with him so he would not be alone. I watched them move away from the car, around the corner of the house to the driveway.

I finished up in the kitchen, and when Gabe hadn't yet come in, I left a note on the dining-room table. Gone to bed. But don't hesitate to knock if there's anything you need. I added, Sleep well, choosing between it and We're so glad you're here.

The girls were in the basement, the television was on, and I called down to tell them, Not too late. Helen said, Susan's already asleep, and Susan said sleepily, No, I'm not. Usually I left the basement door open so I could hear them when they came up, but tonight I closed it.

I went into my room. Tom was already in bed. He was reading a folded-back news magazine, his glasses perched on his nose. On these hot summer nights he slept in his shorts and a thin white tank shirt that exposed his fleshy shoulders, as pink and round as his head. He had

266

the window fan on high and only looked up briefly when I came in, smiled vaguely. I went into the bathroom to brush my teeth and put on my summer nightgown. Then I crossed the room once more and turned the fan down to a low hum. I went through my fusty bedtime routine. Turned the clock around on my night table. Poured some hand cream into my palms and spread it up and down my arms. Placed a pale blue hairnet over the back of my head. Turned off the lamp that had been my mother's in the old apartment and slipped off my glasses. The room contracted and lost every edge. I got into bed and, as was our routine, turned on my side to face Tom as he read. I closed my eyes. As was his routine, Tom lowered his arm to the mattress beside me, giving it to me. I put my two hands on his forearm, moved to put my lips to his skin.

I had turned the fan down low enough so that I could hear Gabe coming in and the girls coming up from the basement. Low enough, too, so that I could ask Tom what Gabe had said while I was in the kitchen, about his routine at Suffolk. Had he mentioned the electric shock? Had he talked about what had brought him there. That terrible day?

I closed my eyes and put my lips to my husband's cool flesh, and he, still reading, brushed the back of his hand against my breast. I had not liked Gabe's friend, and in my distaste, I had gone into the kitchen and lost out on what Gabe had said, about his routine at Suffolk. About what had brought him there. I had turned the fan down low enough so that I could now whisper, 'Who was that guy, that friend of his?'

Tom flipped the magazine closed with one hand and placed it on his nightstand. He took his reading glasses off and leaned toward the light, keeping his arm on the mattress beside me, pulling away just a little to reach the cord. He sat back. It was his habit to ease himself into bed as a man might sink into a tub. He moved under the sheet just a little, keeping his back against the pillows that were piled against the headboard. Again, idly, he moved his hand against my breast.

'Do you remember Darcy Furlong?' he said into the darkness, just above the whirring of the fan. 'From the brewery?'

I laughed. 'That name,' I said.

I let go of his arm and rolled over on my back. He put his hand on my hip.

'Rumors went around about him for years,' he said. 'Foolish things, mostly. Someone found him knitting in the lunchroom. There was supposed to be a tube of lipstick in his desk drawer. He wore polish on his toes — although some of us joked that, hell, if that was true, at least it meant that at some point he took off those damn saddle shoes.' He chuckled. 'Nothing terrible, really. Just small, snide things said about him now and then. But Mr. Heep got wind of it, eventually. He always had one ear to the ground in that way. So Darcy was out sick for a while — some minor surgery, we all signed a card. And during this time Mr. Heep calls us in for a meeting. I told you about this.'

I nodded. I recalled it vaguely. 'Mr. Heep said

he was aware that there were certain kinds of
rumors going around about Mr. Furlong and all
he wanted to know was did anyone have any way
to prove they were true? Anyone have proof?
That's all he asked. Of course, no one did. What
in the world would serve as proof? We saw him in
the office every day. He was a good worker. He
came in on time in the morning and went home
at night. He was a bachelor. His family lived
down South. What else was there to know? And
when no one answered, Mr. Heep said, 'Well,
neither do I, so until someone has proof,
evidence, that what you have to say about Mr.
Furlong is the absolute truth, I want the rumors
to stop. I want an end to them. And I'll fire the
first man who defies me.''

I heard the back door open and close. Heard, I
was certain, Gabe pausing to lift my note from
the dining-room table. I was aware of the
coolness of my words — I had not written, after
all, We are so glad you're here.

I could hear Gabe's footsteps on the bare floor
of the living room as he crossed to the staircase.
Tomorrow I would tell him again that he was
welcome to stay.

'That was it,' Tom was saying. 'The rumors
stopped. Sure, everyone was free to continue to
think what he liked, but no one said a word. I
have to say, I admired Mr. Heep for the way he
handled it. Put a stop to it. Whatever Darcy
Furlong was — fairy or window dresser or
momma's boy, or just a lonely guy who liked
fancy socks and his own routine — what good
was to come of all of us talking about him? What

were we going to discover? What were we going to change?'

In the darkness, I felt him sink himself a bit farther into the bed, as was his routine. I felt myself, my heart, sinking as well. My brother had been the golden child reciting poetry I couldn't understand, the thin seminarian emerging from the shadow of the tall trees, his prayer book cupped in his hands. Not a year in his first parish, he had given my father the last sacrament, even as the poor man's suffering was at its last and terrible height. I had been startled by the ferociousness of his grief — you slept? — when I woke up in the car we had hired from Fagin. I had been at various times annoyed and puzzled by his solitude and his brooding, his vigilance, the way he feared what was ugly or unkind, and the way compassion seemed to upend him — walking out naked and weeping into the ravaged streets where we had been young. My brother was a mystery to me, but a mystery I had always associated with the sacred darkness of the bedroom we had shared in Brooklyn, or the hushed groves of the seminary, or the spice of the incense in the cavernous church, even with his lifelong, silent communion with the words he found in his books. Incomprehensible, yes, but in the same way that much that was holy was incomprehensible to me, little pagan.

And now my heart fell to think that the holy mystery of who my brother was might be made flesh, ordinary flesh, by the notion that he was simply a certain kind of man.

To think that he had walked out that summer day, crying, weeping, naked, and grieving, not for the mortal world, but for himself alone.

I felt Tom lean down in the darkness to kiss the top of my head, and in doing so, he put his hand to my arm, my elbow. 'Now, I'm not saying I know anything about this guy who was here tonight,' he said. 'All I'm saying is, we should let Gabe be. He's been poked and prodded and shocked and, worse yet, talked at till he's blue in the face, out there in that place.' The awful name now forever expelled from our conversation with his turn of phrase. 'I got sick of it myself, and I was only visiting, the way they wanted to reduce everything to a couple of easy words about sex.' He paused, as if to consider. 'I don't know,' he whispered. 'Maybe it's me. Maybe I see things too simply.' He eased himself down, into the comfort and the darkness of our bed. 'Who can know the heart of a man?' he whispered, and pulled the thin sheet up, over my shoulders and his, as was his habit before we went to sleep. 'Especially a man like your brother.'

★   ★   ★

Later, Tom spoke out of the darkness. It was the middle of the night. He had gotten up for some reason — had the phone rung? — and now he was back in the room. Leaning over, his breath warm. He was whispering. Or crying. I came awake to realize he was crying. 'It's Tommy,' he was saying. Our Tommy.

Tommy's drowned, he said. I could barely

make out the words. He hadn't put on the light. His head was heavy now against my shoulder. Drowned or driving, he was saying, drunk driving, I heard, and I heard myself say, 'Oh God.' I got out of the bed, aware, in the darkness, of the heavy weight of him on the mattress. He was crying, speaking, They were bringing him home, he told me. Through the night. Bringing the body home, and I put my hands over my ears at the phrase. I would not hear it. I found myself in the living room where the dull streetlight came through the crisscross curtains in grays and whites. I had forgotten to draw the blinds last night, with that Matt Cain character here in the living room, and now there was a nightmarish tinge to the couch and the coffee table and the lamps, the family pictures on the walls, the sound of my own entreaties, which I might have been speaking out loud, wasn't at all speaking out loud, Make this a dream, O God, too terrible, too cruel.

But it was the very cruelty of it that made me know it was real. Brutal and cruel, the way of all flesh. But to lose a child was the worst of it all. I fell to my knees. There was the smell of dust on the bare floor. I could hear Gabe coming down the stairs, sleepy and afraid. Good Lord, what's wrong. I had my head to my knees, and from somewhere in the darkness I could hear the girls' careening voices, asking, asking, but putting off with their questions the answer they feared to hear. Some general devastation. Don't put on the light, I begged my brother as he came down the stairs. Tommy is dead. My child. They are

272

bringing his body home through the night.

Good God, good God, he said.

There was wailing from the other rooms. The body was coming home, I heard someone say, and I put my hands to my ears. It was a terrible word, used this way. How could it be that I had never heard it before, the cruelty of it, the stupidity. Why hadn't Mr. Fagin, in all his wisdom, banned the term. The body. Stuffed with horsehair. The child warm in my arms. How would I bear it?

Gabe pressed his hands to my ears. This can't be real, I said. Tell me it's not real, make it not real. I had him by the sleeve. I pulled at his sleeve. I said it to Gabe, but he was full of sympathy and utter helplessness. Impossible, I heard him whisper. He was crying. Weeping. Impossible, he said. I was alone. No one had turned on a light.

You could ask, I said. My throat ached. Ask.

I woke slowly to the darkness of the bedroom and the steady hum of the summer fan, which Tom had turned up during the night. I felt the ache in my throat that told me I had been crying in my sleep. The house was silent. Tom was snoring softly beside me. It took a few seconds for the dream's grief to fall away, so real and terrible. I had had such dreams before. My throat still ached with how real it had been.

I wiped my wet cheek with the heel of my hand. It was the middle of a summer night and my husband was asleep beside me. It had been nothing more than a dream of disaster. Overanxious-mother dream of disaster. Fagin's

273

girl hearing in my dreams the long settled echo of other people's grief. Plus dinner table talk of Tommy and Jimmy diving in and out of the salt ocean day after day, hung over and carefree.

Still, it was a terrible thing to say 'the body.'

Still, I had asked and it had been given. His life restored.

Still, tonight I'd have Tom call the restaurant where both boys worked and tell them to get themselves home for dinner this week. 'Your mother is worried,' Tom would say. He would know just how to put it, both joking and sincere: the women must be humored. 'Come home and give your mother a chance to look at you.'

I sat up, reached for my glasses, stood. I walked out into the living room, where I saw I had indeed forgotten to close the blinds against the coming morning's heat. The slatted street-light was exactly as I had seen it just moments ago. I could smell the summer dust on the bare floors. And each of the family photos on the wall — professional portraits already looking dated, graduation pictures from a time already past — was stamped with the same distorting darkness I had seen in my dream. I paused at the foot of the stairs. The walls of the room were lit with lozenges of streetlight, long rectangles and a thin cross. From the bedroom upstairs I could hear my brother breathing in his dreamless sleep. I climbed slowly. When I reached the top of the stairs, where it was darker, I slid my bare feet cautiously along the floor, some intimation of how I must walk now, in my blindness.

I looked into the boys' room, which was dimly

lit by the streetlight, the two narrow beds neat and undisturbed, the scent of boy about it still, but tempered now with the warm breeze, the odor of the day's heat against the roof. I looked into the second room, where Gabe slept, the windows opened, a night breeze stirring. Gabe was on his back, under a white sheet, his arm thrown over his eyes as he used to do. He was awake and he whispered into the darkness, 'Marie?' as I entered the room.

'Are you all right?' I asked him, and he answered, 'Fine. And yourself?' Which made me smile.

I sat on the edge of the bed, felt him move his long legs to accommodate me. 'Bad dream,' I said, and recognized as I said it my own foolish certainty that it had not been a dream at all. I had asked and it had been given to me. Time had relented, doubled back on itself, restored what had been lost.

I saw my brother lower his arm, felt his hand move toward mine over the thin sheet. In the darkness, he lifted my own and held it. His palm was warm and broad. I felt the certainty of it, of his grip. I understood that he knew my dream. That he had felt me tugging at his sleeve.

On the nightstand beside the bed, reflecting the dim lamplight outside, there was a plain glass of water. Beside it, the white-capped prescription bottle Tom had brought home.

I asked him again if he would stay. 'This is a nice room, isn't it?' I said. 'It's always been a great place for guests. Momma stayed here a couple of times. When the kids were young.' I

275

could see the way the streetlight caught in his eyes and on his teeth.

'I remember,' he said softly. He said, 'That fellow who was here, Matt Cain, asked if I was interested in his place. He's got a three-family out in Bay Ridge. The top floor's available. I don't know the neighborhood very well, but I told him I'd consider it.'

'You'll be lonely out there,' I said. I said it abruptly, without thinking. 'It will be a lonely life.'

I did not remember then that the phrase had been used for Bill Corrigan.

'That's occurred to me, too,' Gabe said softly. He lifted my hand and dropped it down again. 'I don't know if that can be helped.' And then he added, 'It won't be like home' — meaning, I knew, everything that once was. And then he laughed a little. 'Remember Momma in her last days? Not home, we had to tell her, but Brooklyn.'

I let go of his hand as I stood. 'You'll be at home here,' I told him.

He nodded, and then he once more lifted his wrist to his eyes. I lingered for a moment at the side of his bed. Without fear or forethought, without intention, not at that moment, I lifted the prescription bottle and slipped it into the pocket of my robe.

The staircase was darker than the rooms upstairs had been. I went down the stairs slowly, carefully, one hand on the banister, one on the wall, walking with the caution of my blind old age.

I might have saved my brother's life that night. I don't know. I might only have dreamed the loss of my first child.

I went down the stairs carefully in the dark, one hand on the banister, one hand on the wall. What light came from the lampposts outside the living-room window was pooled at the bottom of the stairs. I thought of Pegeen Chehab and her last fall. And then of the distance her parents had traveled to bring her to her brief life, sands of Syria and Mount Lebanon and the slick floor of the pitching ship, and then that brief flame in the parlor floor window.

On the day before she died, Pegeen leaned down to me, her eyes sparkling with her plan. She said, If I see him, I'll get real close. I'll pretend to fall, see, and he'll catch me and say, Is it you again? Someone nice.

She told me, poor sparrow, poor fool, We'll see what happens then.

Other titles published by
The House of Ulverscroft:

FLORA

Gail Godwin

Ten-year-old Helen and her summer guardian, Flora, are isolated together in Helen's decaying family house while her father is doing secret war work in Oak Ridge during the final months of the Second World War. At three, Helen lost her mother — and now the beloved grandmother who raised her has just died. A fiercely imaginative child, Helen is desperate to keep her house intact with all its ghosts and stories. Flora, her late mother's twenty-two-year-old first cousin who cries at the drop of a hat, is ardently determined to do her best for Helen. Their relationship and its fallout, played against a backdrop of a lost America, will haunt Helen for the rest of her life.

LOVE ANTHONY

Lisa Genova

Olivia Donatelli's dream of a normal life was shattered when her son, Anthony, was diagnosed with autism at age three. He didn't speak. He hated to be touched. He almost never made eye contact. And just as Olivia was starting to realise that happiness and autism could coexist, Anthony was gone. Now she's alone on Nantucket, desperate to find meaning in her son's short life, when a chance encounter with another woman brings Anthony alive again in a most unexpected way. In a piercing story about motherhood, autism and love, Lisa Genova offers us two unforgettable women who discover the small but exuberant voice that helps them both find the answers they need.